An Improbable Cause

Robin Wulffson

Omega Press

Tustin, California

ISBN: 0-9753595-3-3

Printed in the United States of America

Third Printing

March 2004

To Carole

Prologue

His victim, lying helpless in a small plastic enclosure, weighed three pounds, two ounces. A tear welled up in the corner of one eye. He wiped it away and reached in his lab coat pocket for the pre-loaded syringe. He scanned the room, a sea of tiny infants. The nurses were occupied elsewhere. It took only moments to empty the syringe into the plastic IV container. He slipped out the side door and walked purposefully toward the stairwell. As he exited the building, he heard the loudspeakers blare, "CODE BLUE IN NICU. CODE BLUE..." The door slammed, silencing the rest of the message. He fumbled for his keys; they skittered to the pavement. Sweat formed on his brow; his breath came in short gasps. He retrieved the keys and unlocked the door to his Mercedes S600, pausing for a moment to admire its sleek beauty. "Nice perk," he muttered to himself. As he eased out of the doctors' parking lot his thoughts flowed back to his junior year of med school when he sat up all night with an infant about the same size as his most recent victim. Despite all efforts, which were primitive, compared to today's technology, life fluttered from the frail body in the morning, just after the nursing shift change. On that day, he decided on his choice of specialization; he vowed to devote his professional career to the care of tiny newborns. For many years, he had done just that. He had lost count of the ones he had saved as well as the ones he couldn't. And now, he not only had ceased to try but had embarked on a course that violated the Hippocratic Oath—a vow he had sworn to uphold on the day he received his medical degree. It wasn't just job burnout; it was far more complex than that. How had it happened?

He entered the parking garage beneath his apartment complex. The elevator had broken down again. He took the stairs to his second floor unit. The drab quarters, reeking of dry rot, represented a quantum leap down the status ladder from his former seaside chalet. As part of the divorce settlement, Betty had kept the 7,000-square-foot manse overlooking the Pacific. Good riddance. Who needed a big house and a nagging wife on her second facelift? He sat on the couch and flipped open the small box on the coffee table. He poured a line of white powder on the mirrored surface, rolled up a prescription blank, and inhaled. Ahh. For the moment, all was right with the world. Just for the moment.

A few miles away, another doctor sat regally in his study, sifting through his mail. The usual comfort he felt in his private chamber, which was overfilled with antique treasures gleaned from the four corners of the globe, was displaced by the task at hand; the dunning letters were getting harsher. He stuffed them in a drawer and surveyed his domain, which many locals—he included—felt was the finest piece of property on this section of coastline. Hopefully, his luck would change. Losing streaks don't last forever. He reached for the phone and dialed the Bellagio. His room, comped of course, was available, and a limo would pick him up at the airport. He felt lucky. This weekend, he would make back his losses, and then some. He was sure of it. The phone rang. After apologizing for disturbing him, a nurse informed him that his patient, Mrs. Ogata, was asking for an increase in her pain meds. *Perfect*, he thought. *I can impress old lady Ogata and the nurses that I'm the dedicated Dr. Wonderful, and fulfill another contract. Plus, I can bill for an after-hours hospital visit.*

He snatched Mrs. Ogata's chart from the rack, scanned the corridor, crept past her door, and ducked into another room. Joe said, "Hello doc," as he approached the bedside.

What the hell was the old fool doing awake at one in the morning?

Joe promptly began one of his incessant baseball tales. The doctor stifled a yawn; he hated baseball, and hated old people even more. Joe had enjoyed some success as a first baseman with the Dodgers. After a few years of stardom, the glory days vanished. Three packs a day for decades had resulted in lung cancer, and that was why Joe was hospitalized—to receive treatment that would not cure him, but prolong his miserable life. The cost of Joe's treatment would eradicate his estate and cost his insurance company many thousands of dollars. This was not a murder, but an act of mercy. He emptied the syringe into the IV, feigning interest in the baseball blabber; then departed while Joe was in mid-sentence. He glanced warily down the corridor, strode a few doors down, and entered Mrs. Ogata's room. As he had expected, the rich old bag was thrilled by his appearance. This one needed to be kept alive as long as possible. In these days, affluent patients, with good insurance, were hard to come by. A nurse entered the room, and gasped, "Come quick, he's arrested."

He gave a lackluster performance in CPR. Exiting the room, he thought, *So long old Joe, you've just incurred the ultimate strike-out.*

Chapter One

Melissa Morrison turned off Pacific Coast Highway and headed inland; the trip would cut an hour from her "quality time" with Roger; but hopefully, she'd still have the better part of two hours with her son. Anne Bellingham had been the last of the morning patients—a grand total of five. When Melissa learned that Anne had taken the bus, with several transfers, to keep her appointment, Melissa insisted on driving her home.

Anne smiled in her direction. "I can't thank you enough Dr. Morrison... I know it's a terrible inconvenience."

Melissa returned the smile. "No trouble at all; you're one of my favorite patients."

"You're so nice to all your patients... I'm so lucky to have you as a doctor, any woman would be."

Melissa absorbed the praise, appreciating even more what Anne had left unsaid. Anne was an intelligent woman, well aware of the ebb and flow of current events in the upscale seaside community of La Playa. Since "the incident," as attorneys for both sides referred to Melissa's disaster case, Anne's opinion was not shared by the general population. The patients remaining under her care since "the incident" were either extremely loyal or oblivious to the media barrage. Despite the light patient load, or perhaps because of it, Melissa had reveled in the morning. She had ample time for each patient, a luxury not possible a few months ago. A highlight was the confirmation of an ongoing pregnancy for Mandy Brown. Mandy had transferred from Dr. Morgan Brookhurst to Melissa after suffering her third miscarriage. The arrogant physician had antagonized Mandy by exclaiming that the miscarriages were Mother Nature's way of ridding the body of genetically defective offspring. Glibly, he went on to tell the attractive young woman, "Look at all the fun you can have trying."

After a series of diagnostic studies, Melissa had discovered that Mandy had an intrauterine septum, a thin partition, which divided her uterus down the middle. Apparently, the embryos were implanting on this structure, and due to its inadequate blood supply, failed to survive. Using an operative hysteroscope, a small telescope-like instrument that was inserted through the cervix, Melissa had removed the septum. Shortly after the procedure, Mandy had become pregnant. A month ago, Melissa had done an ultrasound, which confirmed the presence of a viable eight-week pregnancy. A follow-up ultrasound this morning had revealed that all was well. Even though Melissa had scanned many hundreds of patients, she always marveled right along with them at the image of their developing fetus on the screen. She couldn't imagine practicing obstetrics and gynecology prior to ultrasound; she deemed it infinitely more valuable than a stethoscope.

"My house is the second on the left," said Anne.

"Right," replied Melissa, realizing that she had barely listened to Anne's dissertation, lost in thought, during the 15 mile drive.

"I can't thank you enough for driving me home... Could you come in for a cup of tea?"

"I really—"

"Please, Dr. Morrison, just for a minute."

Melissa was about to beg off, but the pleading in Anne's eyes and voice deterred her. She realized that the time spent with Anne would brighten this lonely woman's life. Anne had lost her husband a year ago, and her only child, a son, had been killed in Vietnam. "Okay, just for a minute."

Entering Anne's home, Melissa noted that it was every bit as British as its owner. Decades of living in the U.S. had not

Americanized Anne one whit. If a double-decker bus drove by the window, Melissa would have not at all been surprised. As she suspected the tea-time provided Anne with some much-needed human companionship. Anne's long-time, and dearest friend had died two weeks ago; the loss had overwhelmed her. Melissa listened patiently while she grieved.

After reminiscing on the many intimate moments that she had shared with her friend, Anne focused on the circumstances surrounding her death. "She died at *your* hospital, you know." Melissa winced at her words. She currently felt little kinship for Cliffside Medical Center. Anne continued, "She was healthy as a horse until she got cancer of the bowels."

"Colon cancer?"

"Yes."

"Unfortunately, that disease is often fatal."

"I know, I know. But that's not what killed her. She had a heart attack and died."

"I'm so sorry, but heart disease is a common ailment among seniors."

Anne shook her head. "Common ailment, but not common for her. Her parents lived well into their nineties, and never had a speck of heart trouble, Beth neither. She never smoked, ate healthy, and exercised every day. She could outwalk me any day of the week."

"But she had cancer."

"Right, but they caught it early. She was in the hospital for chemo treatment. She was told that it would give her a better chance for a cure. It didn't. I think she'd be alive today if she hadn't agreed to the treatment."

"It's hard to accept the death of a loved one. Afterward, we all have our 'what ifs.'"

Anne nodded. "Certainly, but I have an uncomfortable feeling about her death... Call it a sixth sense if you will. I visited her the night she died. She was as healthy as she had always been... Laughing, joking. Her doctor came in just before I left, arrogant chap, dressed to the nines. I consider myself to be a good judge of character; took an instant dislike to the man. Beth didn't much care for him either; but in today's times we have little choice of our doctors."

"What was his name?"

"Dr. Silk Suit Smoothie." Anne grimaced. "Just trying to make light of it. I never got his name."

"It's best to focus on all the good times together."

"You're right Dr. Morrison. My goodness, it looks like the pot is empty. Would you care for more tea? I can brew it in a jiffy."

Melissa seized the opportunity to make a polite exit. The visit had taken the better part of an hour; however, she had been enriched by the experience. She now knew how to make a proper cup of English tea, including such details as scalding the pot. Melissa strove for perfection, and now she knew how to make a perfect cup of tea. Exiting the 405 Freeway, the coastal haze, referred to by the locals as "June Gloom," engulfed her. Then, with less than three miles to go, traffic on the boulevard slowed as four lanes funneled into one. As her lunch time seeped away, she crept toward the source of the slowdown—a collection of fire trucks, police units, and several mangled vehicles strewn about the road. As she passed the scene, she grimaced as a body bag was loaded into an ambulance. The sight caused her to reflect on Anne's description of her late friend's hospital experience. One of the positive aspects of Melissa's specialty, obstetrics and gynecology, was that she was rarely confronted with death and serious illness; however, when she experienced those events, they had a tremendous impact. During her medical career, she had been involved in precious few "bad outcomes," as they were termed by hospital personnel; however, each of them had left an indelible mark, particularly the most recent one. She could picture her patient, and friend, as she once was: vibrantly alive; and her current state: nearly dead. As she pulled into her driveway, she drove the dark thoughts from her mind. The sojourn with Anne had left her with about half an hour to spend with her son.

"Mommy," gurgled 18-month-old Roger.

Ada, her housekeeper, with hands on her hips, and just a tinge of irritation, said, "He been waiting by the window all morning."

"Sorry Roger, Mommy's here now."

"Book," said Roger, pointing to the sofa where he had amassed a small pile of his favorites. Melissa munched on a sandwich, and between bites, managed to get through several stories before it was time to return to the office.

During the short drive, Melissa ignored the "June Gloom;" she basked in the warm glow of little Roger. She could still smell his warm baby scent, and the softness of his honey-brown hair, nuzzling against her cheek. Perhaps someday, he would have a father, and a sibling or two; however, to find a handsome prince required a great deal of frog kissing; currently, Melissa had no time for, or interest in, frog kissing. For now, Roger was enough to fill her life with pleasure. He was the love child of a loveless relationship, serving as the lifeboat, which buoyed her through the current turmoil in her life. Without him, she would go under.

Chapter Two

Exiting the elevator, Melissa recognized the two women positioned by her office door. Samantha, the letter carrier, smiled in Melissa's direction. Melissa's patient, Allison, her back tilted rearward to compensate for her advanced stage of pregnancy, deflected her gaze toward the carpet. Samantha said, "Got a couple of certifieds for you. Sign here."

One missive was from the Medical Staff Office of Cliffside Medical Center; the other was from the Cliffside IPA. Melissa thought, *Nothing good ever comes by certified mail.*

As she departed, Samantha chirped, "Have a nice day."

"You, too," said Melissa. *Easy for you to say. Want to trade jobs?*

Allison was still gazing downward. Melissa said, "Hi Allison. How's the—"

"Is Jana here?"

"She should be back from lunch any minute. Can I help you with something?"

"I'll come back later."

Strange, thought Melissa, *Allison is always so effervescent. Maybe her pregnancy is getting to her? Or is it something else?* She unlocked her office door, gathered up the rest of the mail, placed the two worrisome letters on top of the pile, and retreated to the seclusion of her consultation room. Aside from a wall of medical certificates and a filing cabinet, the chamber appeared as a cozy parlor, decorated in flattering tones of rose and blue. A carved country French desk stood to one side, with an upholstered swivel chair in front. Across the room were several patterned wing chairs, which were heavier and sturdier than Melissa would have liked; however, they were a concession to the needs of her obstetrical patients. Extricating oneself from a low, dainty chair was a difficult feat for a woman in the last months of pregnancy. The arrangement facilitated open communication; Melissa refused to engage patients in discussion while they were lying on an exam table, clad in a scanty gown. After their examination, patients were escorted to Melissa's parlor where unhurried conversation took place.

Melissa tossed the pile of mail on her desk, took a seat; she stared at the envelope from the medical staff office.

While reading it, she audibly gasped.

Dear Dr. Morrison:

After thorough review of your medical performance at Cliffside Medical Center, the Medical Executive Committee has determined that your medical performance has fallen below the standard of care and that your hospital privileges should be revoked. This decision is based on three of your cases with bad outcomes: Sanders, Victoria; Sanders, Todd; and Stewart, Monica. Under Medical Staff Bylaws, you are entitled to request a Judicial Review Hearing to contest this decision. Due to the gravity of the situation, this hearing must be set within thirty days of your receipt of this letter. You are entitled to be represented by legal consul at the Judicial Review Hearing. A copy of the Medical Staff Bylaws is enclosed for your review. If you have any questions in regard to this matter, you may contact Herbert Sempres, Esq. at 555-2211.

The letter bore the signature of Dr. Thomas Globerson, the medical staff president.

She felt an intense emptiness. *Revoked. I didn't think they'd go that far.* She dialed her malpractice attorney's number. "Hello. This is Dr. Morrison. I need to speak to Mr. Graber."

"One moment please. I'll see if he's in."

While awaiting a reply, Melissa doodled on a scratch pad

entitled "Morrison Realty." Displayed on the top of the real estate promotional was a photograph of her mother. Melissa was a softer rendition of Grace Morrison. Melissa had inherited the high cheekbones, alabaster skin, enchanting green eyes, and thick auburn hair. Her mother was smiling in the picture but the toughness showed through. Grace's features were enhanced by a recent facelift, meticulous application of makeup, and probably the photographer's air-brush; Melissa's facial grooming was limited to a bit of lip gloss, often applied in her car en-route to the hospital. Melissa drew horns on Grace's face; she added a forked tail snaking over her right shoulder.

The receptionist came back on the line. "I'm sorry; he's not at his desk. Can I take a message?"

"Please have him call me as soon as possible. It's urgent."

After hanging up, she opened the other certified letter bearing the return address of the CIPA, the Cliffside Independent Practice Association. After opening it, she noted the signature at the bottom of the terse missive: Rachel Hornbeak, her former partner—no, partner was not the correct word, employer/slave driver was more fitting.

Dear Dr. Morrison:

This letter is to inform you that the Board of Directors of the Cliffside IPA has elected not to renew your contract. Kindly refer any active patients in your practice to one of the obstetrician gynecologists on the IPA. A list is enclosed for your convenience.

Compared to the correspondence from the hospital, this letter had minimal impact. Referrals from the Cliffside IPA currently represented an insignificant portion of her dwindling practice. She mused, *Isn't it a coincidence? Both these bombs arrived on the same day. The hospital and CIPA are supposedly separate entities. Hmm.* The pile of mail caught her attention. *I wonder what other joyous news is here in today's mail.*

She sorted through the pile. Payments from patients and insurance companies were placed to the left, bills were deposited to her right, and junk mail went into the trash. Melissa was about halfway through her sorting when she heard pounding on the office door. She considered answering it; however, "<u>Personal and Confidential</u>" typed on an envelope commanded her attention. *Whoever that is can wait until Jana gets back.*

Melissa tuned out the pounding and ripped open the envelope. It was from the law office of Roach and Graber. It confirmed an upcoming deposition, an unpleasant event, of which in her opinion, she needed no reminder. She opened her file cabinet, extracted a bulging file labeled: "Legal Correspondence." She added Graber's communication and the two certified letters to the pile and stuffed the folder back in the drawer. "Weasel," she muttered. "Have a nice time in there with all the other weasel letters."

Grateful that the door-pounding had ceased, she returned to her sorting. At the bottom of the pile was a thick Manila envelope from the Cliffside Independent Practice Association. In contrast to the other missive from CIPA, this was sent by regular mail. Inside was a small binder entitled: CIPA Member Physicians. Along with the binder was a memo from Rachel Hornbeak. It explained that the new roster superseded the previous one and reminded all CIPA member physicians that referrals were restricted to those doctors listed in the current roster. It also reiterated that CIPA was an elite subset of physicians that met the strict standards for membership. Following was a listing of some dozen new members as well as two physicians who were no longer members: Dr. Edwin Knox, who had retired; and Dr. Melissa Morrison, whose contract had not been renewed. She leafed through the roster; sure enough, her name had been deleted

She tossed the roster and the memo into the trash; then turned her attention to opening the envelopes piled to her left. Melissa calculated her practice income for the day to be approximately $1,000. She slit open the first bill; it was from her answering service: $123.57. The second invoice was her office rent: $3,125.00. The big-ticket item came next: her quarterly malpractice insurance premium of $22,000.00. To her relief, the remaining bills were small. When she was finished, she envisioned an old-fashioned scale with the payments in the pan to her left and the bills to the right. *I'm definitely in the red here,* she mused. *About $30,000 in the red, and to cap it off, Cliffside wants to kick me off the hospital staff and the IPA. Another banner day. I've had enough bad news in today's mail to last a lifetime. What else could go wrong?*

The office door opened, signaling Jana's return. She heard a muffled conversation—a man's voice and Jana's. She sounded angry. Moments later, Jana entered Melissa's consultation room; tears were streaming down her face. She extended a sheaf of papers. Melissa's face whitened. When she was finished thumbing through the document, she said, "The miserable bastard. How can he take my son away from me? He has never cared about him one bit. Hasn't bothered to see him for a good six months. Sole custody of the child... Mentally unstable... Improper home environment. How dare he?" She reached for the phone and dialed the number of Frank Wendt, her family law attorney.

A moment later she hung up the phone. "He's in court. Possibly... Maybe he's in his office seducing a client."

"Really. Tell me—"

The phone rang; Jana picked up. "Good afternoon, Dr. Morrison's office... "Hi Dr. Hauser. She's right here."

Melissa gave a "T" signal.

Jana said, "She'll be with you in a minute.' She stabbed the hold button, handed Melissa the receiver, and departed.

Melissa took a few deep breaths, blew her nose, and attempted to will firmness in her voice. "Hi Roger."

"What's wrong?"

"Nothing."

"Melissa."

"I can't talk about it now."

"More problems?'

"If life is a bowl of cherries, mine is just the pits."

"Come on Melissa, cynicism is not becoming to you."

"I know. I'm trying not to become a cynic, but it's hard."

"Are you okay, Melissa?"

"I'm fine, just fine. Don't worry about me... Despite my ever-growing mound of luggage I'm not losing it."

"Why not deposit your luggage in the closet and join us for dinner this evening?"

Melissa smiled for the first time in weeks. "That'd be terrific... It's Ada's night off; I'd have to bring little Roger."

"That's fine, he's included in the invitation. How about Pinocchio's?"

"Great idea, Roger will love it. What time?"

"About seven."

"About seven. See you then... Bye."

"About seven" in Dr. Hauser's vernacular meant precisely seven P.M. Melissa stared out her office window. The sun had conquered the morning haze, transforming the Pacific Ocean from listless gray to dazzling blue. This sight plus Dr. Hauser's friendly voice had infused a bit of sparkle into her frame of mind as well. Her thoughts returned to the legal cluster-bombing that she had just received; the sparkle vanished.

Jana buzzed her. "Mr. Wendt on line one."

Melissa gave Wendt a synopsis of the child custody papers. His response was predictable. He first informed her that custody battles were not only emotionally devastating but also incurred significant legal expense. He suggested that, in light of Melissa's current financial situation, it might be prudent for her to relent to Geoff's custody demands. "After all," he soothed, "Look at the money you'd save."

"That's not a viable option. My son is worth everything to me. I'll hock my last possession before I'll give him up."

"Perhaps we could discuss the matter over dinner."

"Mr. Wendt, I've told you repeatedly that I have no interest in extending our relationship beyond a professional level."

"But—"

"I'm placing a copy of the documents in the mail. I want you to get to work on this ASAP."

"I'll need another $5,000."

"I'll get it to you by the first of next week... Goodbye Mr. Wendt."

Why? Why is Geoff doing this? He has no use for the child... He's just trying to harass me. That's it. His timing was perfect. I bet he knew that the hospital letters would arrive today... To be a doormat, one must first lie down, and I'm not lying down.

A few months ago, she had a thriving practice, was financially solvent, and had no difficulty paying her bills on time. However her current problems were eroding her savings, savings earmarked for her son's education, among other things. She had pared expenses as much as possible. After a great deal of soul-searching, she trimmed her payroll. Her front office assistant and her insurance biller were both fine employees; however, the decreased revenues coupled with the drop in patient volume did not justify retaining them. She was back with her one original employee, Jana, who could perform the complete spectrum of office tasks, and functioned as ten employees rolled into one.

Beyond money, which never was a driving force for Melissa, was the searing memory of the two victims of her medical catastrophe. She stared upward at the collection of framed certificates: her medical school diploma; certificates of her internship and residency training; and her certification by the American Board of Obstetrics and Gynecology. Those bits of paper on the wall represented eight years of hard work: four years of medical school; a year of internship; and three years of specialty training in obstetrics and gynecology. *If I had to do it all over again, would I? I seriously doubt it. Maybe I should have settled for a career in the wonderful world of real estate. Mother was right, I would have been successful. But I wouldn't have been happy. Am I happy now? I was happy—briefly—when I came home for spring break to make my announcement. But, Mommy Dearest promptly popped my bubble.*

Chapter Three

Grace Morrison focused her persuasive glare upon Melissa. "I'm terribly disappointed in your decision."

Melissa returned the glare. "Real estate's your passion, not mine. I *will* become a doctor. I have the grades and the qualifications; I'm going to do it."

Grace's husband, Ralph, sat quietly sipping his martini. He rarely said anything; Grace did all the talking for both of them. Grace plucked a cigarette from her pack, lit it with a crystal lighter, and exhaled a cloud in Melissa's direction. Melissa fanned the air. Grace took another drag. Smoke exuded from her mouth as she spoke, her eyes stabbing through the plume. "Whatever for? I've worked and slaved all my life to build up my business to provide you with a nice life, and now—and now—you're turning your back on the opportunity of a lifetime. With your brains and looks, *my company* would grow like gangbusters. Morrison Realty would become a force to be reckoned with. We'd expand up and down the coast, making mega bucks along the way… Mega, mega bucks. In the years you'd spend slaving away to become a doctor, you could be generating a handsome income and enjoying a comfortable lifestyle."

"There's more to life than money and creature comforts… Your business is doing just fine, Mother. You don't need me."

"You're young and full of ideals; all I'm trying to do is smooth out the bumps in the road for you. If you persist in your defiance, you'll look back someday and regret it. Mark my words."

"I've given a great deal of thought to this decision; it has nothing to do with defying you."

"When you were younger, you were more malleable. What has happened? Where did I go wrong?"

"Maybe I grew up."

Grace snapped, "You grow up in the school of hard knocks, not in the college classroom… In many ways, you're still a child with childish thoughts. One of these days you'll wake up from your fantasy and join the real world."

"I hardly think going to medical school is a fantasy."

"It's not the real world, is it?"

"Obviously, we're at an impasse here. Let's talk about something else."

Grace took anther drag on her cigarette, stubbed it out, and lit another one. "How's your love life? Are you still dating that Beta whose parents own that restaurant chain? What was his name?"

"Randolph, *randy* Randolph Bloomington the Third. I dumped the creep months ago."

"Whatever for? He was handsome, rich, and well-connected; a great catch."

"Only if you're fishing for a pot-smoking octopus. When he wasn't trying to get in my pants, he was after me to share in his 'recreational drugs.'" She coughed and rose from the sofa. "Pardon me, but I'm moving across the room."

Grace stubbed out her cigarette. "I probably should quit, but the stress of my business and the heartache you and your brother are giving me makes it impossible… Getting back to Randolph, it's not uncommon for young people to experiment a little as long as they don't get carried away. As for your prudish ways, in today's times I see nothing wrong with offering a free test drive to a good prospect."

Melissa deflected her gaze downward. "I can't believe I'm hearing this. My mother who raised me with Puritanical values now says it's okay to hop in the sack for a 'test drive' if the customer is a man of wealth and position. I'm not a showroom commodity, Mother, available for purchase by the first one in the door who can afford the down payment."

Grace soothed, "Now Missy, there's—"

The opening door disrupted the conversation. Melissa's younger brother, Ricky, lurched into the room.

Grace shrieked, "You've been drinking at the beach again with those bums, haven't you?"

Ricky nodded, releasing a shower of sand from his sun-bleached mane. "Right on, Grace. Your little boy has been misbehaving again. Ain't it a goddamm shame."

Grace growled, "Don't swear at me."

Ralph slammed his glass on the coffee table. "That's right. Mind your tongue, young man."

Ricky smirked and released a bit more sand. "Chill out, you ball-less old leach."

Grace wailed, "Don't talk to him like that."

Ricky widened his smirk. "I'll talk to him any way I please."

"He's my husband and I won't have you speaking to him like that."

"He's no relation of mine. The only thing he has in common with Dad is that he's been neutered by you, Mommy Dearest."

"My god, oh my god," wailed Grace.

Ralph muttered, "Excuse me," and sped for the bathroom.

Grace cried, "Now look what you've done!"

"Golly gee whiz, I'm sorry I caused old glass gut to take a dump." He belched loudly, tromped upstairs and slammed the door to his room.

Melissa was alone with her wailing mother. Grace was sending her "come comfort me" signals, but Melissa sat quietly staring at the floor. After a moment, her mother gave up the sobbing and reached for solace from her pack of cigarettes. Melissa continued her downward stare. *The ultimate dysfunctional family, the ultimate.*

That night was the last one she spent under her mother's roof.

The buzzing intercom snapped Melissa back to the present. "Mr. Graber on line one."

Graber's secretary answered and asked her to hold for a moment. It was an extremely long moment. Melissa's irritation increased as she waited for Graber to come on the line. Apparently, he felt that his time was much more valuable than hers. She was seriously considering hanging up when his sonorous voice materialized. "Dr. Morrison, how are you?"

Why do attorneys always begin a conversation with: "How are you?" If you were fine, you wouldn't be talking to one. "Not good. I just received a letter from the hospital. They—they want to revoke my privileges."

"Not entirely unexpected under the circumstances."

Just the words of encouragement I need to hear. "Can you help me with this, Mr. Graber?

"I'm sorry doctor, but our firm does not handle this type of case. In addition, your malpractice carrier doesn't cover hospital actions against doctors. You need a physicians' rights attorney."

Great. Just great. Another legal weasel. "Can you give me a referral?"

"Certainly, certainly. George Rucker specializes in these matters, and he's local."

"Being local is not a top priority. I want somebody good."

"He's an excellent attorney and the only local man who handles these types of cases. There are others, but they're located in L.A. and San Francisco. If you like, I can give Rucker a call and forward a copy of your file."

"Let me think about it and call you back."

"I must admonish you to move forward on this latest issue. Any delay could further jeopardize your career… By the way, have you received the letter concerning the deposition?"

"It came today."

"Fine. Well I'm due in court."

Before I commit to yet another attorney, I need to talk to Roger. He's always given me good advice, dating back to my med school interview.

The congested freeway traffic did nothing to ease Melissa's tension. It mounted with each mile. With about an hour of driving left, she passed an off-ramp with an adjacent hospital sign. Hannaford College of Medicine was located about three miles to the right. Among the handful of schools that she had applied, Hannaford was Melissa's first choice. She had confidence in her grades and well rounded curriculum. Melissa did not feel the necessity to apply to several dozen institutions as many of her fellow pre-med students had done. She had researched the background of her interviewer, Dr. Roger Hauser. He had graduated with honors from Hannaford, and stayed on for his specialty training in obstetrics and gynecology. He then began private practice fifty miles north of the institution in Santa Rosita.

Melissa was instantly disarmed by a gray-bearded Teddy Bear in a white lab coat smiling at her from the other side of a hopelessly littered desk. On one corner, which was devoid of rubble, was a photograph of an attractive young woman, appearing to be about eighteen. Melissa mused, *She's too young, even for a trophy wife. She has to be his daughter... That's it. She's his daughter. I can see the resemblance.*

Her apprehension continued to melt away under his gentle questioning. After reviewing her college curriculum and outside interests, Dr. Hauser raised his eyes above his half-spectacles and radiated his smile across the desk. "You're extremely well qualified and have excellent MCATs. Tell me, why do you want to become a doctor?"

Melissa returned the smile. *Here it comes: "Why does a pretty girl like you want to subject yourself to the rigors of a medical education?"*

He stared expectantly.

His pause forced her into speech. "I could give you the usual trite response that I want to help humanity, but I won't. If I did, you'd probably tell me that pretty girls should marry well and forget about the demands of medicine."

"I'd be disappointed in my character assessment abilities if you responded tritely. It's difficult to summarize a question like that."

"It is… I really want to have a productive career, one satisfying to me and beneficial to others. A childhood friend of mine had those values. She became a missionary in Africa. That's not something I could do, but I can envision myself as a physician, improving people's health… An area of special concern to me is preventive healthcare."

He nodded. "I share that concern. Billions of healthcare dollars are consumed each year in the treatment of self-inflicted diseases."

"The result of drugs, alcohol abuse, smoking…"

"Exactly." A merry twinkle surfaced in his eyes as he fetched an object from his desk.

She grimaced. *Yuk, a cigar.*

He placed it in his mouth. "Don't worry. I haven't lit one in years. I'm an old-time obstetrician. Do you know why old-time obstetricians smoked cigars?"

Melissa shook her head. "I haven't a clue."

"If a patient's labor wasn't progressing like it should, her doctor retired to the lounge and smoked a cigar. When the cigar was finished, he re-examined the patient… What's the take-home message?"

She responded promptly as if she was in the midst of a quiz show contest. "Don't act hastily if you don't have to, giving a situation more time can often bring a problem to resolution."

His affirmative nod signaled that she had responded correctly. He then popped another question. "Are you interested in any particular field?"

This was not a quiz question but a gentle probe into the outskirts of her well-organized fantasy world, a fantasy destined to become a reality, step by step. "Although it's premature to make that decision,

I have given a fair amount of thought to the matter. My first choice is surgery; my second, OB."

"Why is surgery at the top of your list?"

Melissa looked down at her hands. "I have good hands, good eye-hand coordination. I can do good things with these hands."

"I've always felt that the delicate hands of a woman are best suited for meticulous surgical procedures... Unfortunately, that viewpoint is not shared by a number of my colleagues, particularly those in the surgical arena."

"Female surgeons are a rare breed."

"Exactly. In many centers—Hannaford included—surgery is male dominated. OB, on the other hand, is currently a woman's world... This year's senior residents are all women."

Melissa fixed her gaze on his eyes. "I'd hate to pick a career based on its accessibility to women, rather than where my skills and interests lie... I wouldn't want to compromise on that point."

"Quite so, but unfortunately life is a series of compromises. We all have to make them. OB/GYN is a good field, and if you're interested in preventive healthcare, it's a much better fit than surgery."

"I see your point. By the time they get to the surgeon, the patient is beyond that point. In OB/GYN, you can head off a problem, it's not death and destruction; it's a happy field."

"Most of the time, most of the time." He stared upward as if visualizing imaginary smoke rings. "Occasionally it can be sad, very sad indeed."

"Miscarriages and stillbirths?"

He returned his gaze in her direction. "Yes, and occasionally much worse things. Women still die in childbirth, you know."

Dying in childbirth, I can't imagine anything worse than having a patient die. His words were attacking her perfect world. This could not happen, at least not to her. She launched a counter-attack. "That's a rare occurrence in today's times."

He fired back with a bit of reality. "Rare, but it still occurs. We've made giant strides in OB since I first went into practice.

When I was in med school, a professor of surgery once made the statement, 'You don't have to be smart to go into OB; you just have to be able to get up at night.' That statement was arguably true then, but it definitely is not valid in today's times."

Melissa thrust her chin forward. "I am smart enough and I wouldn't have trouble getting up at night for a good reason."

For a moment, he lost himself in a private thought; he refocused in her direction with the demeanor of a loving father. "You are smart enough, and as you well know, the MCAT tests your *aptitude* for medical school but aptitude alone does not guarantee success. To make it through one also needs a good support system, emotionally and financially."

"My mother has a successful real estate business."

"Your father?"

"He died several years ago. Mother has remarried."

"Does your mother support you in your decision to become a doctor?"

"No. But I'm hopeful that once I'm accepted she will come around. Mother would much prefer that I marry well and not pursue a career as demanding as medicine."

"Your mother is a businesswoman. Why is she opposed to a medical career for you?"

"She wants me to join her real estate company. She's determined that my younger brother should become the doctor in the family."

His bushy eyebrows arched upwards. "*She's* chosen. It sounds like she has a strong personality. What about him?"

"Her personality is strong, but his grades aren't. He's going to City College; trying to improve his GPA."

"Will he?"

She shrugged. "I doubt it. His life-long ambition seems to be to disappoint her."

"And yours is to please her?"

Melissa tensed her jaw. *I gave up on that exercise in futility years ago.* "No. If she gets pleasure from my achievements, that's fine. If she doesn't that's fine too."

He gazed at the picture on his desk. "My wife and I both guided our daughter in the direction of a medical career. Lisa had a definite interest and the necessary skills. But we never would have forced her into it if it wasn't what she wanted."

"Has she gone into medicine?"

"Never had the chance. She died of leukemia two months before her nineteenth birthday... She would have been about your age."

"I'm so sorry."

"Lisa got sick right after this picture was taken. She was our *Schatz*, our treasure, our only child. She skied like a ballerina; put this old keg on legs to shame. Every winter we vacationed at Innsbruck... Until she died. Do you ski?"

"I've been a few times to the local mountains."

The sadness left his eyes; he reminisced on his native Austria. His words propelled her from his office to an alpine ski lodge. Seated beside a crackling fire, they were engaged in relaxed conversation—in German—a language that she had relished in college.

The telephone interrupted. If not, Melissa sensed that he could have gone on for hours about his beloved Austria and more beloved daughter.

After a brief conversation, he turned to her and said, "Well, we're getting off the track a bit. This interview is about you, not me."

She smiled. *That's right, but I love your stories. Wouldn't it be wonderful to have a father like you?*

"Do you have a significant other?"

"No."

"That's probably a plus at this point in your career. What about the future? Do you plan to marry and have children?"

"Yes. At the right time and if the right person comes into my life."

"A medical career is demanding. Have you considered the difficulties of juggling a career, married life, and children?"

These challenges had long been in place in her orderly inner self. She replied, "I have, and I can do it."

He launched another salvo. "Are you aware of the changes in

medicine? Healthcare is big business, regulations and controls are on the rise."

She volleyed back. "The trend toward HMOs and large groups?"

He accepted the volley. "Exactly. I'm a solo practitioner and doctors like me are becoming dinosaurs, like the mom and pop grocery store, and the family farm. It's becoming much more difficult to survive in today's times with my type of practice."

She focused her big green eyes in his direction. "If you had to do it all over again, would you?"

"I don't know, I really don't know."

"What else would you do?"

He gave his cigar a firm chew. "Who's conducting this interview?"

"Sorry." *Darn, I'm messing up.*

His smile dissolved her fears. "It's okay. Your questions are appropriate and legitimate. I've enjoyed my career, all things considered. I still have a few good years left and I'll survive the changes in medicine. I can't imagine being anything else but what I am. In your case, you're coming into a medical world in which the doctor is losing control. It's more restrictive, more demanding, and less profitable. Are you prepared for that?"

"I am."

He sifted through the mass of medical journals, scribbled notes, and drug literature strewn over the surface of his desk. "Aha, here it is." He held up an issue of *Medical Economics*. He plunged into another stack and plucked out another morsel.

Melissa was awed. This was not merely a desk; it was an elaborate filing system in which assorted items had been strategically placed in locations known only to him.

He extended the retrieved treasures in her direction. "Have Nancy make a copy of these articles for you on the way out, they provide a good run-down on the current trends in healthcare, as well as the future outlook. It'll give you a better idea of what you'll be facing."

Melissa shook her head. "*Medical Economics.* I didn't know such a journal existed. I want to practice medicine, not economics."

"Like it or not, economics are a major force driving the delivery of healthcare. Costs are spiraling out of control. That brings us back to the subject of compromises, cost-containment compromises, which impact the quality of healthcare."

She left the office with a feeling that the interview had gone well. She also left with a copy of the articles on managed care, which she filed away somewhere and never got around to reading. Economics in Melissa's world did not extend beyond balancing her checkbook. She wanted to be a doctor and help people. Money wasn't that important.

After Melissa completed her series of interviews, Hannaford remained at the top of her list. The mail check became a vital component of Melissa's daily routine. After several tortuous weeks, a letter from Stanford, her second choice, was in her mailbox.

She was not accepted.

She reread the letter a half dozen times. The wording didn't change. She was certain that Hannaford would reject her as well. She reflected on her Stanford interviewer, a geeky guy with the personality of a doorknob. Perhaps her attitude showed through; he was nothing like the warm Dr. Hauser. But then, maybe this signaled the first of a series of rejections. She had submitted applications at three institutions, three prestigious, Hannaford, UCLA, and Stanford; and one of lesser caliber, Woodruff. An acceptance by any of them would pave her way for a medical career, but what if they all rejected her?

When the letter from Hannaford arrived, she returned to her dorm room to open it in private. She was certain that she would be turned down, just like Stanford. What then? She mused, *I'm not really prepared for anything else with my college curriculum. Biology teacher? No. Research assistant? No. Peddling real estate with Mother? Ugh. After they all turn me down, I'll try again next year. I'll get a TA position or something. I should have heeded Marie's advice and applied to a gazillion schools.*

She stared at the envelope, convinced that it contained another polite rejection.

She was accepted!

She let out a whoop; then reached for the phone and dialed her mother's number. She held out some hope of a positive response.

Grace's voice flowed like honey from the receiver. "Good afternoon, Morrison Realty."

Melissa said, "Mom, I've been accepted to Hannaford!"

The honey evaporated. "Well that's fine. Now that you've proven that you could do it, you can go on to greener pastures. Georgette is leaving the company; you'd like her cozy corner office."

"Thanks, but no thanks. I've been accepted to med school, and I'm going."

"How do you expect to pay for this pipe dream of yours?"

"I was hoping that you would help me."

Grace sighed. "I would if I could. The market's in a slump. I must think of my future, and Ralph's, and Ricky's."

"Judging from the sold signs around the neighborhood, I find that hard to believe."

"Are you calling me a liar?"

"I'm not calling you anything, just passing on an observation… Speaking of Ricky, how's his education coming?"

Grace did not respond.

Melissa said, "Mother, are you there?"

"He dropped out of school. He's going to become a small businessman."

"Doing what?"

"He's opening a surf shop."

"Terrific," snapped Melissa. "What's he using to capitalize this venture?"

"I'm helping out a little with what I can."

I'll be damned, thought Melissa. "Fine, just fine. You have the funds to finance a business doomed to failure, but none to help me in a medical career."

Grace embellished her sighed response with an irritating, chirping intonation. "He's a bright young man who just needs to find his niche in life. It's unfair of you to condemn him to failure."

"I'm not condemning, Mother, just predicting. I wish him all the success in the world."

Grace continued in her annoying tone, "And I wish you success, too. I can't help my motherly concerns. I'm just trying to give you guidance at a critical point in your life, just as I am with Ricky. He's a young man, and he needs to make a living." She snapped, "You, on the other hand, are smart and pretty. You could be a mover and shaker in real estate. And, and you could marry a man of means. You wouldn't have to work at all. Your priorities are all screwed up."

Melissa's anger erupted. "No, Mother. You're the one with screwed up priorities." She slammed down the receiver. *I'll do it, Mother. With or without your help, I'll do it.*

Melissa had long ago given up trying to understand her mother. Grace was a study in paradoxes. Melissa's childhood memories of her mother were that of a softer person. However, any softness abruptly disappeared shortly after Melissa's tenth birthday when her father came home early from work. He announced that he had been fired from his job as vice president with Aetna Engineering. Her mother's reaction was swift and vicious. That day, her father not only lost his job but also relinquished his role as head of the household. He became, in her mother's words, "a spineless weakling." Eventually, he found another job, one with less prestige and a lower salary. Grace embarked on a career in real estate. She did this "to save the family from bankruptcy and ruin." She took correspondence courses to become a real estate salesperson, subsequently became a broker and founded her own company. Her business took off while their family life deteriorated. The fights became less frequent and then ceased. Her father eventually escaped the situation by dying of a broken heart attack. When Grace launched her real estate career, she also launched an assault on young Ricky and Melissa. Her strategy was to mold them into the best of all possible careers, careers that she deemed ideal. There would be no discussion of alternative careers, thank you very much. However, both refused to perform in the puppet show to her ego. The harder she prodded Ricky toward a career of academic achievement, the stronger he rebelled in the direction of self-serving non-achievement. Grace's efforts to direct Melissa toward marrying well and joining Morrison Realty produced a determination in her to succeed in a challenging profession of her choice. Medicine was the perfect option. It required intellect and the development of technical skills. In Melissa's opinion, beauty or even gender made little difference.

It was almost 3:00. Not a single patient had been ushered back to an exam room. As Melissa approached the front office to check the schedule, she witnessed Allison's exit through the waiting room door. She asked Jana, "What's with Allison? I ran into her in the hallway, she barely spoke to me."

Jana averted her gaze downward and whispered, "She's changing doctors, requested her records."

"She's due in five weeks."

Jana continued to stare at the carpet. "She's a legal secretary, you know."

"That's right—I forgot—she is."

"I asked her what the problem was. She told me it was a personal matter."

"She's aware of my problems; that's the only explanation... What's the rest of the afternoon like?"

"Pretty meager, a pap smear and an OB check."

Melissa shook her head. "Makes it hard to pay the rent."

"I know, I know. I could get by on less salary. I know that you've cut yours to the bone."

Melissa shook her head firmly. "No way. I should be paying you more; you're long overdue for a raise."

Jana gripped her lower lip with her teeth. "Things will work out.

I know they will."

"I hope so. *"Should I tell her I'm on the verge of throwing in the towel? She needs to know. I owe it to her so that she can make her plans. Not just yet, Melissa, you've still got a little time.*

Melissa retreated to her consultation room. The gnats of negativity were swarming about her head. *But,* she thought, *they can't get in unless I let them.* She gazed upward at her diploma from Hannaford. The day that she received it was branded into her memory. She could still smell the freshly-mown grass, and her mother's cloying perfume.

Chapter Four

The June sun warmed the assemblage on the lawn in front of the Health Sciences Building. At the conclusion of the exercises, the newly graduated doctors rose from their chairs and sought out family and friends. Clumps of well-wishers formed on the lawn around each cap-and-gown-clad student; Melissa became the focal point for one of these human clusters.

Grace Morrison, in her inimitable fashion, was taking charge of the picture taking as well as posing in the pictures. "Move a little closer, Ralph... No, back up a little. Just our heads and torsos in this shot. Don't cut out the diploma! Okay, tell us when to say cheese... "No. Not yet. I need to adjust my skirt... Now... Ralph, Earth to Ralph, are you there, Ralph?"

Melissa's posed smile gave way to a genuine one as Dr. Hauser approached. *Punctuality is his middle name. He missed the ceremony. And where's Katrina? Something's wrong.*

He extended his hand, interrupting her thoughts. His smile beamed brighter than the sun. "Congratulations *Doctor* Morrison."

"Thank you, Dr. Hauser. Oh, I'd like you to meet my mother, Grace, and her husband Ralph Berman."

Dr. Hauser extended his hand. "Pleased to meet you, Mrs. Berman."

Grace glared. "The name is Morrison, the same as Missy's. Actually it's Morrison-Berman." She crooned, "The Morrison name was a hallmark in real estate circles long before I met Ralph here."

Ralph smiled congenially and extended his hand.

Dr. Hauser grasped his hand and returned the smile. "You must be awfully proud of Melissa."

Ralph opened his mouth to reply but was stifled by Grace gushing, "We certainly are. What a grand and glorious day this is."

"Your little girl did it all on her own, too, didn't she?" said Dr. Hauser.

Grace cooed, "She certainly did. Ralph and I offered to help, but Missy wouldn't hear of it. She's willful and self-reliant; just like her mother. Right, Ralph."

Ralph mumbled a reply.

Melissa winked at Dr. Hauser. He smiled back. Behind the smile, something disturbing was lurking. She asked, "Where's Katrina?"

Roger's smile dissolved. "She's in the hospital. She noticed a small breast lump. We were hoping it was benign, but—"

"Mastectomy?"

Roger nodded. "The good news is that all the nodes were negative. She has an excellent chance for a cure. Anyway, she sends you her best and is so sorry she couldn't be here."

"I'll be up to visit her tomorrow."

"She's being discharged tomorrow... They're in and out so quickly these days, the next day would be better."

Grace tapped her foot.

Dr. Hauser said, "If you'll excuse us for a minute, I'd like a moment with your daughter." Before Grace could reply, Dr. Hauser took Melissa's arm and escorted her to an unoccupied section of turf. When they were out of earshot, he said, "You just took the Hippocratic Oath; it seems to me that your mother has taken the 'Hypocritic Oath.'"

Melissa laughed. "How right you are."

"Your brother; I'm surprised that he isn't here."

"I'm not; he's off pouting someplace. I guess it's hard for him to witness my successes when he has none of his own."

"That's a shame." He reached into his breast pocket and extracted an envelope. "I have a small graduation gift for you."

She sensed something of significant import. "Dr. Hauser, you shouldn't have. You've done so much already...." She opened the envelope, and extracted a small card, framed in gold.

The brief message warmed her to the core.

Congratulations to you, Dr. Melissa Morrison, on this special day. I've watched you grow over these past four years and hope I have the opportunity to continue to watch your bright star ascend. As a small token of our friendship, I have cancelled your debt.

"You can't do that," she gasped.

His eyes twinkled. "Oh, but I have. You don't need to be burdened with repayment of that little bit of money along with those student loans."

She shook her head. "It wasn't a little bit of money; it was almost $50,000."

He shrugged. "It wasn't much really. I consider it a good investment in your future."

Tears welled up. "I'm overwhelmed."

His relish of the moment continued to radiate from his eyes. "Good. Now you'd better be getting back to that family of yours." She kissed him softly on the cheek and whispered, "You are more of a family to me than anyone back there."

He smiled, attempted to blink back his tears, but failed. "Congratulations again, *Doctor*."

Melissa tensed as Grace's voice grated into their private moment. "Missy, oh Missy, we're going to miss our reservations."

He gave her one last smile and departed.

"Dr. Morrison."

The vision of Dr. Hauser trudging across the lawn evaporated. "Huh."

Jana said, "Sorry, didn't mean to startle you. Your attorney's office called."

"Which one?"

"Mr. Wendt."

"What does Frisky Frank want?"

"It was his secretary. She said that there's no need to send any more funds. Your account is fine for the time being."

"Probably wants to stay on my good side, still hoping to lure me on a date."

"Is he a hunk?"

"From his bedroom eyes to his Bally loafers."

"Single?"

"Doesn't wear a ring."

"Why not go out with him. You could use a bit of romance in your life."

Melissa shook her head. "My life's too complicated right now to get into the dating scene. Plus, he's not my type, and too old?"

"How old?"

"Mid-forties, I'd guess."

"Perfect age for me, send him my way. I could use a little spice in my life at present... You think he'd go for a slightly overweight, slightly shopworn goddess?"

The front office bell chimed. Jan said, "Maybe it's a patient." She departed, humming, "Fly me to the Moon."

Melissa thought, *I'd settle for a flight just about anywhere, as long as it's far away from here.*

Jana buzzed. "Dr. Hitchcock here to see you."

"Who?"

She whispered, "The new surgeon in town, remember."

"Right... Well, I guess I can fit him into my busy schedule. Send him back."

Hitchcock strutted into the room and extended his hand. "Hello, Dr. Morrison, I'm John Hitchcock."

Melissa rose and gave him a firm handshake. "Pleased to meet you, Dr. Hitchcock. Have a seat."

He settled into one of her wing chairs and scooted it, along with his plastic charm, forward. "I just finished my training at Hannaford and am coming on board at Cliffside. I'm joining Arnold Hoxie's group."

She smiled weakly. "How nice. I trained at Hannaford."

He nodded. "I know. You are remembered well there. You were the all-time, awesome woman resident."

She gave him another half-smile. *Oh, give me a break.* "Speaking of women, do you have any in the surgical program now?"

He shook his head, without a vestige of sadness. "Nary a one."

"Is Ainsworth still running the program?"

He nodded. "Sure is…"

"I'd imagine he's close to retirement by now."

"Next year."

"Maybe women will have a better chance of getting into the program after his departure."

"Perhaps… Surgery is a tough field for a woman."

Melissa did not reply.

Hitchcock glanced at his Rolex, "Well, it's been a pleasure meeting you, Dr. Morrison. Here are some of my cards. I've got to get my Porsche in for its service."

She took the cards. "High maintenance little beasts aren't they?"

He nodded, "They certainly are; just like a woman."

"Just like a woman." *Peacock Hitchcock—he's a perfect addition to Hot-Air Hoxie's group.*

As Melissa expected, Hitchcock failed to return the chair to its rightful place. She repositioned it and deposited his cards in the wastebasket. She reflected on the fateful day when her dreams of a surgical career went into the trash—literally.

Chapter Five

In her junior year of medical school, Melissa and many of her classmates were stricken with an illness. With each rotation, the student doctor would be enthralled with the current specialty, only to switch allegiance when exposed to the next one. Sometimes, the opposite reaction occurred, when the student found a particular discipline to be an unacceptable choice. After the ailment ran its course, Melissa returned to her original plan, formulated before her first day of medical school. Surgery was her first choice, with OB/GYN still a close second.

Although she had had never met H. Rutherford Ainsworth, on several occasions she had heard him bellowing at his underlings through the closed OR doors. This current first year group of residents boasted a woman—the first in the institution's history. Melissa interpreted this fact as a sign that the old tyrant was softening. As she entered his office, she immediately abandoned that assumption.

"Have a seat," he commanded.

Melissa realized that her car keys were still clutched in her sweaty palm. She placed them on the uncomfortable chair beside her purse, hoping that he didn't notice the move, and her tension, which was mounting by the second.

"So, why do you want to be a surgeon?" he growled.

She gave the same reasons she had given to Dr. Hauser, and got the impression that he had the same level of interest to her responses as if she were reading entries from the telephone book. She went on to reiterate her achievements in medical school, including her surgical clerkship.

"I'm fully aware of your performance here at Hannaford," he snorted. "We already have a woman in our program, and she's proven to be a disappointment. She's only good three weeks out of the month, heh heh."

Wow, thought Melissa, *this guy is a real piece of work*. "I missed only one day of school, when I fractured my clavicle in a roller-blading accident. I wouldn't disappoint you in my abilities to handle the work-load."

"Perhaps you could keep up, but there's the issue of being a team player. In my experience, it's unwise to have two women in the program... They'd fight."

His arrogance infuriated her. She clenched her fists, and replied in measured tones, "I've never had a problem getting along with my peers, regardless of gender."

He gave her a patronizing semi-grin. "How nice; well I'm due in surgery. I'm afraid that's all the time I have. You are well qualified, Ms. Morrison, and I, as well as the committee, will give serious attention to your application."

Melissa thanked him and made a hasty departure, sensing that any extension of the extremely brief interview would increase his annoyance. As she approached her car in the parking structure, she searched in her purse for her keys. *Damn, I left them in his office.*

She sped back to retrieve them. Entering the anteroom, she noticed that his secretary was absent. She knocked on his door, expecting to be greeted by silence.

He bellowed, "Whaddya want?"

"Pardon me, Dr. Ainsworth, but I think I left my car keys."

"Come in and have a look."

He was seated at his desk, clipping his nails into a wastebasket. Apparently this was his important surgical case. She noted her keys in the chair and snatched them up. The clippings were raining down on something familiar: her application. She fixed her gaze on the wastebasket; then looked him squarely in the eyes. "Thank you for your consideration."

He continued with his manicure and did not respond. She controlled an impulse to drop-kick the wastebasket through the window and departed.

The following day, Melissa sought out the lone female surgical resident, finally locating her on the patio adjacent to the cafeteria. Julia Benson was a crumpled wreck with disheveled hair and reddened eyes. "He fired me," she said. "H. Ruthless kicked me out of the program."

"Why?"

"Lack of productivity, inability to get along with the boys, not a team player. A whole litany of reasons, all unfounded."

"Did you protest?"

"To whom? He's king of surgery. No one questions his decisions. I'm outta here."

"Outta here to where?"

"Don't know... There are many other places where the "good old boys surgical club" is crumbling; it'll eventually fall apart here, too. I'll find a place more receptive to women, *and* without a super asshole like H. Ruthless. He's too much."

"You've got that right. He never considered my application."

"Typical, but consider yourself lucky. If you were in his program he'd make life miserable for you... His disciples-in-training as well." She sniffed; then emitted a faint chuckle. "My leaving and you not coming should prove interesting. No lady doctor to sandbag and torment. They'll have to refocus on each other; maybe they'll embark on a feeding frenzy. I'd love to be a fly on the wall and see how it all plays out."

"Sounds more like a shark tank than a training program."

"Right you are, with H. Ruthless goading them on. Is surgery your only choice?"

"Actually, no. I have a strong interest in OB, too."

"Go for it, then. They have a fine program here, and the chairman is H. Ruthless' alter ego. Actually, all the departments at Hannaford are great, with this one glaring exception… Or, you could go elsewhere."

"I like it here, and besides, I might find myself in the same situation at St. Elsewhere." Julia blew her nose. "You might, indeed. If I get accepted to another surgical program, it might turn out to be no better than the H. Ruthless' male chauvinist empire."

Melissa sought the consul of Dr. Hauser, knowing full-well that he was prejudiced toward OB/GYN. Nevertheless, in order to sort things out, she needed his input.

"Why do you prefer surgery over OB?" Roger asked. "Those fine hands and brilliant mind coupled with your interest in preventive healthcare point to OB. You can use those hands to fix people in the OR, and promote preventive healthcare in the office. Something else must be driving you into surgery. What is it?" Melissa did not reply. He continued, "Bet I know what it is? You want to invade sacred turf, turf dominated by men."

Melissa reflected on his words. *He was always good at pointing out the obvious. He's right on target.*

He asked, "Just what are your priorities?"

"I want a fulfilling career; I want to have a family, a fully functional one. I grew up in one that was just the opposite."

"All that and a crusader for women's rights in surgery. That's admirable, but a heavy load. Ponder your priorities and set realistic goals."

"You've never given me bad advice." *Mother forsook her family for a career. I learned by negative example… I could do much better than Mother, of that I'm sure. She was aggressive in her business, made a ton of money, but lost everything else. She failed as a mom, broke Dad's heart, Ricky's a mess. And me? Do I really want to be a women's rights crusader? What would I gain? Answer: The Susan B. Anthony of Surgery Award. What would I lose? Answer: Any hope of a normal family.*

Melissa's interview by Obstetrics and Gynecology Department Chairman Ron Daniels went well, and she was welcomed into the program. She had passed another checkpoint on the road map of her career.

Chapter Six

Jana tapped on the door. "You have a patient waiting."

Melissa's head jerked upward. "Be right there."

Melissa Morrison, M.D. and Jana Nichols, Medical Assistant, were a consummate example of medical teamwork. A patient's first impression of Melissa's office was of Jana. She was a plain person by most beauty standards, but her warm manner made her beautiful in the eyes of their patients. In addition to anticipating Melissa's needs, she always remembered a patient's name, their children's names, and a multitude of personal details. Jana and Melissa conveyed to the patient an image of thoroughness and caring. Patients usually left the office feeling better than when they entered, because their questions were answered and their medical problems handled.

After the patient left, Melissa sought out Jana's company in the front office. On this day, she could not tolerate another moment alone in the solitary confinement of her consultation room.

Jana asked, "What did Dr. Hauser want?"

"Roger and Katrina are driving down today. They're taking me to dinner at Pinocchio's."

"That's a fun place. What are they coming down here for? To cheer you up or what?"

"I'm sure they're trying to cheer me up, but there's probably something else going on with my stoic Austrian friends. I can sense it."

The sight of Monstro's gaping maw evoked chortles of glee from little Roger. His pleasure infected Melissa as well. "Fish," he gurgled. Melissa smiled. "Right, Roger-Podger, it's a big fish." *When he's a little older, I'll explain the difference between whales and fish.*

The Maitre d' approached, garbed as a ringmaster. "Welcome to Pinocchio's."

"We're meeting Dr. and Mrs. Hauser."

The ringmaster fetched a menu from the rack and guided them into the madcap interior inhabited by a diversified collection of servers, their costumes inspired by fairy tales, comic book characters, and occasionally sources impossible to guess. Dr. Hauser waved from a purple-fringed booth. The plump woman beside him turned, extended her arms, and her broad smile in their direction. As always, her pewter hair was pulled firmly backward, and coiled in a tight bun. On someone else, this would convey an image of harshness, but not on Katrina Hauser. When she smiled, the whole face smiled, including the mouth, the eyes, and even the eyebrows.

"Oma," squealed little Roger, magnetically attracted to her outstretched arms.

Katrina snatched up little Roger and kissed his forehead. *"Mein Herrchen, mein liebes kleines Herrchen"* She held little Roger at arm's length and stared at his bandaged forehead. "What has happened, Melissa?"

"We were playing ball with Casper in the back yard. He slipped and hit his head on the walkway. It scared the heck out of me, but he wasn't badly hurt."

Katrina continued her scrutiny. "Are you sure?"

"After I cleaned up the blood I found a clean two centimeter laceration on the hairline—I don't think it'll leave a noticeable scar—a little Betadine and a couple of steri-strips fixed him right up."

The Mad Hatter approached and set up a highchair. When the toddler had been secured, he asked, "Are you ready to order?"

Dr. Hauser replied, "Please give us a few minutes."

"I hate to see *mein kleines Herrchen* hurt," said Katrina. She turned toward Melissa. "But look at you. You've lost weight, *Liebling*, and you look tired, *totmüde*."

Roger echoed, "Dead tired, middle of the night delivery?"

Melissa lowered her eyes. "No. I don't sleep well these days."

"I understand."

She smiled faintly. *You understand, dear Roger. You always have and you always will. The moments that I've shared with you are priceless.*

Roger greeted her with a hug and grasped her suitcase. "Welcome to my humble abode; come on in. Katrina's out shopping. She informed me that she's going to 'put meat on your bones' during your month with us."

Melissa laughed. "I'm thrilled to be here... And the opportunity to spend one of my elective months training at the knee of the world famous Dr. Hauser."

"Humph, world famous. I'm just an old-fashioned doc, struggling to keep abreast of today's high-tech medical world... Now, let me show you to your quarters."

The bright, second-story room had an odor of fresh paint. Roger explained, "Your coming has been a blessing. It prompted Katrina to redecorate this room. It's been a shrine to Lisa far too long... Far, far too long." Roger deflected his gaze out the window. The door opened downstairs. "Katrina's back," he said

"Let me take a good look at you *Liebling*," said Katrina. "Is that a ring I see? When did this happen? You must tell us all about it already."

The telephone rang. Roger answered. After hanging up, he said, "It's the ER. I tried to trade off the day... In any event they've got an ectopic for me."

"Am I not included?" asked Melissa.

"You're not supposed to start until tomorrow. This is your orientation day."

"I'm already oriented, and I'm here to gain experience, not sit around like a slug."

Within minutes, they arrived at the ER, and were approached by a physician in scrubs with a clip board. He began his recitation as he came within earshot. "Hi Roger, we have a 26 year old with a crit of nine-point-three, late menses, and a tender abdomen. Ultrasound shows a hemoperitoneum and a fetal pole in the left adnexa."

"Hi Jim, you sure make life easy for us. Where is she?"

"Cubicle Four. Gotta go."

After examining the patients and donning scrubs, they met Felice, the OR supervisor, at her desk. "You want the scope?" she asked.

"I'm leaning toward opening her; she's got a fair amount of blood in her belly."

"Chicken," snorted Felice.

Roger raised his hands, "I always bow to your wishes, madam, but I need to consult with my colleague here, Dr. Morrison."

Felice said, "Young 'un, isn't she. Pleased to meet you doctor."

"How do you do," said Melissa, extending her hand. She turned to Roger. "I think she's doable through the scope. Let's give it a go."

"OK; how can I resist the request of two beautiful young ladies?"

"Oh lord help me, I need a shovel," said Felice. She hiked her thumb in Melissa's direction. "She's beautiful, but if you think an old OR lizard like me is good looking, you're demented, blind... Or both."

Roger laughed; he turned to Melissa. "We better scrub up girl; times a-wasting."

Although this was her first experience in an OR outside of Hannaford, Melissa immediately noted the similarity that prevails in such chambers throughout the nation. The room not only looked like the ORs at Hannaford but also was laced with the same antiseptic odor. With the onset of the surgery, Melissa's tension vanished; she was now immersed in the world of surgery. After insufflating carbon dioxide, Roger inserted the trocar—an instrument that resembled a honed barbecue skewer—through a small incision below the umbilicus. He replaced the trocar with the laparoscope; then glanced upward at the monitor, which displayed the patient's abdominal cavity. "Whole lotta blood in here," he said, "Maybe we should open her."

"Let's get a better look," replied Melissa. She made a small incision in the lower abdomen for the insertion of a smaller trocar; then removed the trocar and inserted a suction device. Shortly, the fallopian tube appeared on the monitor, rising from the receding pool of blood. Melissa instinctively grabbed the cautery and promptly staunched the brisk ooze of blood from the tube. "We'll need another port." Roger made another incision in the lower abdomen, opposite the other one. "Help me stabilize the tube," she ordered.

Melissa continued the procedure adroitly, with Roger acting as her capable assistant.

As they shed their gloves and exited the OR, Roger beamed at her. "Great case Melissa. You're fantastic. If you hadn't been along, I'd have opened her."

Melissa drunk in the praise, then reddened. "Gosh, I stole your case. You're the teacher and I'm the student. I'm sorry."

"Sorry about what? Laparoscopy was rudimentary during my training. We just looked in and did a few simple things. Nothing like this case here. You taught this old dog some new tricks, Melissa."

"But—"

"Now go get changed, Katrina's chomping at the bit to fatten you up with one of her sumptuous repasts."

During dinner, Katrina promptly guided the conversation in the direction of Melissa's engagement. She asked, "Who's the lucky young man?"

"Geoff Shackleton."

"*Ein Doktor?*"

"No, but he's in the healthcare field. He's president of a managed care plan."

"Which one?" asked Roger.

"OmegaCare."

"That high-rise off the freeway."

"That's the one. They gave him an offer he couldn't refuse. He told me that his job with Universal Health was a dead end."

Roger shook his head. "OmegaCare is the new kid in town, Universal is a seasoned operation. I would think that it would have ample advancement opportunities for a bright young man. He is intelligent, isn't he?"

"Very."

"How did you meet him?" asked Katrina.

"Mother sold his condo in La Playa when he got the job offer down here with OmegaCare. She introduced us. I held Mother's continued attempts to run my life against him. I didn't want to go out with him because of that fact, but he persevered. Called all the time, showered me with flowers. I've never had attention like that before."

Roger said, "Things are falling into place. A new development is going up over the hill, North something, ah yes, North Grove. Both of you would have short commutes. Take a look at the model homes. they're quite nice."

Katrina said, "So. Already you're having them move down the road from us. I want to know is he *ein Mensch?*"

"From all appearances, he seems to be a good man."

Katrina furrowed her brow. Is he *gut* to you, and most important, do you love him?"

"He's very good to me, seems to be everything I'm looking for, ambitious, intelligent, and good looking..."

"Do you love him?"

"I think so."

"So, you think you love him. *Das ist nicht genug.*"

"I know that's not enough. I do have reservations, but I repeat, he's very good to me, treats me with respect... He's almost too good to be true, too good be true."

"A bit of a skeptic, aren't you?" said Roger.

She shrugged. "In today's world, one has to be."

Katrina said, "*Allerdings*. He treats you *gut*, *dann*?"

"Very good. He's a perfect gentleman."

"Any other reservations?" asked Roger.

Melissa screwed up her face. "You're both going to think this is silly, but he has a mustache."

"So, lots of men have mustaches." Roger pointed to his face. "Me, I have a mustache and a big bushy beard."

"The beard and mustache suit you. They give you a—a Santa Claus look." She paused to drink in his friendly chuckle; then continued, "I told you it was silly, but I've had this image of my ideal man ever since I was a little girl and it didn't include a mustache, it gives Geoff a sinister look."

Roger laughed. "That is silly. If it really bothers you, ask him to shave it off."

"It is silly and I wouldn't impose my will on another person for something like that. It's his mustache and if he likes it, he can keep it."

"If his only flaw is a mustache my dear Miss Idealist, methinks you've found a fine young man to share your life with."

"*Jawohl*," added Katrina.

"Hopefully, I have. And Mother adores him, 'a real comer,' using her words."

Roger scowled. "I hate that word, too. There's a certain vulgarity to it... If he has a successful career, it'll be good for your relationship."

"Well if the relationship fizzles, he has excellent genetics."

Katrina gasped, "Melissa."

"Sorry, just thinking of the worst case scenario."

Roger said, "You do have doubts, don't you? You just can't pinpoint them." He raised his index finger as if on the verge of a great discovery. "I could play Sigmund Freud and analyze your sinister mustache statement."

"Go ahead, Dr. Freud."

"It's not the mustache per se that disturbs you. Some part of you is afraid that he is just too good to be true."

"Maybe that's it, but maybe it's just me and my inner feelings of some basic distrust of men in general... I've had some bad experiences."

"You're not married yet," said Roger. "Give it some time."

"The date's been set. Mother's going full bore on this. And Geoff, he's arranged a honeymoon, guess where... He gave me my choice... Austria."

The Hausers smiled and the conversation shifted to their beloved homeland.

Thoughts of Geoff and the wedding faded from Melissa's conscious thought during her month's stay with the Hausers. She was immersed in a parallel universe, a love-filled home, a *functional* family. All three were enriched. Melissa brought her knowledge of the latest surgical techniques, particularly in the field of operative laparoscopy and hysteroscopy. Roger imparted to Melissa a knowledge base accrued from years of experience. Under his tutelage she gained invaluable experience in vaginal surgery. In addition, he calmly tempered her youthful exuberance, which was typical of a physician in training. Melissa also warmed to the medical community that dwelt within the walls of Santa Rosita Community Hospital. She related well with the physicians she met, and with the hospital staff. The crusty OR nurse, Felice, took a liking to her. She mothered Melissa at the hospital in manner similar to that of Katrina at the Hauser's home. Although Melissa's comfort level was with the high degree of specialized care available at Hannaford, Santa Rosita was a well-run, up-to-date facility capable of handling the vast majority of medical situations. And, for the occasional problematic case, Hannaford wasn't that far away. The pace at the hospital was slower than Hannaford, and Melissa felt certain that she could be happy working there, and living in the community.

On Melissa's last day, she and Roger returned to his office after a morning of surgery. He ushered her into his cozy consultation room and asked her to take a seat. His worn leather couch embraced her, almost engulfing her. She sensed a distinct difference in the room. *The desk! He had cleaned his desk. It was a fine old desk... Underneath the mounds of papers was a beautiful mahogany desk. This gesture signified a moment of great import. It had to be related to his oft-repeated offer for her to join his practice after completing her training.*

"Would you be comfortable in this room, sitting where I am?" he asked.

"That's your chair, not mine. We could fix up the utility room for me."

Dr. Hauser fished the ubiquitous cigar out of his desk and placed it in his mouth. "Nonsense. That room's so small you'd have to step out in the hallway if you wanted to change your mind... I repeat, do you think this room is adequate for your needs?"

"Yes, but with both of us here, we'd be tripping over each other."

He wiggled his cigar in reply. "That we would. But both of us wouldn't be here that much... You see, My Dear, I have an ulterior motive. I'm not a spring chicken anymore. I'll phase myself out over the next several years; then the whole shebang will be yours... If you want it, that is."

Her eyes widened. "I do, but I can't. You can't just give away the practice. It's a salable commodity as I understand it."

Dr. Hauser sucked on the unlit cigar. "Yes it is, but I'd prefer to continue part time and see my old patients... Most of 'em are my age, you know. I'll get a kick out of watching you build the practice with a whole flock of new patients, young women like you."

She gasped, "You're being too generous. Work out an installment plan and I'll pay you back."

He leaned forward; his cigar wagged up and down as he talked. "I'll tell you how you'll pay me back. You can mind the store while I take longer vacations, something I've never been able to do. Katrina came face to face with her mortality when she had the mastectomy. I did too. Who knows how much good time we have left? We want to travel and see the world. That's my payment, plus the pleasure of watching you grow a practice. I believe it still can be done, despite the current changes in healthcare."

"But—"

"No buts." He extended his hand. "A bright young woman like you will have plenty of offers. Any physician or group would be a fool not to take you. You have fine hands, much finer hands than these meat-hooks of mine." He held them up for her view. "In addition to those fine surgical hands, you possess another invaluable skill. Do you know what it is?"

She did not reply.

He said, "Well, I'll tell you. As a member of Hannaford's outside clinical staff, I have access to your entire file. It contains numerous references to that talent. You can sense the subtle signs of an impending problem. Any run-of-the-mill doc can diagnose the obvious, but many would miss the obscure. You wouldn't... The Branson case was a good example."

"That wasn't a hard call. You were on the right track too."

"I was, but I had some reservations against opening her, some of my astute colleagues as well... Did you know that I consulted with Becker, and he recommended sitting on her for a day or so."

"That would have been a disaster."

"It certainly would have. Fortunately, I went with your call, not his. In any event, it would be my privilege to work with you, but I suspect you'll get many offers, perhaps some better than mine. You have almost a year of training left and a lot can happen." He extended his hand. "Deal."

She kept her hands folded in her lap. "You're too generous. If I shake your hand that means I'll accept. Nothing better could come along than your offer, nothing."

"Then shake my hand, but the agreement is not binding. A handshake merely means that I'll hold the spot if, and we'll see if you're still interested when you finish your training."

"Why wouldn't I be interested?"

"Many things can happen in that time span." He re-extended his hand. "Agreed?"

"But—"

He placed an index finger to his lips. "Shh."

She shook his hand, the hand that was always there when she needed it.

After finishing with the afternoon's patients, she reveled in her last love-filled evening with the Hausers before returning to Hannaford. While driving back on the freeway, her thoughts were filled with the delicious image of practicing medicine with the most wonderful man that she had ever met.

Dr. Hauser whispered, "Guess what? Your ex-husband just walked in." Melissa dropped the menu on the table and the zany ambiance of Pinocchio's came back into focus. "Huh... Where?"

"Right behind you."

Melissa's first reaction was to lash out at Geoff about his custody demand; then she reconsidered. This was a rare evening out; she did not want to spoil it with an encounter with Geoff in the presence of her dear friends, and more importantly, little Roger. She snatched up her menu and engrossed herself in it, reading and rereading the entries. Everything about the man was a source of irritation: the voice, the smirk, and especially his deviousness. She ticked off in her mind the reasons she loathed him beginning with their wedding night and ending with the dishonesty that had not only catapulted her into a multi-million dollar lawsuit but also threatened to destroy her medical career. She should have sought an annulment after that appalling wedding night.

The wedding and reception passed in a blur of yellow roses. The pastel blooms lined the pews and dominated Melissa's bouquet, which was caught by Jackie, one of Grace's abrasive real estate cronies. Jackie had alienated herself from Melissa by joining Grace in congratulating her for snagging "Geoff the Golden Boy." The limo eased out of the parking space; Melissa gazed backward and blew a kiss to Roger and Katrina. She continued looking in that direction until they rounded a corner. Geoff attacked her, not only physically but also with his breath, which exuded booze and the stench from the celebratory cigar that she had asked him not to smoke. While fending off the thoroughly drunk "Golden Boy," she agonized on how to handle her first sexual experience with a man who had considerable knowledge in that arena. Her fear mounted, together with her resistance to his advances. She considered slapping him in the face and jumping out of the vehicle. "Wait until we get to the hotel," she said. Her words calmed him—for the moment.

As soon as the bellman left, Geoff grabbed her forcefully.

"I need to use the bathroom," she pleaded.

"Time for that later, babe. I've waited a long time for thish. I want you now."

"Please... Please stop."

"Come on babe; letsh get it on." He grabbed the front of her dress—the one that her mother said was the most smashing on the planet—and ripped it, and her bra, forcefully down to her waist. With another violent movement he removed all but her panties. Another sweep of his hand took care of this last item. He fumbled off his clothing, experiencing difficulty with his belt buckle. She seized the opportunity and ran for the bathroom. Geoff partially extricated himself from his pants. He lunged toward her, tackling her on the cold tile of the bathroom floor. She felt an intense pain, then another, and another.

He was soon finished. Geoff lumbered off to the bed, and within moments, the air resonated with his snoring. She rose shakily, supporting herself on the sink. She felt a warm trickle run down her leg—a mixture of blood and semen. Nausea overcame her;

she crept toward the commode. After the last wave of retching passed she climbed into the shower; she scrubbed her body until she was reddened all over. She had waited all these years for this? Maintaining her virginity had not made her much of an oddity in high school; a minority maybe, but definitely not an oddity. Scholarship was her passion, not pimple-faced gropers. In college she quickly earned the reputation as the Ice Maiden. The young men who might have had a chance of melting her armor were scared off, and the ones who took her stance as a challenge repulsed her. In med school and her residency, the intensity of the work-load left little time in her book for anything else. In addition, she had little social contact aside from male classmates. One of her criteria for a husband was a non-physician, a two-physician household would be a disaster; it couldn't work. And now this—a wedding night from hell. How could she have been so naïve? She had experienced the fairy tale in reverse; the handsome prince had become a grotesque frog.

The following morning, he awakened her with a gentle kiss on the forehead. She rose up from the couch with a start and glared. "Golden Boy" was tarnished beyond repair. His unshaven face was puffy; his eyes reddened. The stench of his breath was unbearable; even worse than the previous evening. He mumbled, "I'm so sorry honey, so very, very sorry. I had too much to drink…"

She drew back and deflected her gaze toward the wall. "You raped me."

"Aw honey. You're so beautiful. It was the liquor not me."

"It *was* you, Geoff. You did it, not the liquor. That was the most horrible experience of my life."

She continued to stare at the wall until he left for the bathroom. Her torn clothing, strewn about the room, contrasted sharply with the room's pristine décor. She gathered up her entire going-away wardrobe, including the shoes, and dumped the collection in the trash. She sat on the couch and sobbed.

She was still crying when he returned from the bathroom dressed in a crisp blazer and slacks.

"I'm leaving you," she said.

He promptly unleashed his stockpile of charms upon her, begging for one more chance. He made numerous references to the fun they'd have exploring Austria. The fact that "the trip was already paid for" had no impact, but the destination did. In addition, she pondered the embarrassment she would experience when family and friends learned of the wedding that fizzled on the launch pad. That would be humiliating; however, far less humiliating—and painful—than the recent sexual encounter with "Lecherous Geoff."

He kneeled before her with moist eyes. "I love you princess. Please give me another chance. Please, it'll never happen again. I promise."

The word, princess, reverberated through her inner-self. It evoked childhood memories; in that fantasy world, she was a princess. On many occasions, she dressed in her princess outfit, forcing little Ricky into servitude as her little page. And more importantly, her father often called her his little princess. His death had left a tremendous void, a void that needed to be filled. Could Geoff fill that void? Maybe. She stared at Geoff as if he was a frog under a dissecting microscope. "Did you ever play Monopoly?"

"What?" Yes, as a kid, but—"

"You've used your 'get out of jail free card.' You won't get another. Now go downstairs and get some coffee. I need to shower and dress."

Vienna and Salzburg dazzled Melissa with their old-world charm; the cities were even more intriguing than she had imagined from Roger and Katrina's descriptions. She was fascinated with the honeymoon location, but not her companion, even though he was on his best behavior. He curbed both his drinking and his sexual appetite for the duration of the honeymoon. Another attempt at intercourse was out of the question. She was too sore and too afraid. Upon their return, in light of his dramatically improved deportment, she decided to give the relationship a little more time. In the following months she attempted to follow his guidance in the new world of sex; however her first experience with him had left an indelible impression. Contrary to the protagonists in the romance novels that she avidly read as a teenager, there were no fireworks. Romance novels were just that, works of fiction, fabrications intended to entertain the reader. Welcome to the real world; there are no fireworks.

A familiar voice assaulted her. "Well, well, well. Small world isn't it?"

Melissa elevated her head from the menu and turned in the direction of the intrusion. Waddling beside Geoff, in all her immensity, was Dr. Rachel Hornbeak. Melissa had not seen either of them for several months. Rachel had gained weight and Geoff had lost, particularly in his face. Melissa smiled, not from pleasure, but at the contrast between svelte Geoff and gross Rachel. She tried to will the smile off her face, but chuckled instead. "Hello Geoff, Rachel." .

Geoff snorted, "We came here to discuss some business over dinner."

Melissa nodded. "It's okay, Geoff, we're divorced. You're free to date whomever you please."

"Oh cut it out, Melissa." Geoff turned to little Roger and chucked him under the chin. "Do you want to come and live with daddy, little man?" The toddler burst into tears, raised his pudgy arms in defense. Geoff retreated.

Melissa hissed, "It'll be a frosty day in hell before he spends one night under your roof. Now, get out of my sight before I throw something at you."

"Let's find our table," huffed Rachel.

The ringmaster, menus in hand, was pretending to ignore the conversation. He smiled broadly. "Right this way."

"Seat the lady," said Geoff. "I need to use your men's room." The ringmaster made a sweeping gesture. "Around the bar to your left."

Dr. Hauser's eyes followed Rachel's waddle until she was well out of earshot. "So that's the infamous Dr. Hornbeak. You described her as unattractive but that was inadequate—she's coyote ugly."

"Coyote ugly?" said Melissa, visualizing a slender animal, which in no way resembled the porcine Rachel.

Amusement twinkled from his eyes. "Coyote ugly is, when you wake up in the morning and look at the girl nestled in your arm, you gnaw it off so that you can leave without wakening her."

Melissa and Katrina laughed heartily, stimulating an encore from little Roger.

Dr. Hauser said, "It looks like she slept in that dress, it's covered with hairs." He chuckled. "Coyote hairs."

Melissa laughed. "Horse hairs."

"What?"

"Her horse, Golden Boy; the main passion in her life."

He shook his head. "Golden Boy must be a Clydesdale to handle her weight." Laughter erupted again.

Katrina asked, "Do you really think they're dating?"

Melissa said, "No, I was just hurling a barb at him. Geoff was probably telling the truth—not that he does that often—they probably are discussing business over dinner."

"What kind of business?" asked Dr. Hauser.

She shrugged. "Who knows, who cares."

Little Roger banged the table for attention. "Go Potty."

Melissa rose. Dr. Hauser wagged his finger. "I'll take him."

Little Roger trudged off with his Opa. When they were out of sight, Katrina asked, "What was that business about little Roger living with him?"

Melissa slammed her water glass on the table. "I didn't want to ruin our evening. Geoff is suing me for full custody."

"*Lächerlich.* He has no love for the child."

"Ridiculous is right. I'm sure he's just doing it to harass me." Her voice dropped to a whisper. "That's the only explanation."

"It is."

The two women sat quietly for several minutes, tuning out the zany surroundings of Pinocchio's.

When Dr. Hauser returned with little Roger in tow, Melissa asked, "What brings you down to this neck of the woods?"

"House hunting," said Katrina. "Roger sold the practice."

Dr. Hauser explained, "I've been offered an insurance review job down here. I can call my own hours, no more night call."

Katrina said, "You never complained."

"No, but I'm too old for that anymore."

"How wonderful," said Melissa. "I'll have more time to spend with my two favorite people."

"We thought so too," said Katrina. "We'll have much more time to be together. *Nicht wahr?*"

Melissa asked, "How's the house hunting coming?

Katrina replied, "Great. We put in an offer on a nice one, already."

"Where?"

"Emerald Canyon," said Dr. Hauser.

The Mad Hatter returned and asked, "Are you ready to order?"

Dr. Hauser nodded. "The three of us will have the linguine in clam sauce, and the little fellow will have a child's portion of the spaghetti."

"He'll make a mess," said Melissa.

"I'll take care of that," said Katrina. She wagged her finger at little Roger. "*Essen, nicht fressen.*"

Melissa echoed in English, "Don't eat like a pig."

Little Roger giggled and banged his spoon on the high chair tray. His rapping attacked Melissa's overtaxed nervous system and she jerked her head upward. Geoff passed by, ignoring them. Melissa wondered what had occupied him for so long in the men's room. The white flecks on his mustache explained. Geoff, still staring straight ahead, flicked his tongue upward and removed the particles. When he was out of earshot, she said, "So that explains the weight loss. Dear Geoff has given up martinis for nose candy."

"Nose candy?" asked Katrina. "What kind of candy does one put in the nose?"

"Cocaine," explained Melissa.

"*Ach, schrecklich.*"

"Right; frightful, the habit certainly is, and so is he. The man is totally disgusting."

Dr. Hauser patted her hand. "Don't let seeing them spoil our evening. They're both out of your life now."

Katrina nodded. "*Ja, ja. Du, vergiss nur, vergiss nur.*"

"I'm trying to forget them. I was just reminded of my knack for making bad decisions."

"Rachel or Geoff?" asked Dr. Hauser.

"Both of them, unfortunately, both of them."

She asked herself, *Who was the bigger mistake of my life, Rachel or Geoff?* She answered the question. Geoff was the bigger mistake of the two. In both cases, her instincts told her that she was making a blunder. Furthermore, her mother had been the instigator of both relationships. Perhaps the explanation was that somewhere in her inner-self there was a little girl who strove desperately to please her mother. And perhaps she had only married Geoff for his genetics. Her treasure of a child would not exist if she hadn't married him. In this sense the marriage had not been a mistake. In all other ways it had been a terrible decision. The marriage was a mistake, Rachel was a mistake, and the day she had been talked into persevering with a doomed marriage was a mistake.

She spotted Dr. Hauser sitting at a small table in the corner of the restaurant. He rose to greet her. She hugged him. "Sorry I'm late; there was an accident on the freeway."

"No need to explain. I'm thrilled that you could meet me for lunch. It's a rare treat."

"A rare treat for me, too."

"In a few months, you won't be fighting the traffic between Hannaford and here."

She forced a smile and nodded.

He closed his menu and placed it on the table. "You didn't drive up here for a casual lunch, did you?"

She gazed downward.

"Out with it Melissa. What's wrong?"

"I never could fool you, could I?"

"Not for a minute."

"I'm getting a divorce."

"Has he mistreated you again?"

"He's been very good to me. Flowers, little gifts sent in the mail, sweet cards." *All outward signs of affection.*

"What is it, then?"

"He lost his job with OmegaCare; profits have dropped since he joined them and he's being held responsible."

"The healthcare field is a tough business."

"It is, but he fouled up by the numbers. His business day ended at noon with two martini lunches. It's his own fault."

"He's unemployed?"

"No, he wangled himself into a new position, Mother helped him. He's now with the Cliffside IPA, Vice President in Charge of Utilization, a pay and prestige cut, but a job... His third in three years I might add. Hopefully, he learned his lesson and will shape up his act. Anyway, I've had enough; he can move to La Playa and do his thing. I'll go into practice with you."

"You're caught up in a tug of war, going into practice with me, or preserving your marriage."

Melissa nodded. "I chose you, I definitely chose you."

"Do I get a vote in this matter?"

"No. My mind is made up."

"A marriage is a lifetime commitment... Mine has been anyway. I would hope that yours could be, too. Go into practice in La Playa. Don't throw your marriage down the drain after just a few short months. You'll regret it."

Melissa blinked back her tears. "I made a commitment to you, too."

"Your marriage vows take precedence over any commitment to

me."

"What about your plans to take some time off? I want to pay you back for all you've done for me."

He patted her hand. "You've already paid me back... I have a contingency plan anyway."

"And what might that be?"

"I'm doing some insurance review. In time, I can do more; then phase out the practice."

"That sounds like a poor second choice."

"Maybe, maybe not. There are a lot of pluses to having regular hours. In your case, La Playa is a nice place to live, less smoggy and congested than around here. Have you researched practice opportunities in the area?"

"Not really. Mother and Geoff have done a bit of unsolicited research, but I haven't."

"You'd better get cracking, girl; you have less than two months to find a job."

"I thought I already had a job, with you."

"You did, but current circumstances prohibit it."

She felt something extremely valuable and irreplaceable slipping from her grasp. "I'd still rather leave Geoff and go into practice with you. I have a sneaking suspicion that I'm being set up by Mother and Geoff."

"How so?"

"Mother adores Geoff. She takes his side in everything. Mother has found—according to her—the world's most perfect doctor to go into practice with, Dr. Rachel Hornbeak. Do you know her?"

"No, but your mother may be on the right track with this one. A number of women OB/GYN groups are forming and they all seem to be doing well in these days of managed care."

"Maybe so, but if I can't go into practice with you, my instincts tell me that I'd be better off joining a big HMO."

"Some of them have hiring freezes at present. The new managed care plans are competing with the private sector and the HMOs for patients. They are presenting the image that you can have a private physician, quality care and economy."

She asked, "Can they succeed in that?"

Dr. Hauser shook his head. "I doubt it. I suspect that there's a big discrepancy between their idealism and reality. I don't have a lot of faith in managed care in its present form, but I do have a lot of faith in you. You'll do well, I know it."

"Melissa?"

"Huh?" she replied.

Dr. Hauser peered at her from across the table. "You keep zoning out on us. Your situation is really getting you down, isn't it?" Tears welled up. "I'm thinking of calling it quits. The hits just keep on coming, and…"

"You mean Geoff's custody demand?"

"Yes, and…"

"And what?"

She whispered, "I—I received a letter from the hospital today… They want to revoke my privileges."

"I'm surprised that they would take such drastic action based on one bad outcome."

"Correction, three bad outcomes."

"Okay, three bad outcomes, none of which were your fault. A good outcome is never guaranteed. Surely your colleagues can understand that."

"Apparently they don't… At least those in positions of power on the Medical Executive Committee; the OB/GYN Core Committee, too."

"You were given an opportunity to contest the charges, weren't you?"

"They offered a hearing. I accepted." She blew her nose. "I received a referral from Mr. Graber for an attorney to handle the matter. Do you by chance know a George Rucker?"

Dr. Hauser shook his head. "No. I don't know many

attorneys."

"He specializes in physicians' rights, and appears to be the only game in town."

"Have you met with him?

"No. I wanted your input first."

"Consult with him then, but trust your instincts."

"I've been down that road before."

He patted her hand. "I know you have, but you are smart and perceptive."

"Maybe so, but I feel that this thing has taken on a life of its own, it's consuming me."

"Only if you let it," said Katrina.

"Hang tough," added Dr. Hauser.

"Maybe I'll move to Oregon, live in a beach shack, and write poetry."

"Cut it out," said Dr. Hauser. "What a ridiculous statement. I know you too well, girl. You're by no means the Bohemian type."

Melissa smiled. "The Oregon idea was just a joke, but I do think I'm going to call it quits."

"You're not a quitter," he replied.

Katrina said, "*Ja*, you need to see this thing through. How can we help? Do you need money?"

Melissa replied in a small voice, "I'm fine. I have enough in savings to see this thing through. Your love and support is all I need for now. Without it, I couldn't make it."

"Your mother?" asked Katrina.

"She's no help… And is bombarding me with 'I told you sos.'"

"Consider the source and ignore it," said Roger. "You can make it, we're sure of that."

"I'm trying to, but it's hard; so very hard." Melissa stared at them with overwhelming love. *I wish I shared their confidence… Well, enough of this doom and gloom.* "Katrina, tell me about your house."

Katrina's soft brown eyes took on a glow, as she related the potential home's many fine features. Melissa was caught up in Katrina's enthusiasm. Soon the Hausers would be local. Happy times were ahead… *Maybe.*

Chapter Seven

The previous evening with the Hauser's had been refreshing. Roger and Katrina could always cheer her up and their support gave her the courage she needed to persevere. She descended the stairs with a bit of a bounce in her step. Her mood brightened further when Roger smiled at her from his highchair. He gurgled, "Mommee."

Ada was busy spooning him his breakfast. She did not turn around, but mumbled, "Good Morning Miss Melissa."

"Good Morning Ada." *Something's wrong.* Melissa fetched a mug of coffee and took a seat at the table. The newspaper wasn't there. Ada always placed it on the kitchen table. Melissa asked, "Where's the paper?"

Ada muttered, "No paper."

Ada possessed a childlike simplicity. She was not capable of lying.

In a commanding tone, Melissa said, "Ada."

Ada turned in her direction. Tears were streaming down her face. Melissa made another firm inquiry about the paper. Ada rose, sheepishly fished it out of the trash, and placed a hand on her shoulder. She whispered, "*Muy malo.*"

Melissa winced at her photograph on the front page. She was reclining face-up on a chaise lounge clad in a bikini. Two pictures flanked hers. One displayed a wasted remnant of a woman in a hospital bed, her features obscured by a respirator. The other depicted an infant on life-support. The headline screamed: TRAGIC OUTCOME, TWO IN COMA. An angry scowl hardened on her face. When she finished reading the article, she reached for the telephone. She dialed Graber's number.

"Sorry, he hasn't come in yet," replied the brusque voice.

Roger gurgled at her in a vain attempt to attract her attention. She was far too upset to respond.

Ada asked, "What you like to eat? I fix you something nice."

"Nothing, thanks, just the coffee."

She sipped her coffee and reread the article. After her second cup, she found the courage to drive to her office. Her image in a bikini filled her thoughts during the short drive. Two blocks from the office, a horn blared. She looked up with alarm and discovered that she had drifted across the centerline. She gripped the wheel and wrenched it sharply to the right, narrowly avoiding a head-on collision. Beads of perspiration formed on her brow; she drove slowly and carefully the remainder of the distance.

Entering her office, she instantly noticed the two men seated in her waiting room and sensed that they were not the husbands of patients. They had a disquieting intensity about them. They rose, one holding a camera and the other a tape recorder. The man with the tape recorder approached. "Dr. Morrison, we're from the *Daily Breeze*. Would you care to make a statement about—"

"No, no statement." She held up her hands to shield her face from the repetitive flashing of the camera. She brushed past the two men and entered the business office. Jana rushed to her side; the two women took a defensive stance.

"Dr. Morrison, is it true—"

Melissa interrupted, "Any statements will be made through my attorney, Mr. Graber. Jana will give you his number. Now if you'll excuse me, I have to begin my office day."

Jana scribbled the number on a slip of paper and thrust it toward the man with the tape recorder. She then opened the waiting room door and gestured toward the hallway. "Out!"

The telephone rang; Jana sprang to answer it. "Good morning,

Dr. Morrison's office..." The other line rang. "Please hold.... Thank you for holding... Hi Betty... Oh, I see, do you wish to reschedule... Thank you for holding... Do you wish to reschedule..."

Melissa retreated to her consultation room, leaving Jana to her task of handling patient cancellation calls. A few minutes later, Jana buzzed her. "Your mother on line two." Melissa stared at the blinking button in preparation for the assault. The flashing continued relentlessly; it would not go away. She gingerly plucked the receiver from its cradle.

Grace screeched, "Missy, my god, Missy, what have you done now? The Morrison name trashed and defiled on the front page of the paper."

"It's me on the front page, Mother, not the Morrison name."

The decibel level of the screech increased. "It's you half naked on the front page, along with the fine Morrison name. Why did you pose for such a picture?"

Melissa snapped, "I didn't pose for the picture. Geoff bought me that bikini and took the picture. He must have given it to the paper."

"I can't believe he'd do a thing like that. You're upset and just lashing out."

"Darn right I'm upset. The article is bad enough, but Geoff has to be responsible for that picture. There's nobody else..."

Grace wailed, "You've ruined your life and now you're dragging me down in the muck and mire along with you. Morrison Realty will no longer be a respected name in this community. Where did I go wrong? I tried so hard, so very hard."

"You'll survive, Mother. You always have and always will. I venture to say that your business is doing much better than my practice at this point."

"I tried to give you guidance and you ignored it. When you persevered in having a medical career, I backed you all the way. What did it get me? Grief and heartache, that's all. I found a nice young man for you to marry and you drove poor Geoff away with your selfishness. Then I used my influence to find you a position with a respected physician... You failed in that venture too. And now this, posing naked on the front page. How could you do this to me?"

"You know, Mother, I could use a little support in this matter. You'll not goad me into another comparison of two versions of reality, yours and mine. Now you must excuse me, I'm wanted on the other line." Melissa stabbed the disconnect button, thereby sparing herself from her mother's final words of reproach. She pressed the intercom and asked, "Who is it?"

"Mr. Graber's office on line two."

Graber's secretary answered and, as expected, asked her to hold for a moment. Finally, he came on the line. "Dr. Morrison, I assume that you are calling about the article in the paper."

She suppressed her irritation with the delay, and said, "I'm mortified, Mr. Graber. My alleged malpractice case is spread all over the front page, and the picture, the picture is a cheap shot. They're displaying me as some sort of monster bimbo doctor."

"Do you have any idea where they got the picture?"

Anger welled up from within; she struggled to modulate her voice. "My ex-husband must have given them the picture."

"Why would he do such a thing?"

"Because he's an evil man and wants to hurt me in any way he can. I was sunning myself in the privacy of my patio. I want to sue the paper for libel, slander and anything else you can think of."

"You'll have to prove malicious intent and substantiate damages."

"Damages, hah, that's an understatement. The phone's been ringing off the hook with canceling patients."

Graber soothed, "Dr. Morrison, try to stay focused. Our first priority is to pare this action down to a reasonable amount. Must I remind you again that the plaintiff is asking for $10 million, and your coverage limit per claim is $1 million. Remember, prioritize, prioritize."

The syrup oozing from the receiver was nauseating. She willed firmness into her voice. "I didn't do anything wrong, Mr. Graber.

I'm focusing on the fact that I didn't do anything wrong. I'm still hopeful that we can obtain information that will vindicate me.

Graber sighed, "Dr. Morrison, this is a tremendous uphill battle. Somewhere along the way, you must endeavor to look at the situation realistically."

"Do you believe in my explanation of the situation, Mr. Graber? Do you?"

He soothed, "Of course, of course. By the way, have you contacted George Rucker?"

"I have an appointment with him tomorrow."

"Good, good. Well, I'm due in court. If you come up with any information of significance between now and then, don't hesitate to call."

After the phone clicked in her ear, Melissa said, "Good-bye, weasel."

Graber's admonishment to "look at the situation realistically" chipped more chunks of her confidence away. She forced him out of her mind and sought out Jana's company. She found her busy with the phone, quietly trying to convince a patient not to cancel. The appointment book contained a succession of lined-out entries. This not only signaled a patient who would not be returning but also a patient who would not refer her friends to the office. Jana hung up the phone and crossed out another name, Anne Bellingham. Melissa stared at the lined-out entry and recalled sipping tea in Anne's cozy parlor not so long ago.

The large gaps in the schedule added to Melissa's melancholia. By three p.m., she had seen the third and last patient for the day. She was contemplating leaving for the day when Jana buzzed her. "Mrs. Hauser on line one."

Melissa willed a pleasant tone into her voice. "Hi Katrina, what's up?"

"We got the house already. We are so happy."

"Great."

"*Liebling,* what's wrong. Your voice is so sad."

I guess she missed the morning paper. Well, thank God for small favors. "Nothing, I'm just a bit tired."

Jana entered. Melissa said, "Hold on a second."

Jana said, "Your housekeeper on line two. She's in quite a state."

Melissa bade Katrina goodbye, promising to call back later. She picked up the phone and was assaulted with an incoherent babble, a mélange of Spanish and English. She said, "Ada, slow down. Whatever is the matter?"

"Lady here at house. She look all around. I try to stop her. She say you bad mother."

"I'll be right there."

Standing in Melissa's living room was a skinny study in angles clad in an ill-fitting black dress. "Who are you?" asked Melissa.

The woman thrust a card in her direction. "Anita Grandolfo, Social Services. I'm doing an in-home evaluation and must ask you a few questions, Ms. Morrison."

"It's *Doctor* Morrison, and I must ask you to leave. What right do you have to barge into my home and snoop around?"

"Every right granted by California Law when a child's well-being is at stake."

"Is this related to my ex-husband's custody demand?"

"Most definitely. I spoke with him this morning, and I must tell you I share his concerns regarding the child's welfare."

"There's nothing wrong with my son."

"What about the head injury?"

"He fell in the backyard."

"I see. Where did you have him treated?"

"I took care of it myself."

Grandolfo jotted rapidly in her notebook. "When was the last time you took him to a physician?"

"About a month ago for a routine visit?"

"The physician's name?"

"Look, I've had about enough of this. Kindly leave before I call the police."

"That's a good idea. Your lack of cooperation justifies me requesting removal of the child from the home. I can summon a police officer to assist me in that action. I'd advise you not to challenge my authority. I'm well within my rights as a county officer."

"You better be right in that regard. I'll check."

"I'm sure you will. Now, once again will you furnish with the name of the child's doctor?"

"Kathy Anderson."

"I'll be in contact with her to review records."

"Whatever for?"

"Other signs of battering."

"Are you insinuating that I'd hurt my child."

"Most definitely. I'm going to recommend an independent physical exam for the child in addition to the standard psychiatric evaluations."

"What standard psychiatric evaluations?"

"For the child, you, and your maid."

"Ada is not a maid, she's my housekeeper and Roger's nanny."

"Is she a citizen?"

"She's working on that. For your information, she has a valid green card. What about my ex? Will he be required to undergo a psychiatric evaluation also?"

"Most definitely."

"That ought to be interesting for whoever unbolts his head and looks inside."

Grandolfo shook her head while scribbling in her pad. "The evaluation is not a violent act, just questioning and testing. You obviously have a lot of anger towards Mr. Shackleton. He struck me as a perfect gentleman, and a concerned father."

"Inseminating and fathering are separate entities. Have you asked him how often he visits *my* son?"

"That's one of the issues. He told me that you are openly hostile to him and thwart his attempts at visitation."

Melissa shook her head. "A total lie."

"There're always two sides to every story, Ms. Morrison. According to Mr. Shackleton, you're on the brink of losing your medical license because of extreme negligence and incompetence. I saw the article in the paper, by the way."

Melissa tapped every resource to control her rage. "You obviously have a built-in bias to this situation, Ms. Grandawful—"

The name is Grandolfo."

"Sorry. Do you have any more pertinent questions or are you going to continue with your inflammatory prejudices?"

"Just one more question, and I'll be on my way. How much time is the child under your supervision and how much time with the Mexican maid?"

"I told you, she's a housekeeper and a nanny. She's Salvadorean not Mexican."

"Whatever. Kindly answer my question."

"Ada watches Roger during the day. I'm home with him in the evening and weekends, unless I'm called out for a delivery."

"The Mex—er—housekeeper, does she live here too"

"Most of the time. She has one day off a week."

"Anybody else stay at the residence? Significant other, boyfriend, girlfriend?"

"Absolutely not."

"Well, good day, Ms. Morrison. I'll be in touch."

After Grandolfo departed, Melissa called Wendt's office and queried him about the visit. He informed her that the woman was within her rights.

Melissa said, "You mean to say that she can barge into my home unannounced, pass judgment on me, and threaten to remove Roger from our home?"

"She can. These custody battles can become extremely nasty. Are you sure you want to proceed with this matter?"

"Most definitely."

"We need to discuss this further. How about dinner this evening?"

"I think not." *I'll give the man credit for persistence.* "I can meet at your office."

"Tomorrow morning? I could order in a breakfast."

"I have a commitment—with another attorney—in the morning. Late afternoon would work for me. I must remind you once again to keep our relationship on a professional level."

"You're breaking my heart, Dr. Morrison. Strictly business, then; about four?"

"Four would be fine."

Hanging up, Melissa thought, *Attorneys, they're taking over my life. Tomorrow I have the distinct honor—correction, misfortune— to consult yet another stalwart member of the legal profession. I can hardly wait.*

Chapter Eight

George Rucker's office *was* local; less than two miles from the hospital. Melissa took a seat on a vinyl sofa in his waiting room and selected a magazine. She fully expected to thumb through it and several others before being summoned. To her surprise, he appeared in the doorway. "George Rucker at your service; come on in."

He reminded her of the salesman from whom she bought her first car, the "pre-owned creampuff" that suffered a fatal oil hemorrhage on the freeway two months after the purchase. After she took a seat, he said, "I received a copy of your file from Roach and Graber, spent yesterday evening reviewing it. The major issue here is the lack of any documentation that you desired to admit the patient the day before the incident."

"It disappeared; I definitely documented my desire to admit the patient."

"They sanitized the chart; do it all the time."

"Sanitized?"

"Yes, sanitized. I'm quite familiar with Cliffside and their administrative policies. They play a mean game of hardball... I've defended several Cliffside physicians in similar cases."

"What was their outcome?"

He exuded sincerity. "I'd be a liar if I told you that I was able to prevail for my client in all cases. However, in two cases I did. In one, the charges were dropped. In another, they were reduced to a year of probation."

"What are my chances?"

"Hard to tell, Dr. Morrison. But, trust me, I'll do the best I can for you, the best I can."

Melissa wanted to believe him. She scanned the diplomas on the wall. He attended Westwood Law School, an institution she had never heard of. She then fixed her gaze back in his direction and asked, "The hospital attorney; what do you know about him?"

"Herb Sempres has been with Cliffside since dirt, knows where all the bodies are buried."

"Literally or figuratively?"

"Both."

A wave of fear attacked her. *Dead bodies. There's something evil going on at Cliffside. It's not just about me, and it's not just the IPA. Or maybe this thing is getting to me.*

Rucker interrupted her thoughts. "Let me explain something about the process. The Judicial Review Hearing is conducted in the evening, and each session—typically there are three—lasts three to four hours. During the first session, the hospital will present its case against you. During the second, we present our case. And the last session is a summation. After that, the panel of physicians will deliberate."

"Who sits on this panel?"

"Sic physicians selected from Cliffside's staff. One of them will be an OB/GYN. That person will be the most crucial member of the panel."

"Do I have any say in the selection?"

"Of course. Another key member is the hearing officer."

"Educate me."

"He is an attorney who serves as a referee. He has no vote on the outcome, but in his capacity as a legal expert, has considerable influence on the physicians."

"What happens if I lose at the hearing?"

"Good question. We can appeal to the Cliffside Board of Directors, but they usually rubber-stamp the JRH findings. After that, the case can be taken to our court system."

"Assuming an unfavorable outcome, other than losing my ability to practice at Cliffside, what else could happen?"

"Negative findings will be reported to the National Practitioner Data Bank. The information will become available to all hospitals in the U.S., as well as state medical boards, including the California Medical Board."

"The California Medical Board. What action could they take?"

"Anything from a slap on the wrist to revocation of your license. Of course, you'd be entitled to a hearing before any restriction of your license could be imposed."

She reflected on his words. *A succession of hearings, all leading my career in a downward spiral... Just what I need to cheer me up. Lose this one, prepare for the next one; then lose at that one, ad nauseum. Things definitely seem to be spinning out of control. Could this man stop the steamroller? Maybe I should get a second opinion? Perhaps a more capable attorney could be found elsewhere.*

Despite some lingering doubts, Melissa's overall impression of Rucker was that he was competent in his field. She told herself, *I really don't have the time or energy to travel outside the area for a second opinion. And, his claim to be familiar with the hospital and its attorney is a plus. And, he spent last evening studying my file.* She asked, "Will you take my case, Mr. Rucker?"

"I will, Dr. Morrison. I took the liberty of having my secretary draw up a retainer agreement. Please have a look at it."

She scanned the document. The words "an initial check in the sum of $10,000 leapt off the page. "I—I don't have my checkbook with me, Mr. Rucker."

"Not a problem. You can drop it off in tomorrow's mail."

She left holding the hope that she had not purchased a pre-owned vehicle destined to self-destruct on the freeway. Her medical career was in his hands.

A week later, she was digesting the latest issue of *Obstetrics and Gynecology* when Jana buzzed her. "Mr. Rucker on line two."

It actually was Rucker, not his secretary. Melissa was pleased.

"Dr. Morrison, I've received a list of the proposed panel members. Let me read them off to you. The names were somewhat familiar, all physicians with whom she had a nodding acquaintance. She had no objections until he announced the last name. "They have proposed Dr. Rachel Hornbeak as the OB/GYN on the panel."

"Tell them no way. That woman hates my guts."

"Sempres told me that would be your reaction. Their second offering is a Dr. Morgan Brookhurst."

"Ditto for him. I need to be assured of some degree of impartiality."

"I'll convey your feelings. In addition, I've lodged an objection to their proposed hearing officer. Stan Thornton was an associate of Sempres for a number of years. I've told them he was unacceptable."

"It sounds like they're trying to stack the deck against me."

"I told you they wouldn't play fair. Oh, and one other thing. I found their amended charges to be defective. I offered a continuance, but Sempres assured me he could have everything in order for the hearing. Well, I've got to go. Call me if you have any questions whatsoever."

"I will." *I'm impressed. I think I've found a winner.*

Jana buzzed, "You're having a real legal-eagle day. Mr. Graber's secretary on line one."

Melissa grimaced in dread of another conversation with the man, and paused for a moment before reaching for the phone.

"Dr. Morrison, this is Jennifer, Mr. Graber's secretary."

"Good morning."

Jennifer's voice possessed the solemnity of a funeral director. "I have some bad news to convey… Mr. Graber has suffered a major heart attack."

Despite Melissa's dislike of the man, the news saddened her. She felt a twinge of guilt over her negative thoughts toward him. "I'm sorry to hear that. How is he doing?"

"He's in Cardiac Care at Cliffside. We're hopeful of a good

recovery at this point." The somber tones were replaced by a synthetic cheerfulness. "In any event, I'm calling about the upcoming deposition. Ms. Thatcher will be attending the deposition with you."

Melissa's innate suspicion of the legal profession surfaced. "Is she new with your firm?"

"Yes, but she is well-credentialed."

"What about Mr. Roach?" Jennifer sighed, "His calendar is a disaster, a virtual disaster ever since Mr. Graber's heart attack. Ms. Thatcher needs to be brought up to speed on the case. Would you be able to clear your calendar for a meeting on the morning prior to the deposition?"

"No problem." *The way my calendar looks, I could clear out the entire month.*

"Fine. I'll let Ms. Thatcher know. Good Day."

After she hung up, Melissa added another concern to her pile. She was now being assigned a new, and probably inexperienced, attorney. Despite her dislike of Graber, he had a good reputation for defending physicians involved in malpractice litigation. Hopefully this new attorney would be of the same caliber. Ms. Thatcher—a woman—that was probably a plus. Perhaps a woman would be more sympathetic. Maybe this new attorney would actually believe her. Once again, she successfully willed the gnats of negativity out of her presence. *With my string of bad luck with attorneys, I'm due for something better. Hope springs eternal.*

Chapter Nine

Entering the law office, Melissa once again shooed off an attack from the gnats of negativity. She was somewhat intimidated by the opulent surroundings. Several large sofas and a number of chairs graced the expansive waiting room. They beckoned: come and have a comfortable seat here, but don't stain my pristine surface. At one side of the chamber, a spiral staircase ascended to another entire story, which according to the building directory, was also occupied by the firm. Melissa mused, *No wonder my malpractice premiums are so high, it must cost a bundle to pay the rent and staff this place.* On the wall adjacent to the staircase sat a stunning receptionist. The young woman was perched behind a high desk; she apparently served as the gate-keeper to the inner sanctum. She nodded to Melissa; then retreated back to the telephone. "One moment please... Good morning, Roach and Graber... Just a moment and I'll connect you."

Adjacent to the secretary's rookery was a small table adorned with two silver urns, cups, and saucers. Melissa approached the assemblage. *I could use a cup of coffee.*

A young woman appeared. The combined effect of the sky-blue eyes, the freckled face, and the blond pageboy conveyed the image of a fresh-scrubbed farm girl. She extended her hand. "Hi, you must be Dr. Morrison... I'm Rebecca Thatcher. Please call me Becky."

The gnat swarm materialized. *I don't believe it... Becky Thatcher. She's too young, very sweet... And inexperienced. I bet she's fresh out of law school.*

"My office is down the hallway to our left. Would you care for a cup of coffee?"

"No thank you."

"Right through this door." Becky gestured to a nearby chair. "Have a seat."

Melissa picked up one of the business cards on the desk and stared at it. Becky said, "My parents were big fans of Mark Twain I guess. I considered changing my name when I enrolled in law school but decided to keep it. It's a name that people won't easily forget."

"They sure won't. I understand that you're new with the firm."

Becky leaned forward and whispered, "I am, but don't worry, I'll do my best for you... I did pretty well in law school."

Melissa scanned the wall behind the desk. She noted a diploma from Harvard Law. As she suspected, Becky was in this year's graduating class; however, some accompanying documents suggested that she had made her exit emblazoned with honors and awards.

Becky said, "I'll also have you know that I never, ever lost a case in moot court. Some of those hot-shot guys just hated me."

Melissa felt some of her tension wane; she contemplated teaming up with a young professional woman who probably understood all too well some of Melissa's academic challenges. Melissa typically began relationships in her Ice Maiden mode; however, certain individuals melted that aloofness. Her armor was beginning to soften. Melissa smiled. "I like you, and that's a compliment. I've met a number of attorneys in the past few months; most of my experiences have been negative. I like you though."

"I'll let you in on a secret. I don't like most attorneys either."

Another layer of armor peeled away. "You're new here; that reminds me of the day I started practicing medicine. My first patient and my first lawsuit. That was one memorable day."

"I guess that's as good a place to start as any. Why don't you tell me about it?"

Melissa nodded. "I arrived at the office a half-hour early. I wanted some time to get organized before the patients began arriving."

Melissa entered the waiting room and felt a surge of warmth. She mused, *I've arrived, I've finally arrived. In a few minutes, patients will enter this room and wait for me to tend to their needs. I'm a doctor now with private patients. I wonder who my first patient will be? She'll always be special, that first patient.*

The room was professionally decorated with a feminine flair; a bit ostentatious for Melissa's taste, but nicely done. The overall effect was one of soft warmth. A smiling woman in a pink smock entered the room holding a crystal vase containing a small bouquet of cut flowers. She extended her hand. "Hi, Dr. Morrison, I'm Jana. We met briefly when you interviewed."

"Hi Jana... Looks like we're the only ones here."

"Right." She placed the vase on the coffee table, straightened the adjacent magazines and continued, "Let me show you around. Your consultation room is right down the hall here."

Melissa stifled a gasp. "Wasn't that room occupied by Dr. Evans?"

Jana muttered, "Dr. Evans is no longer with Dr. Hornbeak."

Melissa tensed. "Oh... I thought she was on the verge of a partnership arrangement. What happened?"

"Let's continue the tour." Jana gestured to a doorway. "Next door is the ultrasound room... It doesn't get much use these days."

Melissa examined the machine with approval. It was one of the latest models and of high quality. She averted her smile from the machine to Jana. "Well, I have a special interest in ultrasound. I think we'll be using it more."

Jana tensed. "Have you discussed that with Dr. Hornbeak?"

"No, but—"

"A tech comes two afternoons a week. She does the scans on our private patients. More and more of our patients are from the Cliffside IPA. We have to send them to the hospital for their ultrasound, in the rare instance that we can get an approval. Anyway, the other exam rooms are fairly standard. The colposcope is in that one over there."

After the tour concluded, Jana asked, "How about a cup of coffee?"

"Love one."

Jana fetched two steaming mugs and followed Melissa into her new consultation room. Melissa took a seat and surveyed the chamber; the warm glow returned. *This is my consultation room and my goal of becoming a practicing physician is at hand... Wait a second, Melissa, this room was recently vacated by a physician who two years ago sat at this desk and contemplated her future.* The glow faded, and Melissa found herself staring at the coffee mug. She took a sip. "Good coffee."

Jana smiled. "Thank you. I grind the beans fresh each morning. Dr. Hornbeak considers it an unnecessary extravagance; I consider it a necessity. I'll forsake a lot of things in my life, but I won't forsake a good cup of coffee in the morning, even in these days of austerity."

Melissa sensed that Jana's initial defensive posture was softening; she launched a probe. "Speaking of austerity, my husband is a vice president in the Cliffside IPA. According to him it's a medical utopia at an affordable cost. I really didn't get a chance to discuss the IPA with Dr. Hornbeak during the interview. Can you tell me something about it from the medical perspective?"

Jana wrinkled up her nose. "Austerity takes on a whole new meaning with CIPA; it's bare bones, no frills, basic care. The plan gets so much per life per year."

"Patients are termed 'lives' in the managed care world."

"Right, they used to be called patients, but now they're called lives. The IPA makes money if a patient receives minimal, or better yet, no services for the year. If a patient—er life—requires a major hospitalization, the IPA loses money. The plan relies heavily on family physicians to serve as gatekeepers."

Melissa nodded. "The gatekeeper's role is to keep the life out of the castle."

"You're catching on. They get their money up front, and there's no incentive to do anything extra for the patient."

"They have to take care of pregnancy."

"Yes, but as cheaply as possible. At least our OBs are better off than the gyns. They can deny a hysterectomy but they can't deny a pregnancy."

"I have strong feelings about providing quality, thorough care. La Playa is an affluent area and I've heard that Cliffside Medical Center has the highest of standards."

Jana shrugged. "Only if you are among the rich and famous and have private indemnity insurance. Otherwise you receive medicine for the masses."

"I would think that a hospital in an upscale community such as La Playa wouldn't need to become involved in medicine for the masses."

"Being on the coast has its drawbacks; freeway access is lousy and half the population is fish. That limits their marketing area, and they market heavily to keep their beds filled. More and more of them are being occupied by managed care patients."

"I'd rather have solid middle class patients than the rich and famous anyway."

"The patients are fine; it's the medical services that are limited."

"Well, if a patient of mine needs a procedure, I'll see that she gets it. I'm not afraid to buck the system."

The sound of lumbering footsteps loomed; Rachel appeared in the doorway. "Jana," she bellowed. "So there you are. The goddamm phone's ringing off the hook. What the hell's wrong with you?"

Jana, unruffled by the outburst, replied, "The exchange is still picking up. Sue and Judy are not here yet; I was orienting Dr. Morrison."

"Well, check in with the goddamm exchange and orient her between phone calls."

Melissa forced a smile on her face. "Good morning Dr. Hornbeak."

"Morning," humphed Rachel. She turned on her heel and waddled off.

Melissa sat at her desk, sipped her coffee, and reflected on the wisdom of her decision in joining the practice of Dr. Rachel Hornbeak. *You've done it again, haven't you, girl? From now on, follow your instincts and don't listen to Mother, or Geoff. Her friendly manner during the interview was just a front... Like her waiting room. She swears like a sailor, looks like a water buffalo, and exhibits all the charm of a rattlesnake.*

"Pardon me," said the voice with a smile. Melissa looked up to see Jana standing in the doorway. "You have a new patient, Monica Stewart, an add-on. Left lower quadrant pain of two days duration and spotting." Melissa reached for the chart. "It might be a good idea to get a pregnancy test."

"It's positive."

"Hemoglobin?"

"Thirteen-point-two."

"You're a whiz."

"Thank you. Can I show her in?"

"Sure."

"Oh, I might add, she's a CIPA patient."

Monica entered, surrounded by an aura of toughness; she appeared older than her 23 years. She responded to Melissa's greeting with a grunt, and chewed her gum with gusto while her history was taken. Monica continued to smack and crackle during the pelvic exam. "Does it hurt here?" asked Melissa.

"Nah."

"Here?"

"Nah."

"Here?"

"Ooh, yeah, a little. *Smack.*"

After completing her examination, Melissa stripped off her gloves and said, "I believe that you need to have an ultrasound. Let me check on the arrangements."

Monica sat upward, baring her voluptuous breasts. Apparently proud of her endowments, she made no attempt to draw the gown around them. She thrust her chest forward and asked, "Can I get dressed?"

"Wait just a minute; we'll let you know." Melissa exited the exam room, followed by Jana. When they were out of the patient's range of hearing Melissa said, "I'd sure like to scan her."

"You suspect an ectopic?"

"Right. Based on her symptoms, it might be in her left tube."

"She's an IPA patient; we'll have to get approval and send her to the hospital."

"That's a shame with a perfectly good ultrasound machine right here. How long will the approval take?"

"Best case scenario, a few days. Worst case scenario, never. Only bona fide emergencies can be done stat."

"What if we declare it an emergency?"

Jana shook her head. "Tough to do with this patient's symptoms."

Melissa thrust her chin forward. "I think I'll have a word with Dr. Hornbeak."

"Be careful."

The voice boomed through the closed door. "You ripped me off on the last shipment of oats, buddy boy. You better make up for it this time or your ass is grass... You better!"

Melissa heard the receiver slam down, and knocked. Rachel neglected to turn the volume control down on her vocal chords. "Come in."

"Dr. Hornbeak, I have a patient with a possible ectopic. She's an IPA patient and I understand that I have to get approval for an ultrasound."

Rachel rolled her eyes much like an impatient schoolteacher confronted by a slow student. "Right you are."

"I was wondering if I couldn't do a quick scan on the office machine. I'd sure like to know if she has a gestational sac and have a look at her left adnexa."

"It'd be nice, but you can't. We've got to play by the rules."

Melissa furrowed her brow. "I can't see how—"

"Look, if CIPA finds out that we're doing unauthorized ultrasounds, my ass will be in a sling... Yours too."

"The machine's just sitting there. What if I just do a quick scan and we don't charge for it?"

Rachel shook her head, setting her double chins into motion. "You're just not getting the message. CIPA will yell 'foul' if we start doing free scans. The IPA feeds me a lot of patients. I don't want to antagonize them."

"If that's the case, why not send her to the hospital. I would think that CIPA's budget could handle a medically indicated scan."

Rachel snapped, "What part of the word 'no' don't you understand? We've already been paid for the patient. We'd be spending our own money for the scan. The less we spend on the patient, the more money we keep. Get the picture?"

"I get a picture of bargain basement, poor-quality medical care."

"Right you are, sweetie. It's the only way to play the medical game in today's times and make a profit." She glanced at her watch; then glared. "And time is money; you're wasting my time. And yours. I hope this isn't going to become a routine, running to me with questions with every goddammed patient you see."

Melissa shook her head. "No, it definitely won't."

Melissa strode down the hall to where Jana was standing and said, "Have the patient dress and I'll see her back in my office."

Monica took a seat and asked, "Like, I thought I was gonna—*smack*—get an ultrasound to see if my baby's okay?"

"Unfortunately, you're on the Cliffside IPA. We'll have to get approval."

"Like I ain't no rocket scientist—*smack*—like wasn't that an ultrasound machine in the room next door?"

"It is, but unfortunately, with your insurance plan, we have to get approval and have it done by the hospital."

"What a hassle."

"It is and I'm sorry." Monica whined, "I wanna know if my baby's okay, Doc."

"I do too. The odds are your baby is fine. Also, there's a small chance that you could miscarry."

"Like, cuzza the bleeding?"

"Right, there's also a chance that you might have a tubal pregnancy. That chance is a little higher in your case because you have a history of pelvic infections; your tubes might be damaged."

"Bummer. Won't an ultrasound like tell for sure?"

"Possibly; it depends upon how far along you are. Now here's what we're going to do. I'll submit a request for the ultrasound. I want you to have a blood test for pregnancy called a quantitative beta HCG and a repeat test in three days. We should then be fairly certain if the pregnancy is progressing normally."

"Like, I already know I'm pregnant and like, I hate bein' stuck with needles." She spat her gum out into her hand. "Got any place that I can park this?"

Melissa produced a wastebasket. Monica deposited the wad, retrieved two fresh sticks from her purse and resumed chewing. Melissa replaced the wastebasket underneath her desk and continued, "The blood test for pregnancy will give us a number. The second test will give us another number. If the second number is double the first, the pregnancy is normal."

"Like, it's still a hassle."

"I'm sorry for your inconvenience but it's the only way to diagnose your condition. The lab is right downstairs. I want you to have your blood drawn on the way out. Okay?"

"Yeah."

"I also want to make you aware of the symptoms of a tubal pregnancy. If you experience pain, dizziness, or heavier bleeding, I want you to call me right away."

"Yeah—*smack*—what happens if, like, the pregnancy is in the tube?"

"You'll need surgery."

"Bummer... Bein' cut open."

"Hopefully that won't be necessary."

"It better not!" Her gum smacking intensified as she lost herself in thought. The smacking ceased. "Can you, like save the baby, if that happens?"

"No, all we can hope for is to save the tube for future pregnancies. Here's a request for the blood test and the rest of your prenatal lab work. We'll call you when the approval for the ultrasound comes through and I want to see you back in three days after you've had the second test. Also, I want you to call me right away if you experience an increase in your pain or feel uncomfortable in any other way."

Jana tapped on the door. "You're getting backed up, doctor."

During the next hour, with Jana's capable assistance, Melissa was able to catch up with the heavy patient load; then maintained the pace for the rest of the morning. By one p.m., she finished with the last morning patient. She and Jana were the only ones left in the office. Jana extended a printed sheet. "Monica's quant beta just came through on the computer. It's seven-thousand-three-hundred-and-twenty-six."

"With a value like that we should definitely see a gestational sac." Jana nodded. "The presence of a sac would pretty much rule out an ectopic wouldn't it?"

"Pretty much. Hopefully she can get her scan soon. The result sure came through quickly."

"We're hooked up to the hospital computer... Great for labs and op reports."

"Very efficient, I like that. Say, where can I get a bite to eat around here? I missed breakfast and my stomach's growling."

"Mine too. There's a nice deli down the street."

"Sounds good. Why don't you join me?"

Jana smiled. "I'll check out with the exchange."

They ordered their meal at the counter, walked a short distance to an outdoor dining area, and took a seat at a small corner table. They sat quietly munching on their sandwiches, inhaling the crisp salt-tinged breeze from the nearby ocean. After a while, Jana interrupted the silence. "Your first morning went well. The patients really like you."

"I've got to give most of the credit to you. You anticipated my every need and that of the patients."

"Thanks for the compliment. I think we make a pretty good team."

"We do. How long have you been with Dr. Hornbeak?"

"Three years... It's a record. Most don't last long."

A seagull hopped hopefully toward their table. Melissa threw a bit of bread in its direction. She stared at the seagull for a minute; then deflected her gaze toward Jana. "I can understand why. Does she always talk to you like that?"

"Only when she's upset about something." She chuckled. "Dr. Hornbeak's frequently upset about something. I just ignore it. It really doesn't bother me and I can't afford to lose my job. I've got a kid to support and no husband."

"That's a heavy load."

"It is. Do you have kids?"

"No. My husband isn't ready for children yet and today is the first day of a real job. I need to settle in first."

Jana stared at the horizon. "It's a long road to becoming a doctor. I had those aspirations once... But they're long gone."

"Too bad."

"I got married my first year of college, two months later I missed my period. My husband decided it was too much for him to handle. He did the macho thing and rode off into the sunset."

"A not uncommon scenario. Were you using birth control?"

"He was supposed to be taking care of that... That's what I get for trusting him. I grew up real fast the day he walked out on me."

"Have you thought about furthering your education, it's never too late."

"Too late for me, but not for Sandy."

"Sandy?"

Jana smiled. "My daughter. She's a junior in high school, straight

A student. She's got a good crack at a scholarship. Who knows, we may get a doctor in the family yet."

"So she has an interest."

"Most definitely. Last summer she worked in the office; followed Dr. Evans around like a puppy dog." Jana grimaced.

Melissa's curiosity was piqued with the mention of Dr. Evans. She had formulated a conclusion but needed its confirmation. *Go easy Melissa, if you want an answer.* "Dr. Evans seemed nice when I met her, appeared very competent."

"She's a terrific doc, patients loved her."

Melissa gave her softest look. "One of this morning's patients told me that she left town."

Jana glanced around; she whispered, "This is just between you and me. Promise?"

"Promise."

"She was hopeful of a partnership with Dr. Hornbeak but it never happened. She was fired, given the sack just like any other employee."

"I thought so. I think I've made a mistake in joining her practice. I don't think I'll give her the opportunity to fire me... I'm seriously thinking of quitting. The only reason I joined her in the first place was on the recommendation of my mother and my husband. I should have known."

"Try and give it some time. She's had a rough life, went through a nasty divorce several years ago, and has never gotten over it."

"I bet your divorce was no picnic, either... But it didn't make you mean as a barracuda... Lets change the subject; talking about her will ruin my lunch."

Jana chuckled. "I really like you, Dr. Morrison. You think straight and have a lot of spunk. Besides, you treat me with respect and that means a lot."

"I really like you too, but I won't put up with many more outbursts from that woman."

"Dr. Evans had a short fuse—they locked horns a few times... More than a few. I think you can handle her better. Give it a go for a while. Please?"

"I have my limit too. One might call it a point system. As you know, we've already locked horns once. A few more and I'm out the door."

"Then you'll stay aboard for a while."

"For a while." Melissa glanced at her watch. "We better finish up here, almost time to go."

As Melissa finished her sandwich she reflected on her current situation. She had entered into a contract, and a contract was a commitment. Because she honored her commitments, she *would* give the situation more time. Plus Jana was a real gem; she and Jana would make a great team.

The afternoon passed smoothly; the following day as well. Melissa noted that her patient load was heavier than Rachel's but she didn't mind. The office pace was much more manageable than the hectic tempo of her residency. She felt herself settling into the office routine and some of her initial misgivings began to wane. Midway through her third day in private practice, she noted that Monica Stewart had not kept her ten o'clock appointment; she reached for the phone. "Monica, Dr. Morrison. How are you doing? Any more pain?"

"Nah. It went away. I feel fine."

"I'm glad that you're doing better. You missed your appointment with me this morning. Could you come in this afternoon? I'd like to reexamine you."

"Like, I'm kinda busy. Me and my boy friend are gettin' married."

"Congratulations."

"Like, it's no big thing. We've been livin' together three years."

"Did you get the second blood test?"

"Nah—*smack*—like, the lab chick stuck me five times for the first one. Like, no way was I gonna do that again. Anyways, what about the sonogram?"

"The approval hasn't come through yet, but as soon as I get off the phone with you, I'm going to inquire about it."

Monica's voice rose in a shrill crescendo. "Like, this hassle is bumming me out. Anyways, my boyfriend has good insurance, not a bogus one. We're getting married Saturday. I'm gonna find myself a good doctor that won't hassle me, an *older* doctor with more experience."

"I'm not trying to hassle you, Monica. I'm trying to provide you with the best care I can within the limitations of your insurance."

Monica slammed the receiver.

Becky finished the line on her pad and glanced upward. "It sounds like the managed care concept is a bit frustrating for all involved."

"Right. The patient, the physician, and the hospital."

"Give me some specifics."

"The plan receives a healthcare dollar; administration takes their cut first and distributes the remainder to the healthcare providers: physicians, hospitals, labs, etcetera. The physician receives lower reimbursement than the going rate, ditto for the hospital, the patient receives restricted services. Everybody loses except for the administrators, they skim as much as 35 percent of the healthcare dollar right off the top."

Becky shook her head. "How can they be competitive?"

"In a sense, they aren't. Employers get lulled into signing their employees up with the IPA because it's cheaper than indemnity insurance. The patient—or life—is placated by low deductibles and/or a minimal co-payment. For example, CIPA's co-payment is five dollars per office visit."

"What motivates physicians to join if the fees are reduced?"

"Their patients are being swallowed up by these plans. It comes down to survival in tough times. Cliffside has an innovation, which makes it more attractive to physicians, the bonus system."

"How does it work?"

"Hospital and patient costs are physician generated; the concept is to reward the physician for not admitting patients, and if they are admitted, to discharge them as soon as possible. Bonuses also are accrued for not ordering x-rays or other tests."

"I get the picture. The bonus system, in a sense, gives the physician a piece of the action, just like the administration."

Melissa nodded, "That's the idea. Unfortunately, cost containment has its downside. A perfect example is my ectopic pregnancy case. If I had been able to do an ultrasound exam, the incident never would have occurred."

Becky poised her pen above the pad. "Why don't we continue with your recollection? Was that the last contact with the patient?"

"Yes. Two weeks later I got a call from an irate colleague."

The voice blasted through the receiver. "Dr. Morrison, this is Dr. Brookhurst. I have a former patient of yours here in the ER, Monica Stewart."

"I suspected an ectopic, but she failed to return for follow-up. She told me that she was going on her husband's insurance and would be changing physicians."

The voice dripped with sarcasm. "Well, she has changed physicians. In addition, she's got a hemoperitoneum, *doctor*, most likely from a ruptured ectopic. I'm pumping some blood into her and taking her to the OR. Did you bother to do any lab work on her?"

"She had a quant beta of seven-thousand-and-something."

"Ultrasound?"

"We didn't do one. She was an IPA patient and we needed approval."

"You could have made the diagnosis two weeks ago if you'd bothered to do one, doctor. Sheesh, ghetto medicine at it's finest."
Click.

Becky continued writing while she spoke. "Did you talk to Dr. Brookhurst after the surgery?"

"Yes, after half a dozen phone calls. He was rude and judgmental. He did a left salpingectomy."

"Removal of the tube?"

"Right. Her attorney alleged that the tube could have been saved if the surgery had been done earlier."

"Could it?"

"Possibly, but unlikely. According to the op report, she had extensive PID and severely damaged tubes."

"PID?"

"Sorry, pelvic inflammatory disease. Her tubes were scarred from previous pelvic infections."

"I see. Does hemoperitoneum refer to internal bleeding?"

"Right. The tube ruptured and the patient bled internally."

"How was the patient's recovery?"

"Fine, just fine... Until she developed hepatitis from the blood transfusions. She was a pretty sick cookie for a while."

"What was the final outcome?"

"She eventually made a full recovery... The case resulted in a $250,000 settlement."

"Not a good start for your first patient in private practice."

"No, not a good start."

"Now, before we discuss the current litigation why don't you fill me in on a few details. Your marriage failed sometime after the first case."

Melissa sensed that Becky was probing into the plaintiff attorney's allegation that she was stressed out and indecisive as a result of personal problems. The question jabbed; however, she controlled her annoyance with the realization that all aspects of her personal life were under scrutiny, and it was essential for Becky to be apprised of them. Little Casper came to mind and evoked a faint smile as she replied, "Because of a dog and a diaphragm."

"A dog and a diaphragm?'

"Right, a dog and a diaphragm. I bought a puppy shortly after we were married... I came home from work one day to find that Casper had chewed up my diaphragm. Maybe he mistook it for a miniature Frisbee."

"A miniature Frisbee?"

"Casper loves to play Frisbee. Anyway, getting back to my story, I wasn't that concerned. It wasn't getting much use anyway."

Becky looked up from her notes. "Give me a time reference?"

"I had been in practice with Dr. Hornbeak for about six months. This would place the event approximately two years in the past. Geoff came home at one a.m., woke me up. He had gotten bombed again. His usual custom was to hit the bed snoring, but not this time. He made an amorous advance. I protested, told him Casper had chewed up my diaphragm and this was my ovulation time. He's very strong; I finally gave in to him."

"So that was the end of your marriage?"

"The beginning of the end. The next morning, he was very sweet and apologetic."

Geoff soothed, "I'm sorry, princess. I had a bit too much to drink."

Melissa replied acidly, "It's not the first time, and I'm sure it won't be the last. This is the second time you've raped me."

"Aw come on, Miss, we're married. It wasn't a rape."

"It was; it definitely was. You didn't hurt me like you did on our wedding night, but it was still rape in my book."

He gazed into her eyes and placed his arms on her shoulders. "I'm really sorry. I've got a lot of business pressures right now."

She tensed and drew back, forcing the removal of his arms. "That's no excuse to get drunk and attack me like an animal. Now I'm going to be sick all day."

"Are you sick now?"

"No, but I will be after I go to the office and take the morning after pill. I don't think either of us is prepared for an unplanned pregnancy."

"Isn't that hormones?"

"Correct you are."

"I thought you couldn't take them because of that blood clotting problem you had."

"The risk is small, less risky than being pregnant."

He placed his arms around her. She tensed, but did not pull away. He said, "I'm awful sorry, Honey. You know, if you are pregnant, I think we can manage. What do you say? If it happens, it was meant to be."

She willed the tautness from her body, turned and stared into his eyes, looking for signs of insincerity. There were none. She smiled faintly. "I want children, but are you sure that's what you want?"

"Damn sure, Honey; damn sure."

A primitive maternal instinct welled up, an instinct that overruled her skepticism.

Becky handed Melissa a Kleenex and said, "A pregnancy arose out of that evening."

"It did."

"What was Geoff's reaction?"

Melissa blew her nose. "I planned a special dinner, complete with a chilled bottle of sparkling grape juice. I left word for Geoff to come home early if possible. He didn't. He finally rolled in at 11..."

Melissa sat up on the couch and gave Geoff a visual strafing. "Where have you been?"

His liquor-laden breath accosted her pregnant nose. "Out with the guys."

"Did you get my message?"

He nodded, with a tinge of sheepishness. "Yeah."

"Why didn't you come home?"

"I was afraid you might have bad news."

"It's not bad news, Geoff. I'm pregnant. We're going to have a baby."

He shook his head and frowned. "To me that's bad news. I don't think I'm ready for fatherhood."

"It's a little late to change your mind isn't it?" He gave her that hateful smirk. "You often repeat the quote, 'It's a woman's prerogative to change her mind.' Well, it's a man's prerogative too, Miss. Go have an abortion."

The last vestige of love and any other positive emotion toward Geoff vanished as she reared up and slapped him. "You bastard. You know my feelings about abortion."

He clenched his fist; then returned it to his side. "Well Miss, the choice is yours. Have an abortion or I'm walking out."

"I'll help you pack in the morning. You can use the couch tonight."

Becky shook her head. "What a loser... After your son was born, did he come around, show interest in the child?"

"Somewhere between slim and none. Until recently. He's suing me for full custody."

"Why the change?"

"As far as I can tell, just to push my buttons."

"Has he?"

Melissa reached for a tissue. "Yes."

"Being a single mom and a physician must be rough."

"It is, but until this custody thing my family life has been great. I'm managing just fine without Geoff... Actually Geoff's departure simplified my life. My son, Roger, is a delight and I have a wonderful housekeeper, Ada." Melissa smiled. "My family is made up of little Roger, Ada, and an Italian Greyhound. In addition, I'm blessed with two wonderful friends, Roger and Katrina Hauser. They're like grandparents to little Roger, and parents to me."

"Sounds like a nice family unit to me. Well, we need to get back on track. You mentioned that you began private practice with Dr. Hornbeak. Are you associated with any other physicians at present?"

"No, I'm in solo practice."

"How long were you associated with Dr. Hornbeak?"

"Two years, I lasted—er—it lasted two years. My partnership meeting turned out to be a boot out the door. I had a bad feeling about that meeting. I pretty much knew what was coming."

Rachel reclined back in her chair and placed her hands behind her neck. One of the buttons on her blouse popped from the added strain and plinked onto her desk. She pretended not to notice and returned her chair to the upright position.

Melissa controlled a chuckle by deflecting her gaze toward a picture of Golden Boy displayed prominently on the desk. The portrait was a new addition since the last time Melissa had been invited into Rachel's sanctuary. She couldn't remember the last occasion; it had to have been more than a year ago.

Rachel stared at the button for a moment and then said, "Well, Melissa, it's decision time. Our two-year anniversary is at hand. What do you think of our association at this point?"

Melissa hoped she was concealing the humorous aspect of the popped button. She stifled a grin when she recalled the games of tiddly-winks she had played as a child. "The practice is growing and I enjoy my work. In a way, even though we are in practice together, I don't think we really know each other very well, nor have we explored our common interests."

"Common interests." Rachel hammered her desk with a clenched fist. "We have damn few common interests, except for the fact that we both got rid of sonofabitch husbands and simplified our lives. Mine left me with a horse and yours a kid. Horses are less trouble, much less trouble. I didn't have to take a week off from work to take care of a sick horse."

The combined effect of Rachel's fist striking the desk and the verbal jab created a disconcerting tension. Melissa strove to conceal her disquietude and replied calmly, "Roger had no one else to care for him. It was my vacation for that year."

A reddish hue bloomed on Rachel's corpulent face. "An unplanned vacation, and a damned inconvenience. I worked my ass off that week."

Melissa nodded. "I know, and I'm sorry it inconvenienced you. The way I look at it, that's the advantage of a partnership... Security when family emergencies occur."

Rachel yelled, "Listen girlie, when I was a resident, and while building this practice up from nothing, I didn't have the luxury of time off for family emergencies. I was the only woman in my training program, and I was treated like shit... I bet your program was mostly women."

"Yes, but—"

"A sweet young thing like you wouldn't have made it when I trained. You couldn't have handled the flack from all the bastards in the program, professors, attendings, fellow residents. Wanna know how much time I got off? I got one damned week of vacation a year. That was it. Any additional time off was unheard of especially for a woman. Anyway, my asshole husband gave me the clap. I felt like hell and knew something was wrong, but couldn't get the time off to have it checked. The bastards accused me of malingering when I passed out while on call at three in the morning."

"How terrible."

"Oh my, my, yes; very terrible. I can't have kids because of that, but I don't give a shit. Who the hell wants kids?"

"I'm so sorry," said Melissa. "Today's training programs are more humanitarian, and there is more acceptance of women. The misadventure you experienced wouldn't occur today. Your diagnosis would have been made earlier."

"Speaking of prompt diagnoses, you screwed up on your first patient. Missed an ectopic and got your ass sued."

Melissa's tolerance was spent. She could not bear any more verbal abuse. "I get the drift of this conversation, Rachel. This isn't a partnership meeting, it's a firing."

Rachel snarled, "goddamm right it is. You're outta here, babe. Don't let the door hit you on the ass on your way out."

Melissa stared at her calmly. "I would like the opportunity to take the charts of the patients that I accrued since I joined you."

The redness intensified on Rachel's face. She reared up, popping a second button, and roared, "They're my patients now, not yours, every goddamm one of em. Now get out!"

Rachel followed her into the hallway.

Melissa turned and said, "I'll just gather my certificates from the wall and leave. Don't worry, I won't steal anything."

Jana and the rest of the staff looked on with stunned silence.

"What the hell are you standing around and gawking for?" snapped Rachel. "Get your asses back to work."

After collecting her personal items, Melissa returned to the front office. Rachel's imperious presence prevented her from doing anything but muttering a simple good-bye to Jana and the others. Rachel hurled a final insult with the demand of her key to the office. Melissa contemplated chucking it at her; however, she maintained control, removed the key from the ring and placed it on the counter.

Arriving home, Melissa allowed Roger's cheerfulness to distract her from her concerns. All along she suspected that a partnership with Rachel would never become a reality. The shock of the meeting waned, and was replaced with relief. Now that their relationship was terminated, she could make plans to go forward in her medical career, a career not encumbered with the overbearing Rachel.

After dinner, she tucked Roger into his crib, read him a story, and tiptoed out of the room. The doorbell rang; Roger stirred, but did not awaken. Melissa hurried to the entrance before the bell could ring a second time. She opened the door to Jana. "I hope I'm not intruding."

Melissa shook her head. "Not at all; come on in. Would you like a cup of tea?"

"Love one."

"Make yourself comfortable, I'll put the kettle on."

When Melissa returned, Jana said, "I quit my job."

"You didn't! Was it because of what happened today?"

"Because of everything. Today was the last straw. I told her that she was the bitch of the universe and quit. I think Sue is going to quit... Brenda as well."

"What are you going to do?"

"I figured that you'd need a good medical assistant."

"I do, but I haven't sorted out what I'm going to do yet. I have no patients and, even if I did, no place to see them."

"You do have patients."

"No I don't. Rachel has custody of all the records. If my patients inquire about my whereabouts, I'm sure she'll tell them that I left town."

Jana extended a thick Manila envelope. "That she will, but I have a complete listing of all your patients. As soon as you locate an office, I'll begin calling them."

"But how?"

"I knew this was coming. I began this little project a month ago. Given the choice, the patients will pick you, I'm sure of it."

"All along, I was skeptical about a partnership. I guess I just didn't want to accept the obvious, plus the last few months have been hectic."

"Boy, that's an understatement. You took all that extra night call while the witch took off doing lord knows what."

"In addition to extracting the last pound of flesh out of me, she kept me too busy to look for another opportunity." Melissa thumbed through the typed list of names and was impressed by the graphic representation of two years in private practice. She was interrupted by the whistling of the teakettle and rose to attend to it.

After pouring the tea, Melissa said, "I can't thank you enough, you're a lifesaver."

Jana nodded. "A lifesaver for both of us. I'm so happy to be rid of that shrew." She raised her teacup. "Here's to the burgeoning practice of Dr. Melissa Morrison."

Melissa raised her cup. "Here's to the partnership of Melissa and Jana. We're going to do it, the two of us."

Jana took a sip of tea and grimaced.

"What's wrong?" asked Melissa. "Something wrong with the tea?"

"The tea's fine. I hurt my arm today."

"How?"

Jana rolled up her sleeve, exposing a purple bruise.

"That looks nasty; how did it happen?"

"When I told Rachel I was quitting, she chucked a medical dictionary at me."

"What a bitch!"

"What a bitch!" exclaimed Becky, turning her legal pad to a fresh page. "It sounds like Jana is a real gem."

"That's for sure. I owe much of my success to her. It was a little rough at first, but the practice thrived."

"You continued on with the Cliffside IPA?"

"Rachel did her utmost to kick me out—she's their medical director—but I persevered. I did notice that I received mainly problem patients and OBs in their third trimester."

"The last three months. I would think that would mean less work for you than seeing a patient all the way through."

"Not really. Most of the visits are in the last trimester, and labor and delivery is the most significant part of OB care. I much prefer to see a patient early-on. It's better for the patient and the physician. The reason I received mainly third trimester referrals is a monetary issue. The IPA structures their physician reimbursement by trimester. The reimbursement is much less for patients first seen in the last three months."

"But you did well despite the types of patients referred to you?"

"Yes. In addition to the managed care patients, I drew a large number of women from the private sector, more than when I was with Rachel."

"Then, up until the Sanders case, the practice thrived."

"It did well. I managed to pay off my student loans and accrue a nest egg—a nest egg that has kept me from going under—at least for the time being. Then, Vicky Sanders came to my office, and everything went to hell in a hand-basket."

Chapter 10

"You have a new patient," said Jana. "An IPA patient."

"Third trimester?" asked Melissa.

Jana chuckled. "You must be psychic. She's due in six weeks, complains of a headache and an upset stomach."

"Urine dip stick?"

"Trace protein; negative glucose."

"Blood pressure?"

"One-thirty-two over eighty-four. Can I show her in?"

A flood of memories hit Melissa as Vicky Sanders entered; their friendship spanned kindergarten through high school. Melissa left home to attend UCLA, and Vicky enrolled in the local city college. While there, she met and fell in love with an intense young man, Jim Talley. After a brief engagement, they married and left to do missionary work somewhere in Africa. She was no longer Vicky Talley. That concerned Melissa; however, of more concern was Vicky's appearance. Her eyes lacked the bright sparkle that Melissa remembered so well. Her pregnant abdomen stuck straight out, contrasting sharply with her gaunt features. All of her energy was sapped by the developing baby within.

Vicky brightened briefly at the recognition of an old friend; she appeared equally surprised at the unexpected reunion. "Wow, you're a doctor now... *My* doctor. I thought the name was a coincidence... You were going into real estate."

"That was Mother's plan, not mine."

"Good for you. It took some spunk to buck her."

"Spunk that you gave me."

"Being one of five kids gives that to you I guess."

"Gosh, it's been years since I heard from you."

"A lot has happened. I—I lost Jim three years ago… As of next Saturday." Tears welled up. "He was killed in a plane crash, shot down by militant rebels... If the girls hadn't been sick with the flu, we'd have been with him."

Melissa handed her a box of tissues. "I'm so sorry."

After dabbing her face, Vicky said, "I was blessed during the time I had with him. And God blessed me with two beautiful children. Melissa will be eight next month, and Mandy is five-and-a-half."

"You've remarried."

"To a plumber. What do you think about that?"

"Just like your dad. That's fine, just fine."

"I've been blessed again with Ben."

"Are you here to stay?"

"Yes. I returned shortly after laying Jim to rest."

"Why didn't you call?"

"I called your mom's office a number of times, and asked for your number. I was told that she was with a client and would return the call. She never did. Funny thing, several times I could have sworn it was your mother who answered the phone."

Melissa hoped her anger was not visible. *She often does answer the phone. She never approved of Vicky, the plumber's daughter, but that's no reason to act that way. If Mother had bothered to get to know Vicky and her family, she would have realized what gems they were.* She asked, "How are your parents?"

"Doing great. Dad sold his business and they moved to a ranch in Montana. I stayed with them when I got back. They helped me heal… And I met Ben through them, he bought Dad's business."

The conversation had tired Vicky further. She slumped back into the chair. Melissa returned to her role as an obstetrician and asked, "Have you been seeing a physician during this pregnancy?"

Vicky's voice lacked inflection. "Yes. Until I quit my job and went on my husband's insurance. He belongs to this Cliffside thing, and let me tell you, it's been a real ordeal to get to see you. It's taken more than two months.

If mother had the common courtesy to give her my number, I would have gotten her in much sooner. "Who was your doctor?"

"You probably know him, Dr. Brookhurst."

"Yes, I know him. You're not feeling well, are you?"

"I'm exhausted, got this nasty headache and my stomach hurts. I never felt like this with my other pregnancies."

"Your blood pressure is up just a little. Do you recall what it was in Dr. Brookhurst's office?"

"I don't know... Normal, I guess."

"I'll check on that. Jana will show you into an exam room and I'll be with you in a minute."

At the conclusion of the exam, Melissa asked Vicky to sit back up on the table. She tapped Vicky's knee with a reflex hammer and remarked, "Your reflexes are normal, that's good. I'll see you back in my office when you're dressed."

Melissa returned to her consultation room and dialed Brookhurst's number. "This is Dr. Morrison. Could I speak to Dr. Brookhurst?"

"He's with a patient. Can I help?"

"I have a patient in my office, Vicky Sanders. She transferred to my care from Dr. Brookhurst. I wonder if you could pull her chart and tell me what her blood pressure readings were?"

"Just a minute."

Finally, the woman came back on the line. "I'm sorry, Dr. Brookhurst will not release any information until he receives written authorization."

Melissa, realizing that the woman was just following instructions, curbed expressing her annoyance. "I'll fax you an authorization. Could you fax back her prenatal record? The patient is here in the office, and I need those records stat."

"I will."

As she hung up the phone, Vicky took a seat. Melissa turned

in her direction. "I was just on the phone with Dr. Brookhurst's office. They're going to fax over your records. You'll need to sign a release."

Vicky nodded. Melissa continued, "I think you may be developing PIH, pregnancy-induced hypertension. It's a condition commonly referred to as toxemia."

"Hypertension… That means high blood pressure, doesn't it? Is my blood pressure high?"

"It's not high for many individuals, but it may be high for you. Also, I'd like you to go to the hospital for some laboratory tests and a non-stress test."

Vicky's head snapped upward. "Will I have to stay there?"

"Not necessarily. I just want to be sure that you and the baby are okay."

"I don't want to go to the hospital. I don't feel well, just want to go home and lie down."

"I know you don't feel well; that's why I want you to go to the hospital and have some tests… Okay?"

"Okay."

"I'll meet you there in a few hours."

After the last patient for the day left the office, Melissa asked Jana again if the records had been faxed from Brookhurst's office.

"Not yet," she replied.

Melissa dialed Brookhurst's number. His answering service responded. "They've left for the day?"

"Could you reach Dr. Brookhurst for me?"

"He's signed out to Dr. Claypool."

"I have a question that Dr. Claypool will not be able to help me with. Could you try Dr. Brookhurst and have him call me at the Cliffside LDR? It's important."

After receiving an assurance from the woman that she would make a concerted effort to contact Brookhurst, Melissa concluded that his behavior was running true to form. Brookhurst was one of those individuals who plodded through life accompanied by his own private rain cloud. His practice was not successful because he valued his time off over his availability to his patients. He was not a member of CIPA because he chose not to be. The meager reimbursement a physician received for IPA patients demanded a high volume and long hours. The sour grapes that Brookhurst picked were the harvest of his laziness and lack of ambition. Melissa moved Brookhurst up several notches on her "losers list" and left for the hospital.

As usual, the Cliffside LDR floor was abuzz with activity. The hallway was flanked with doorways to chambers, decorated in a country inn motif. Each room contained a bed that could accommodate the laboring patient and convert to a delivery table. Opposite the bed, was an isolette, the tiny bed symbolizing the ultimate purpose of the room. The chamber contained a fetal monitor tucked in an end table. The equipment necessary to assist in the labor and delivery process—available for retrieval at a moment's notice—was hidden in several decorative wooden cabinets.

A lusty cry followed by whoops of joy emanated from one of the rooms. The newborn cry always brought a smile to her face every time she heard it. She paused at the doorway for a second to enjoy this pleasurable sensation; then her thoughts turned to her patient. Although Vicky was not in labor, her evaluation was taking place in one of the LDRs. She entered Vicky's room and asked, "How are you feeling?"

Her faint reply lacked conviction. "A little better."

Melissa retrieved a folded pile from the bin beneath the fetal monitor and thumbed through it. She smiled at Vicky. "Your baby looks good on the monitor."

"Fine. Can I go home now? *Please?*"

"Let me check on the lab results, and I'll get back to you."

Melissa took a seat at the Nurses' Station. Vicky's nurse, Sarah, placed a pile of computer printouts on the counter. Melissa scrutinized the information; she turned to Sarah and said, "These tests are a bit worrisome. Her liver enzymes are a bit high, and her platelets are a little low. I suspect she's an early PIH. I want to admit her."

"She's an IPA patient, we'll have to get approval from Utilization."

"I know. Could you give Bridget a call for me?"

Bridget Middlemas, R.N., was called "Middlemouse" frequently behind her back and sometimes to her face. The diminutive woman was constantly treading on the demilitarized zone between irate physicians who requested hospital services for their patients and the administrators of CIPA whose priority was to contain healthcare costs. Bridget arrived at the LDR promptly, realigned her glasses on her ski slope of a nose and myopically scanned Vicky's chart. She shook her head. "I'm sorry, Dr. Morrison, she doesn't meet the criteria for admission with PIH at this point." She pointed to the chart notation, which indicated two previous full term pregnancies. "Look, she's a multip. PIH is mainly a problem with first pregnancies, primagravidas."

"True, but this is a pregnancy with a new husband. That places her risk right up there with the primigravidas."

"It does... But she doesn't have hypertension."

"She's a small woman and this BP may be a significant change for her."

"What were her prior BPs?"

"She just transferred to my care. Her previous care was with Dr. Brookhurst. I've attempted to obtain that information, but it's unavailable at present."

"Too bad."

"Isn't it. Look, I know you have to follow the IPA guidelines, but I feel strongly that she should be admitted. I won't give up until I talk to your superior."

"I thought you'd say that. I really wish you wouldn't." She screwed up her face and cringed. "He'll yell at me for not handling the situation. I can't stand him yelling at me."

"I know that you must adhere to your guidelines. I'm doing this all on my own. I'm concerned about this patient and I intend to be her advocate. Ignore him if he yells at you."

Middlemas shook her head. "I can't. I just can't."

The Cliffside IPA was housed in the medical office building adjacent to the hospital. Melissa took a seat in the anteroom and thumbed through a stack of propaganda material lauding the innumerable benefits of the Cliffside IPA. Before she lost interest in comparing reality with glossy hyperbole, Geoff's secretary ushered her into his spacious accommodations.

He sat reclined back in his chair, his lizard shoes propped up on a large ebony desk. He was gazing at a detailed Ferrari model, prominently displayed on one corner of the desk.

Melissa said, "Am I interrupting something?"

He averted his eyes and smirked. "Well, Miss, what a surprise. What can I do for you?"

"I have a patient I'd like to admit, even though she doesn't exactly meet—"

Geoff shook his head, widened his smirk. "Miss, we have an RN to make those decisions. Did you talk to her before barging in here?"

"I did, but according to her guidelines, she couldn't authorize an admission."

"That's what guidelines are for. That stupid little mouse, I'm going to give her another talking-to."

"Leave her out of it. It was entirely my decision to come here. Bridget is an RN but I'm a physician. Doesn't that count for something?"

His tone became even more condescending. "Of course it does. However, need I remind you that those guidelines were developed by physicians, your colleagues, I might add. These guidelines strike a balance between cost containment and medical necessity."

"This patient really worries me. I suspect that she's on the verge of a serious illness, PIH."

"Let's cut to the chase here. Does she have it by the criteria or doesn't she?"

"I'm awaiting some prior BP values. When they arrive, my guess is that she'll meet the criteria."

He placed his hands behind his neck, reclining even further backward. Melissa was hopeful that gravity would prevail, dumping him on his plush carpeting.

He leaned forward a bit. "Well, my guess is when you get them and if she meets the criteria, we'll admit her, not before. We cannot admit a patient because of your emotional feelings. This is a hospital, not a hotel, and not a charity."

"I was afraid that that would be your response. You always were a jerk." She gave him a pseudo-smile. "Tell me, how's the job here working out? Are you keeping out of trouble?"

His smirk widened into a grin. "Most definitely. Things are on the upswing for me." He removed his feet from the desk, leaned forward with an aura of confidentiality and said, "Be sure to catch the business section of tomorrow's paper... Now I have work to do. Be a good little Miss, trot back across the street and send the patient home."

"Damn you, Geoff. I'll discharge the patient, but I will do two things. First I'll write a note in the chart that I disagree with the decision not to hospitalize, and I'll dictate a discharge summary to that effect. If you are going to make medical decisions, you must accept the responsibility for them."

"My, my, my. Little Miss Crusader Rabbit is becoming a thorn in the side of efficient cost-effective care. I sit on the physician review board now. Your CIPA membership comes up for scrutiny soon. It doesn't pay to be on my bad side."

"You don't have a good side, Geoff, just a bad side and a worse side." She slammed the door on her way out.

Melissa took a seat at Vicky's bedside. She thought back on past conversations with Dr. Hauser. He had practiced medicine in an era when the doctor's decision was the law and challenged by no one. Medical decisions were now made by a jerk with the shoes, and the medical logic, of a lizard. She said, "Vicky, I think you are in the early stages of PIH, or toxemia. Unfortunately, your condition doesn't qualify for admission at this point. Therefore, we must do the next best thing. I want you to go home and go to bed. Can you do that?"

"Uh huh."

"Do you have help at home?"

"Ben... And my little Melissa, she's mature beyond her years."

"I can't wait to meet Ben and your children. I might mention that they're welcome to accompany you on your office visits."

"That's nice."

"I want to recheck you in the office tomorrow morning. Call at nine and set up an appointment. Also, if your headache increases, you see spots before your eyes, experience dizzy spells, or feel bad for any other reason, I want you to call me right away."

"Okay."

After dinner, Melissa pored through her collection of scrapbooks and annuals. Despite Grace's repeated attempts to thwart a relationship with a girl from a family "beneath our station," Vicky and Melissa had shared many good moments. Melissa enjoyed her visits to Vicky's home. If given the opportunity, Melissa would have moved into the love-filled dwelling; thus escaping the lackluster environment that prevailed in the Morrison house. During dinner at Vicky's home, each child in turn was encouraged to recount the events of his or her day. Vicky's parents listened with genuine interest to every detail. After dinner, the entire family participated in doing up the dishes. Then it was game time, Monopoly being a favorite. Camaraderie prevailed over capitalism in the game; winning or losing was of little consequence. At Melissa's home, when her father was alive, he made gentle probes during dinner into how Melissa and Ricky's day had gone. Grace barely listened to them; then promptly steered the conversation back to her real-life Monopoly Game in the world of real estate. Monologues such as "the sweetheart deal I closed on Bay View Drive," and "that bastard Lathrop stole my sale," dominated the conversation.

When Melissa lost her father, Vicky and her family were a great comfort. In an attempt to boost her spirits, they gave her a puppy. Grace's approval of Happy was even less than it was of the plumber's family. A few weeks after receiving the gift, Melissa returned home from school to find Happy gone. Grace "got rid of the miserable cur." Melissa never knew by what means. The puppy disappeared the day after he had soiled the carpeting for the second time.

Vicky's gaunt features haunted Melissa as she attempted sleep. Despite sleeping fitfully, the optimism that comes with the dawning of a new day mellowed her worry. She sipped her coffee and engrossed herself in the morning paper. Melissa rarely read the business section; however midway through her scanning, she recalled Geoff's comments and turned to that section. His picture was on the first page. It was a small article at the bottom of the first page, but page one nevertheless. She gasped when she read the headline: GEOFFREY SHACKLETON NAMED CEO OF CLIFFSIDE IPA. Below the headline was a sub-head: Bruce Wickerstrom Resigns amid Allegations of Diminishing Profits and Mismanagement. The article went on to state that Shackleton also was assuming the duties of Director of Media Relations for the hospital.

Ada responded to Melissa's gasp. *"Que?"*

"Geoff's now in charge of the IPA."

"Que?"

"Sorry Ada, he's the new honcho of Cliffside IPA, it's an insurance plan. It says here that he's going to turn the plan around and make it profitable—hah—I wish him good luck." Melissa chuckled. "Maybe he can turn it around; the man's head is screwed on backwards."

Ada gasped, "His head is on backwards?"

"Not really, just making a joke."

"Si. You better finish your coffee and go, you be late."

On her drive to the hospital, Melissa engaged in a private bet with herself. *I wonder how long Geoff will survive as captain of the Good Ship CIPA. My guess is less than six months—yes, less than six months before the captain is keel-hauled and fed to the sharks. How much do you want to wager, girl? Ten million?* Upon entering the office, she presented the business section to Jana. After digesting the article, Jana shook her head. "Do you think he can handle the position?"

"I doubt it. I'm not really the vindictive type, but I hope he goes down in flames... I'll enjoy that."

"I bet you will."

"Say, has Vicky Sanders called to make her appointment?"

"No. Do you want me to give her a call?"

"It's early yet. Give it an hour or so. She might be sleeping; she needs her rest."

Jana traced her finger down the appointment book. "Your morning is heavily booked. Is the afternoon okay?"

"I'm worried about her. Work her into the morning schedule."

"Will do. By the way, we haven't received the records from Dr. Brookhurst as yet. I'll give them another try."

Later that morning, Jana approached her. "There's no answer at her home."

"Her husband's work number?"

"Don't have one... Her registration form is incomplete, she overlooked about half the questions."

Another sign that she's ill. "Keep trying. I stressed to her that she should rest in bed. I wonder where she can be."

"I'll keep trying."

"Fine. I've got to run home and check Roger over the lunch hour. Ada called and said he's tugging at his ear again, might be another infection."

Melissa's lunch break was absorbed by a trip home to check on Roger, leaving no time for any other activity. Upon her return, she hastened to the appointment book and noted that Vicky's name was not present. Jana appeared in the corridor. "There's still no answer at Vicky's residence, but we finally got her records."

Melissa thumbed through the information. "Hmm, just as I

suspected, her last BP in Brookhurst's office was ninety over sixty. She does have a significant change. Try her again?"

Jana replaced the receiver a few moments later. "Still no answer."

A steady flow of afternoon patients distracted Melissa from her concern. After the last one left her office, she tried the number one last time; then announced to Jana, "I'm going to stop by her house."

Melissa turned off the boulevard and Vicky's street came into view. She pulled over in response to the wail of a siren; a paramedic vehicle sped by in the opposite direction. Apprehension erupted. She pulled up in front of Vicky's house and sped toward the door. There was no answer. She raced next door and rang the bell. A woman answered. Behind her were two young girls. The eldest bore an incredible resemblance to Vicky as a child. Melissa said, "I'm Dr. Morrison. Vicky Sanders is a patient of mine and I came by to check on her."

"Well, she sure needs a doctor. They just took her to the hospital. She had a fit. Lucky I was home to take the children."

"No!" shouted Melissa. She raced back to her car.

Three blocks from the hospital, her pager fired off. She recognized the number in the display: Cliffside Emergency Room. She slowed for a red light, scanned quickly for cross traffic, and seeing none, pressed the accelerator again.

Most of the ER staff was huddled around Vicky. Melissa spotted Dan Hawkins, one of the ER physicians, and asked, "How is she?"

"Apparently she had a seizure at home, appears post-ictal."

"BP?"

"One-ninety over one-thirty."

"Four grams of mag sulfate and five milligrams of Apresoline, IV stat," shouted Melissa. "How's the baby?" A nurse replied, "FHT is ninety with the Doppler, we don't have a fetal monitor down here."

"As soon as the mag is hung, let's get her upstairs."

The medication was promptly administered, and the gurney was propelled to the LDR. Three minutes of fetal monitoring was all that was required to confirm Melissa's suspicion. Vicky's baby was dying inside her uterus.

"We need to do a stat section," said Melissa. "Who's in the house?"

"Dr. Brookhurst's around," replied the nurse.

"Anybody else?"

"No."

"Then get Brookhurst."

"He's not an IPA doc—"

"Get him," snapped Melissa. "We'll need a neonatologist, who's on call?"

"Dr. Linsey. I'll page her."

Melissa was pleased that Tara Linsey would be attending to the premature newborn. In addition to being an excellent neonatologist, Tara was the only physician on Cliffside's staff with whom Melissa had formed a close bond. Like Melissa, Tara was discouraged from a medical career by her parents; however, once she entered medical school, her parents fully supported her decision. Another positive aspect of Tara's life that was missing in Melissa's was that Tara was happily married to a terrific guy.

A good barometer of an efficient surgical team is the time it takes to do a crash section. Vicky was given a general anesthetic and a quick prep. Seven minutes after Melissa called the section, she delivered the baby through the uterine incision. Melissa handed the limp bundle to Tara. She placed the infant in the isolette and ordered, "An amp of bicarb... Laryngoscope... Epinephrine... What's the heart rate?.. That's an improvement... Keep bagging.... Come on little guy."

Melissa's ears listened to the drama unfolding a few yards away while her hands sutured the uterine incision."

"Whoops," shouted Marmor, the anesthesiologist. Dr. Alan Marmor was a man who rarely spoke during cases. Melissa couldn't recall him—or any other anesthesiologist—saying "whoops." Marmor's next statement explained. "She's arrested, get the paddles." Melissa dropped the needle holder, cupped her hands over Vicky's chest and began cardiac massage. Marmor filled several syringes from the multitude of vials in his cart. After injecting them into Vicky's vein, he grasped the paddles from the circulating nurse. "Stand clear, everybody." Vicky's body convulsed, her body heaved upward as the electrical charge surged through her chest. All eyes were on the EKG tracing: a flat line. Melissa replaced her hands on Vicky's chest and resumed the cardiac massage. Marmor rammed a large syringeful of whitish fluid into the IV, hurled the empty syringe to the floor and growled, "Damn, we're losing her, let's zap her again."

"Damn, we're losing him," screamed Tara.

Vicky's chest convulsed again. This time, a spike materialized on the monitor. Melissa returned her attention to the uterine incision. The monitor continued to beep reassuringly as she closed the surgical layers in Vicky's abdomen.

Tara approached. The surgical mask obscured most of her face; however, there was disconsolation in her eyes. "We've got a live baby, APGAR one and three. Doesn't look good." She then turned to join the two nurses in escorting the infant to the NICU, the Neonatal Intensive Care Unit.

"We've got a bleeder here," snapped Brookhurst. "Another... Damn, she's bleeding from everywhere."

"She's got DIC," said Melissa. "Let's get some fresh frozen plasma and cryoprecipitate up here stat."

Becky gazed softly at Melissa. "What a nightmare. Let's pause for a moment. How about a cup of coffee?"

"I'd love one."

A minute later, Becky's secretary appeared with a small tray. Melissa accepted the cup and sat quietly sipping the warm brew, inhaling its aroma and saying nothing. Becky looked on with misty eyes. When Melissa finished her cup, Becky asked, "Do you want to continue, or do you need more time?"

Melissa looked up at her. "Let's go on. I need to get through all this. A lot of the rest you already know."

"Right. But first fill me in on some medical terminology. What's PIH?"

"Pregnancy induced hypertension. The lay term is toxemia."

Becky made a note in her tablet. "And DIC?"

"Disseminated intravascular coagulopathy. It's one of the manifestations of the disease. Simply explained, the blood quits clotting and patients stricken with it begin bleeding from everywhere. It's an obstetrician's nightmare."

"You were able to control the bleeding."

"After a monumental effort we did... Just barely. She almost died on the table and her current status is probably worse than death, her baby's too."

"I agree, worse than death. Both are in a chronic vegetative state, irreversible brain damage."

"Neither of them have a life, no life at all." Tears began to flow.

Becky extended a Kleenex, gazed upward as she spoke. "In addition to the humanitarian aspects of a young mother and child lying comatose, we have to deal with the monetary issues. A dead baby or a dead mother, command much less monetary redress than a live one."

"The cost of their continued care."

Becky returned her gaze to Melissa. "Right. Anyway, let's continue. Did you ever find out why there was no answer at the patient's residence?"

"She transposed a digit when she entered her phone number on our registration form."

"Not an uncommon mistake."

"No."

"You haven't mentioned Vicky's husband."

"I talked to him at the hospital for a brief moment before the surgery, and at length afterward. I also spoke to him by telephone twice afterwards. When the realization that he had a comatose wife and baby hit, he was overcome with grief, lashed out against me, the hospital, anything medical... I can certainly understand his feelings."

"Beyond his grief and the status of his wife and child is the need to cope with her two children, who now for all practical purposes have lost both their parents. And it's another reason the damages are set at $10 million. On a brighter note, from your description of events so far, I can't see where you've deviated from the standard of care. However, I have reviewed the hospital records and I can find no documentation of your desire to hospitalize the patient the day prior to the incident."

Melissa's face reddened. "They destroyed them, the bastards destroyed them. I wrote a complete note in the chart and dictated an even more detailed discharge summary. The note disappeared from the chart and there is no record of my dictation in the transcription department."

"If what you say is true, that hospital is pathetic, truly pathetic."

"It is and they are."

"Including your ex-husband."

"My ex-husband in particular. If he had an ounce—I take that back—a nanogram of decency in his body, he would have substantiated our conversation."

"Could he be responsible for the disappearance of the records?"

"He could indeed."

"You mentioned that he's now the CEO of CIPA. How's it doing with him at the helm?"

"Surprisingly, it's doing very well. Their last quarter was the best ever."

"Maybe he has good management abilities."

"If so, it's the first time in his life."

"What about this Middlemouse nurse? You mentioned that you discussed your desire to admit the patient with her."

Melissa laughed. "Middlemas, you're saying it too. When I

realized that I had a problem with the hospital, I—"

"When was this?"

"When the OB Core Committee called me in to discuss the case. Their demeanor gave me a bad feeling. I located Middlemas later that day, skittering down the hallway."

"Hi Bridget, do you have a second?"

Middlemas continued walking. "I'm real busy right now, and–_"

"I just need a moment. I'm sure you recall the day I admitted Vicky Sanders for observation."

"Umm... Yeah."

"Then you must recall that I desired to admit her."

Bridget's face blanched; she assumed a slumping position, staring at the floor. "I don't recall exactly, I—umm—do recall that we both agreed that she didn't meet the criteria for admission... That's all I—umm—can remember."

Melissa glared at her. "Bridget, you and I both know full well what happened that day. This is important, my career's on the line."

Bridget glanced upward briefly. She was on the verge of tears. "Mine is too, Dr. Morrison. I'm awful sorry."

Melissa maintained eye contact. "You certainly are. You know, Bridget, one of these days you might have to tell the truth about that day.

Bridget repeated, "I'm sorry," and trudged off.

Becky said, "It appears that this woman has been intimidated by the IPA, the hospital, or both; thus, she can be intimidated by others. We'll depose Nurse Mouse, see if she wants to perjure herself." Becky thumbed back through her pages of notes. "This nurse, Sarah, she took care of Vicky on the day prior to the incident. We'll depose her as well."

"You'll have to find her first. I was told that she resigned from the hospital and has left the state. Nobody knows where she is."

"This is beginning to sound like a conspiracy."

"You're right. It is." Melissa stared at Becky. *She believes me, she believes me.*

"What is your opinion of the neonatologist? What's her name again?"

"Tara Linsey."

"Do you have any criticism of Dr. Linsey's care of the infant?"

Melissa shook her head. "None whatsoever. Tara is an excellent neonatologist. There are three in the group, and she's my favorite. The other two are Chuck Ainsley and Larry Stafford. Chuck is a good neonatologist, but lacks in bedside manner. Larry Stafford is older and many staff doctors feel he's suffering from job burnout. And possibly other things."

"What other things?"

"They're just rumors."

"What kind of rumors?"

"Chemical abuse, cocaine. Some of my colleagues dispute them. But many—me included—think the man has a problem."

"A number of professional people have collapsed under stress and gotten involved in chemical abuse, happens in our field too."

"I'm sure that it does. Neonatology is a high-stress field. The babies they save give them a boost; however, the ones they lose hit them hard. After a while it grinds them down."

"Well, we're getting off track a bit, let's go on. I understand that you are facing a hearing at the hospital."

"Yes, a Judicial Review Hearing. I'm fighting a battle on many fronts."

"Has a date been set?"

"Next week." She retrieved a card from her purse. "Here's George Rucker's card, he's representing me at the hearing."

"I'll give him a call. That's next week. Tomorrow is your

deposition with the Sanders' attorney, Marvin Golub. You've had your deposition taken before?"

"Once, for my ectopic pregnancy case."

"How did you do?"

"My attorney really didn't prepare me. I thought it would be more like a courtroom situation where I could explain my side."

Becky's face hardened; the country girl image disappeared. "It's not a courtroom situation at all. It's a fishing expedition. Golub will attempt to strengthen his case through his questions. I've researched his *modus operandi*. He will probably use a friendly approach at first and then attack like a pit bull when you least suspect. During his friendly mode, he'll try to put words in your mouth."

"I'm aware of that. I believe I profited from the last experience. I'll do better this time around." *I hope.*

Chapter 11

Becky and Melissa sat at a long rectangular table in Roach and Graber's conference room. Three walls were paneled in oak; the fourth provided a superb view of the surrounding community of La Playa and the nearby Pacific Ocean. Cliffside Medical Center was visible through the morning haze. Melissa stared at the hospital and the adjacent building housing Cliffside IPA; she visualized Pandora's Box.

A secretary knocked on the door and asked, "Are you ready?"

Becky nodded; a minute later, the court reporter trundled her stenotype machine into the room and set it up at one end of the table. Marvin Golub entered; he flashed a plastic smile and took a seat across from Melissa and Becky. "My, my. This is a first, I've never conducted a deposition with even one beautiful young woman, but two, mind you, two beautiful young women."

They both gave him a half-smile. The court reporter drank in the scene with a faint smile of her own. Golub continued with his unappreciated overtures until Becky interrupted him with a demand to proceed with the business at hand.

Melissa focused on Golub's flashing teeth as the deposition began. *Shark's teeth. He's a shark. Watch out, Melissa and don't be disarmed by the phony smile.*

The initial questions were all benign and easy enough to answer: where she attended medical school; her specialty training; and her board certification. Melissa patiently and calmly answered the questions pertaining to her background. She controlled a grimace when Golub asked, "Are you married, Dr. Morrison?"

"No."

"Do you have any children?"

"A son." She conjured up an image of little Roger and for a moment the conference room blurred.

It returned abruptly into focus when Golub asked, "Were you married in the past?"

"I'm divorced."

"It must be difficult, managing a medical career and a child without a spouse, very stressful." He looked at her expectantly.

Melissa said nothing. *Ask a question and I'll answer it, but don't put words in my mouth.*

Golub continued, "When you began your private practice, were you associated with any other individual or group?"

"I was associated with Dr. Rachel Hornbeak."

"Are you still associated with Dr. Hornbeak?"

Melissa stared at Golub. *You already know the answer to that one, don't you?* "No, I am no longer associated with Dr. Hornbeak."

"How long were you associated with Dr. Hornbeak?"

"Two years"

"What happened to the relationship?"

"It didn't work out. We went our separate ways."

"It didn't work out... Were you terminated by Dr. Hornbeak?"

"You might say that."

"On what grounds?"

"Objection," said Becky. "That calls for speculation on the part of my client."

"You may still answer the question," said Golub.

"I will not speculate."

Golub frowned, then moved on to the events surrounding Vicky's visit to Melissa's office and her subsequent hospital evaluation. Each of his questions stirred up a bit more sadness, a melancholia that increased with each of his painful jabs.

Golub looked up from his pad. "You claim that you desired to admit the patient and that you were thwarted by the Cliffside IPA Guidelines. Would you please locate any documentation in the hospital record?"

"There is no record in the hospital chart, other than the repeat dictation."

Golub furrowed his brow. "You state that you protested the discharge but the only documentation is a discharge summary dictated three days after the delivery of Todd Sanders. Why didn't you dictate a summary on the day you allege that you protested the discharge?" He thumbed through the hospital chart. "That date would be the day prior to the incident, March nineteenth."

Melissa replied calmly and deliberately, "I placed a written note in the chart, but it disappeared. I dictated a discharge summary, the transcription was lost."

He shook his head. "How unfortunate. Do you have any idea who could have removed a portion of a hospital chart and destroyed a transcription?"

"That would call for speculation; if I had any definitive facts, I would share them with you."

"Would you care to share your speculations with me?"

"No."

"Dr. Morrison, are you under psychiatric care?"

"No."

"Hmm. Have you seen a mental healthcare professional in the past year?"

"No."

"Do you have any appointments scheduled with a mental healthcare professional?"

"I have an appointment to see a psychologist."

Golub gazed upward. "Why are you seeing a psychologist?"

"It was required of me because of a child custody battle."

Golub focused his gaze on her. "Did your ex-husband, Mr. Geoffrey Shackleton, initiate this custody battle?"

"He did."

"What are his demands?"

Melissa winced slightly. "Full custody."

"I see. What are your current custody arrangements?"

"Mr. Shackleton has visitation every other weekend if he so desires."

"Are you willing to compromise on the current custody arrangement?"

"No."

Golub scribbled some notes; then placed a coda on the deposition when he asked, "Have your privileges to practice medicine ever been restricted in any fashion or revoked?"

"No."

"Is any such action pending?"

Becky said, "Objection. This information is privileged pursuant to Evidence Code one-one-five-seven."

Golub responded with a faint smirk and placed his pen on the tablet. "No further questions."

After Golub and the court reporter departed, Becky placed a sheaf of papers in her brief case and snapped it shut. She turned to Melissa and said, "You did well. You held up just fine."

"Thank you." Melissa bared her teeth. "My, my, I've never been in the presence of two such beautiful ladies, yuk."

"Yuk is right. I'll call you tomorrow. We have a few things to go over." She glanced at her watch. "Whew, I've got to run."

"Me too. I'm meeting two of my most favorite people for dinner. They know the deposition was scheduled for today. They're taking me to Pinocchio's to cheer me up."

"I've heard of it. It is a cheer-up kind of place."

Chapter 12

Melissa strolled through Monstro's mouth with her spirits on the upswing. She was relieved to find that she had arrived ahead of the always-punctual Hausers. However, her relief was transformed into an intense disquietude with the passage of time. She handed another breadstick to little Roger, rechecked her watch and scanned the room again. "More," squealed Roger. Melissa retrieved another breadstick from the dwindling supply; he snatched it from her grasp. His pleasure over a simple bit of bread cheered her. A familiar voice distracted her. "Hi Melissa. How's my little man?"

"Opa," squealed Roger. "Where Oma?"

Dr. Hauser took a seat. "Sorry I'm late."

Melissa smiled. "No problem... Where's Katrina?"

Roger stared at the table. "She's a little under the weather."

Melissa recognized Roger's charade, and replied with one of her own. "Nothing serious I hope."

"She's having some trouble bouncing back from her chemo."

"What chemo? You never told me. When?"

"Last week. You have enough on your mind at present. I didn't want to—"

"It wouldn't have been any trouble. Katrina is precious to me. Is it a recurrence of her breast cancer?"

He nodded.

"Did she have the chemo at Hannaford?"

"No, here at Cliffside."

Alice in Wonderland approached, and asked, "Are you ready to order?"

"Give us a few minutes please," said Melissa. "Why Cliffside?"

"They have a good cancer center at Cliffside. Besides, we're now on the Cliffside IPA with my new job."

"Dammit, Roger. You know my feelings toward the IPA. How's Katrina?"

"She's weak; her white count went down to the cellar. Not to worry, she's a tough Austrian. She'll bounce back."

Melissa's eyes watered over; she angrily blinked back tears. "For a recurrence of breast cancer, she needs more than a tough Austrian constitution, she needs state-of-the-art medical care, something I've found lacking in the super-economy managed care environment that prevails with the Cliffside IPA."

"From all appearances, she's getting the best of care. As far as economy goes, I've discussed the possibility of a bone marrow transplant with her doctors."

"I'm sure they said no."

"On the contrary, they assured me it was a covered benefit on the plan."

Melissa shook her head. "I'll believe it when I see it. That type of treatment costs $50,000 or more. I can't believe they'd shell out that kind of money, it takes an Act of Congress to get approval for a $200 ultrasound exam."

"I'm acting as Katrina's advocate. Everything's going to be okay. Now let's order and I want you to tell me how your day went."

Melissa's thoughts of the deposition had been totally thrust aside; they rose to the surface for a moment but she forced them away. "She's got an advocate in me too. I'm worried about her, Roger, very worried."

"So am I, but she'll pull through, I'm certain of it. Now, tell me about the deposition."

"I just want to enjoy your company and relax, Roger. It was just another lousy legal day. It's behind me... Another lousy, weasly legal day is behind me."

"You're due for a few bright spots. Tomorrow is another day, perhaps something good will come to you."

Melissa choked back her tears. "I haven't had a good day in so long, if I had one, the shock might do me in."

Roger squeezed her hand. "Good days will come. I just know it."

Little Roger squealed with delight. Pinocchio paused for a moment to do a shuffle dance; then hastened away to take an order. Melissa thought, *He's got no strings to keep him down, but I do. I'm not living a fairy tale, and there's no happy ending in sight.*

Chapter 13

The following morning, Melissa pulled up in front of the bookstore. Her thoughts were of Katrina and what type of book she would like to read. *They just moved in to a new home, perhaps a landscaping book... I bet she'd like a good novel. I'll check the best seller section.* She unfastened her seat belt and flung the door outward.

Bang.... Chunk.

The noise startled her, jerking her head in its direction. A crumpled, fluorescent green heap lay in the road beneath her opened door. Entwined with the mound was a bicycle. The crumpled heap looked up at her and spoke. "You doored me, what'd you do that for?"

"I'm terribly sorry. Are you okay?"

A muscular young man picked himself up from the asphalt. His bright blue eyes strafed her. "I think so... But my bike, my bike is trashed."

"I'm so sorry. I'll pay for the damages. Don't worry about the bike. Let me have a look at that knee."

"It's okay, just a little road rash. Are you a nurse?"

"I'm a doctor."

His jaw dropped. "You're kidding."

"No, really, I'm a doctor. That knee needs some attention."

He stared down at his bicycle, picked it up and attempted to wheel it forward. The pretzeled front wheel grated harshly against the front fork. He shook his head. "My bike needs attention, too. It's not ride-able."

"I really feel terrible about this. Can I give you a lift somewhere?"

"I rode here from Solomon Beach."

"Solomon Beach... That's a good twenty miles from here. You rode all that way?"

"Uh huh. And I was planning to ride back until..."

Again, I'm so sorry. Let's get your bike in the trunk."

Melissa scanned the road before pulling out into traffic. She noted a vehicle approach from the rear and waited patiently for it to pass, then cautiously eased out into the lane. She smiled at him. "I'm sorry. I just didn't see you."

He smiled back and pointed to his brightly-colored jersey. "I guess I'm hard to spot in this outfit, blend right into the roadway."

His voice was devoid of sarcasm; Melissa sensed that he was attempting to make light of the situation. She laughed. "Yeah, right. I was preoccupied. I've got a lot on my mind these days; wasn't paying attention when I opened the door on you. I was thinking of a sick friend... I was going to buy her a book to cheer her up."

"Then I bumped into you and you forgot all about it."

Melissa laughed at his soft humor. "I did."

"Say, you never bought the book. Do you want to go back?"

"No, I'll stop by on my way back." *My, it's refreshing to meet someone so nice... Especially after I dumped him onto the asphalt.*

"You sure?"

"Sure."

"Hey, let me introduce myself, I'm Ryan, Ryan MacKenzie."

She smiled. "Melissa Morrison." She then deflected her gaze back to the roadway. *Pay attention to your driving, Melissa. That's all you'd need to do to cap off your day, crack up your car and inflict more injuries onto this nice man.*

She continued to focus on her driving until he remarked, "Say, could I ask a favor of you?"

"Sure. What?"

He gestured. "See that bike shop up ahead. I'd like to drop off my bike. Maybe they can fix it so I'll have it for the weekend."

"No problem."

He exited the shop looking like he had lost his last friend. She assumed that his bike was totaled. It looked like an expensive one, and her budget didn't have any room for unnecessary expenses. She asked, "Is the bike seriously damaged?"

"No, not that bad. The bad news is it won't be ready until Tuesday. I'll miss both of my club's weekend rides."

She reflected that it might have been better if she'd totaled the bike, then she could have returned to the shop with him and, despite the impact on her dwindling finances, purchased a new one. She groped for an appropriate response; then replied, "I'm sorry, I really am."

"It's okay. It's okay."

He was obviously pouting. It was not okay. She was responsible for damaging his bike, skinning his knee and ruining his weekend. He stared out the window and she abandoned attempts at further conversation.

"Pull over there," he said. "Thanks for the lift."

"It's the least I could do." *That knee of his needs attention. Should I offer to tend to it? He seems friendly... And harmless. But you've been fooled before by a friendly facade, haven't you girl? Well, here goes...* "Say, I'm really concerned about that knee of yours. I'd like to offer you my medical services."

"I'll be all right."

"Without proper medical attention you won't. You've got road grime embedded in it. It could infect and if it's not cleaned properly, you'll have an ugly tattoo."

"I guess you know your business."

He unlocked the door to the condo. She was instantly impressed by its neatness *and* the bicycle. Adjacent to the fireplace, leaning against the wall, was a tandem; the bicycle was as spotless as everything else in the room. A large seascape hung above the fireplace; it depicted a sandy coastline interspersed with volcanic rocks, clumps of kelp, and bits of driftwood. The shore was under attack by powerful spindrift-rimmed rollers. Several seagulls wheeled above the spray, struggling against the wind. She said, "I like that painting. Is it by someone local?"

He smiled. "Yes. It was painted by an emerging artist. I got a terrific deal on it. Don't you think it captures the local coastline?"

"It does. I really like it." She wondered if his smile was directed toward her or the painting. Possibly it was intended for both. She scanned the room. "Very nice place. I'm surprised that your wife would let you keep a bike in the house, though."

"I'm a bachelor. I guess one of the advantages of that status is complete freedom in the room decor. The salt air here at the beach is bad for a bike, it'd rust... What gave you the idea that I was married?"

"Your place is so neat. My stereotype of a bachelor pad is nothing like this."

He chuckled. "Too nice a place for a piggy bachelor man?"

She laughed. "Right."

"Well, you don't match my stereotype of a doctor. My image of a doctor is a fatherly, middle-aged man, not a..."

"Not a young woman like me."

"Yeah. Anyway, since I am now aware of the fact that you are a doctor, I'm going to take you up on your offer. What do you need for my medical treatment?"

"A small basin, hot water, soap—and some antiseptic—if you have any."

He returned with the requested items and gestured toward a doorway. "Let's go in the bathroom."

He took a seat on the tub and extended his leg toward its interior. She soaked up the soapy water in the washcloth. "Sorry, this is going to hurt a little." He grimaced in anticipation, then relaxed as she gently dabbed his knee with the cloth. She sensed that he was enjoying her ministrations. When she finished, he complimented her for her gentle touch and asked, "Would you care for something to drink, soda, lemonade?"

"Lemonade sounds good."

He ushered her back to the living area and left for the kitchen. She scanned the bookcase for clues about Ryan. She noted a novel here and there, but the bulk of his library consisted of books with topics such as: "Advanced Systems Programming," and "C++ Language Reference." Upon his return, she asked, "Are you a computer programmer?"

He nodded toward the bookcase and replied, "How'd you guess?"

She laughed and took the glass extended in her direction. "Mmm, good lemonade."

"Is it sweet enough for you? I like it on the tart side."

"Perfect," she replied, taking another sip.

"Do you work out of Cliffside Medical Center?"

Melissa nodded. *For the time being, anyway.*

"I'm with RAM-Tech; we installed the computer system for the hospital. What do you think of it?"

"It's a nice system from my limited perspective—I'm not that computer literate—just use it for lab results and op reports."

He appeared a bit exasperated by her response, as if he'd received the same on many occasions in the past. "It's a good system; it can do more than that, much more."

"I'd like to learn more about it; unfortunately, I have too many other things going on in my life just now. I like all the graphic features. I understand the term for that is user friendly. Did you design all that?"

"Our company did. We focused on attracting the user to the computer. The GUI helps a lot to accomplish that."

"The what?"

"Sorry. GUI stands for graphical user interface."

"Shows how much I know about computers."

"Computers are indispensable. I couldn't live without one."

His voice rose in volume as he expounded on the topic. Melissa could not follow Ryan's "Ode to a Computer," which was liberally infused with technical jargon. She searched for a means to steer him from the topic. *The tandem. I bet that will work.* "Say, why not ride that bike tomorrow?" He stared fondly at the bicycle and appeared to be considering her suggestion. *Aha,* thought Melissa, *I've discovered another of his passions.*

He said, "Haven't ridden it for a while. I bought it to lure my girlfriend into cycling. It didn't work, we broke up. I guess I could take it to the ride tomorrow and go trolling."

"Trolling?"

"Trolling. Ride around the parking lot and troll. I'd probably wind up with a troll, though... Nah, that's not my style. I guess I'll do something else this weekend." His pout returned.

"I've never ridden a tandem... It looks like fun. I haven't been on a bike since college. It was an old clunker that I rode back and forth between the dorm and the campus, nothing as fancy as this one, though."

He smiled at her, then at his bike. "This is a great tandem, Ergo Shifters, Campy equipped."

"All gibberish to me. It looks like an overgrown mountain bike."

His smile broadened. "It's a mountain bike tandem. I haven't done much off-roading with it, or on-roading for that matter."

Yes indeed. I've definitely struck a nerve here. He knows not one, but two foreign languages—computer-ese and bicycle-speak.

He gave the saddle an affectionate pat; then turned in her direction.

His sky blue eyes were captivating. *Hmm, he's very shy... But very nice. I bet he's trying to get up nerve to ask me to ride on his tandem.* They exchanged smiles. *Here goes,* she thought. *I'm by no means the forward type, but I don't think he has the nerve to ask me.* "Here's an idea... You want to have a bike ride tomorrow, and I've never been on a tandem. If you don't mind an inexperienced rider?"

A boyish grin materialized. "Would you? That'd be terrific."

"I don't have a fancy bicycle suit like yours, just a tee shirt and shorts."

"That's okay... Say, just a second. I'll be right back."

Several minutes later, he returned with a turquoise jersey emblazoned with a large toucan and a pair of black cycling shorts. "I bought these for my girlfriend's birthday, but we broke up before I could give them to her. I think they'll fit you okay. That way, you won't come across as a Fred."

"They look like they'll fit just fine. What's a Fred?"

"A novice cyclist."

"I see."

"Oh, one bit of advice, these shorts are designed to be worn without underwear." His face reddened. "Underwear can chafe you."

He's blushing. Yes indeed, he's blushing.

His face reddened further. "I—I'll pick you up at ten after eight."

Recollection of red-faced Ryan caused her to smile spontaneously on several occasions throughout the remainder of the day. She awoke the next morning with a smile as his blushing image came to mind. Then, she was hit with a bit of panic. This outing would mark her first date since the meltdown of her marriage more than two years ago.

Chapter 14

A few minutes before eight, Casper barked frantically at the sound of the doorbell; he leaped with impatience for Melissa to open it. Ryan was standing in the entrance wearing a toucan jersey identical to the one he lent her. "I hope you don't mind... Tandem teams usually wear matching jerseys." His face reddened.

"Not at all. After all I don't want your friends to think I'm a Fred. Hey, we're toucans, two can on a tandem."

He laughed and the redness faded. Casper wagged his tail, begging for attention. Ryan stroked him under the chin. "Hi there little fellow. Are you wagging your tail or is your tail wagging you?" He looked up at Melissa. "Cute dog. What kind is he anyway?"

"An Italian Greyhound."

"A super compact model of a Greyhound."

Melissa laughed, "Right."

"What's his name?"

"Casper."

Little Roger appeared from around the corner, clutching Ada's hand. Roger broke from her grasp and ran to Melissa. She gathered him up. "This is my son, Roger, and my housekeeper, Ada."

Ryan smiled at Roger. "Hi Guy," then turned to greet Ada.

"Bye-bye car," said Roger, his voice filled with anticipation.

Melissa placed him in Ada's arms and said, "Mommy's going bye-bye car. I'll be back soon." Roger began to cry, arched his back and stretched his arms in her direction. Melissa gave him a kiss, turned to Ryan and said, "We'd best get going."

As Ryan pulled away from the curb, Melissa said, "I was married briefly."

"Cute little guy."

"He's the greatest, the greatest." *Hmm. He still appears warm and friendly after meeting Roger. That's a good sign... He's nice, extremely handsome, and very bright, but my life is complicated enough right now without adding a romantic entanglement. Things are platonic right now, let's keep it that way.*

Melissa helped Ryan remove the tandem from the roof carrier and noted the approving glances of the predominantly male group of lycra-clad cyclists. After he adjusted her saddle and the straps on her helmet, he said, "Let's take a practice spin."

He straddled the tandem and held it while she mounted. After a few practice starts and stops, he remarked, "You're a natural at this."

"Thank you. I've never been on a bike that I couldn't brake or steer. I guess I'll have to get used to that."

He laughed. "Most new stokers experience that sensation."

"Stoker?"

"Stoker refers to the rider on the back. My designation is captain.

Captain and Stoker... Hmm... The only stokers I've heard of were soot-stained slaves that worked in the ship's engine room shoveling coal into the boilers. Slackards were whipped unmercifully... Here's another nice mess you've gotten yourself into Melissa.

A loud voice interrupted her thoughts. "It's nine o'clock, let's roll."

Melissa was a quick learner. She rotated the pedals and pushed forcefully downward as Ryan mounted and simultaneously thrust downward on a pedal. The tandem rolled smoothly forward with the rest of the pack. The group halted briefly for a red light then took off again. She gazed at Ryan's muscular back. Her initial apprehension was waning. "This is fun and we seem to be keeping up okay."

"Just wait," said Ryan. "The first five miles are a warm-up, just wait."

She didn't have long to enjoy the leisurely pace before the metallic clanking of shifting derailleurs heralded the end of the warm-up phase. The distance between them and the pack widened. She sensed that Ryan was working much harder than she was; she compelled her legs to pedal more forcefully. They caught up with the group at a red light; then dropped back again. Ryan eased up on the pedals and gasped, "It's okay, let 'em go. We'll catch up to them when we regroup."

"Okay," she panted. "This is a real workout."

The parking lot was strewn with clumps of cyclists, munching on Power Bars, sipping water, and cracking jokes. Ryan braked to stop and held the bike steady to aid her dismounting. Melissa grasped the water bottle from the rack and drank thirstily. Several minutes later, her breathing returned to normal. Then, to her dismay, the cyclists began to mount their wheeled steeds and roll out of the lot.

Ryan asked, "Want to rest a while longer?"

"I'm okay. Let's go."

"You sure?" Not wanting to disappoint him, she nodded a reply and mounted the instrument of torture. He turned to her briefly with a smile as they exited the lot. "Well, one plus, the ride back has some good downhills, great for tandems. I'm sure you noticed that the ride here was a bit of an uphill."

"I noticed, and so did my out-of-shape body notice." *It darn near killed me. I'll probably suffer a cardiac arrest on the way back.*

The pack took on the form of a giant multi-colored beast and rapidly gained momentum. The faster pace on the level terrain refreshed her. She concentrated on her pedaling and thought, *Legs, do your stuff. Show these guys that you're not a Fred.*

They rolled onto a long downhill grade; the tandem began to fly. Ryan continued to apply force to the pedals and Melissa did likewise. "Tandem left," yelled a rider as they sped to the front of the pack. Melissa was exhilarated by the speed and the rush of the air. She turned her head to the rear and viewed a string of riders on their tail. The front wheel of the first bicycle to their rear was inches from their rear wheel. Melissa turned and shouted to Ryan, "Why do they follow us so closely?"

"They're drafting on us, sucking wheel in bicycle talk... Bump!"

"What?" A jolt stuck her from below. "Ow."

"Your visibility is restricted back there. I'll try to give you as much warning as I can."

"I'll be prepared next time."

Ryan's strength and Melissa's determination kept them with the pack all the way back. They triumphantly returned to the ride start in the midst of the front riders. Melissa's jersey was soaked with sweat and her spirit filled with elation as she gulped down the now-warm water in the bottle. For the first time in recent months, she wasn't focused on the multitude of problems in her life.

She plopped down in the passenger seat and said, "I really enjoyed that, the return trip in particular. Downhills certainly win out over uphills in my book."

"Quite right, but for every uphill there's a downhill. You appreciate them more when you earn them... That's good cycling philosophy."

"It extends beyond cycling, that philosophy has wide applications." *Including my life.*

He smiled. "I guess that makes me a 'cyclosopher.'"

She asked, "A what?"

"A cycling philosopher."

"Right. You are. In any event, that was the most fun I've had in a long time."

"You did very well."

"You did most of the work. I know I held you back."

"Not really. I felt the power in those legs. With a little training, you could easily hold your own with this group."

"How far did we ride?"

"Thirty miles."

Her eyes widened. "That's the furthest I've ever ridden. We make a good team, two can."

"Two can… You can share the backseat of my tandem anytime… Hmm—say—would you like to ride again tomorrow?"

"I'd love to but my housekeeper has the day off. I don't have anybody to watch my son."

"Too bad."

He became silent, lost in thought, for the next few miles. Melissa groped for words to console him, but found none.

He broke the silence. "Say, I have an idea. I have a trailer. Kids love riding in it. It's a bit more work pulling a trailer, but—"

"Is it safe?"

"Very safe. We always pick a route with good bike lanes and little traffic."

She envisioned another pleasant interlude from her disaster-ridden life. "Okay, let's do it." *Why would a bachelor own a bicycle trailer?* "Do you have a child?"

"No. I bought the trailer for my ex-girl friend's dog." He pursed his lips and adopted a French accent. "Fifi zee poodle… Fifi didn't take to cycling any more than Brenda did."

Melissa sang to herself in the shower and relived the pleasant morning. She savored the memory of them speeding along, leading the pack; the exhilaration of that moment had cleansed her mind of demons. That night, instead of the customary nightmares, she dreamed of a poodle with pink fingernails crying in a bicycle trailer. She awakened refreshed, but aching from various muscle groups, particularly her thighs and buttocks. A long shower helped; she would rise to the occasion and embark on another cycling adventure.

Chapter 15

The group of riders assembled in the parking lot was larger than the previous day. Melissa spotted a number of tandem couples. Ryan said, "Our club has a variety of rides, ranging from fifteen to sixty miles." She gasped. "You're not planning to do sixty miles, are you?"

He laughed. "No. I think the twenty mile breakfast ride is more our speed. I think you'll like it. It's a social ride with a slower pace than yesterday."

Social and slower suited her just fine. Her aching muscles could not perform at yesterday's level. She interrupted Roger from his investigation of the parking lot and plopped him in the trailer. He began to fuss; she feared that they'd soon be pedaling down the road with Roger howling from the confines of the little yellow trailer. Ryan produced a Teddy Bear from the trunk and wiggled it in front of Roger. "Bear," chortled Roger, reaching for the toy.

"The bear will work as a temporary distraction," said Ryan. "Once we get rolling, I can assure you that he'll be a happy camper."

"I hope you're right. Roger's a good little guy, but he has a ballistic mode."

Ryan shrugged. "All kids do. I—"

A loud voice interrupted him. "Breakfast riders roll on out."

They were surrounded by a congenial group composed largely of tandems. Behind many of them were trailers similar to the one connected to Ryan's machine. Melissa glanced back at Roger. He was enraptured with the scenery rolling by. Couples on the tandems shifted position frequently and engaged in mini-conversations. Melissa joined in this activity, totally disengaged from the ongoing pressures in her life. They approached a long uphill segment of Country Club Drive. As the grade increased, she was distracted from viewing the adjacent golf course. She concentrated on her pedaling, and panted, "My legs sure can feel the difference pulling the trailer."

The single bikes and several tandems pulled ahead; Ryan puffed, "Uphill on a tandem with a trailer is a piece of work. Not to worry, we'll catch them on the downhill."

"Ah, a bright spot at the end of my tunnel. Despite the upgrade, this is a nice quiet road, no traffic."

"Few cars, but there is a hazard up ahead, the golf cart crossing. Those guys have a predilection for charging in front of us; assume we're stationary objects... Looks like we've got a possible golf cart encounter up ahead."

Melissa spotted the golf cart approaching at a tangent from the right. "I don't think they see us."

"Right. If we don't make eye contact, it's brake time." The driver turned in their direction. "Ah, he's seen us... Damn! Stopping!" Ryan abruptly braked the tandem, dropped his right foot to the ground, and balanced the heavy bike. "Idiot," he shouted.

The cart did not slow. The driver and the other three occupants glared in their direction. As the cart bumped over the other side of the bike trail, the driver raised his middle finger and yelled, "Keep your fucking bike off the road, asshole!"

Melissa recognized the voice, and the face; they belonged to Geoff. The others also were familiar. Ken Baker, the hospital pathologist sat beside Geoff. Baker's sallow complexion, a result of dwelling in the basement lab among chemicals and tissue specimens, appeared even paler alongside his tanned companions. In the back seat sat Larry Stafford, the senior neonatologist at Cliffside. Stafford's disheveled appearance contrasted sharply with that of the nattily attired golfer beside him. Jim Kerr, at all times, was impeccably dressed in the latest fashions. Kerr was the senior oncologist at Cliffside. Among other functions, he and his colleagues administered chemotherapy to the cancer victims at the hospital.

Ryan mounted the tandem, thrust downward on the pedal and muttered, "What an idiot."

"That idiot is my ex-husband." *Now why did I blurt that out?*

"Charming fellow."

Melissa hoped that the encounter would not tarnish her new relationship. She really couldn't blame Ryan if it did. She was a single mom with a huge collection of luggage, including an obnoxious ex-husband. He obviously was unaware of her current legal nightmares—that knowledge would kill any hope of a continued relationship. But what he already knew was enough. His silence confirmed her suspicions. She was certain that they would finish the ride with a bit of polite conversation here and there; he would drive her home; then disappear from her tangled mess of a life. She mused, *All things considered, he seems too good to be true, just like Geoff... Once burnt twice careful. But, he is much sweeter and softer than Geoff. He has a little boy charm to him, a trait completely lacking in Geoff. He's a bit hung up on computers; I'd hate to compete with a computer for a man's affections.*

His voice interrupted her thoughts. "One of the guys in the backseat looks familiar. I've seen him someplace before."

Relieved that Geoff was not the topic of conversation, she replied, "They're all doctors, except for my ex-husband. I guess he's reached a new plateau in his life, hobnobbing with doctors." *Damn, Melissa, leave Geoff out of the conversation. Don't say another word about the jerk.*

"Well," panted Ryan, "We're reaching a plateau on this ride, here comes our downhill."

Their speed rapidly increased, both from the force of gravity and their pedaling. As their speed increased, her irritation ebbed. The other riders were queued up behind a red light at the bottom of the grade. Ryan began to brake; the light turned green; he released his grip on the levers. They roared past the others with their accrued momentum. They eased up on the pedals and the other riders soon caught them. The terrain leveled off, making for easy pedaling and relaxed conversation. As he had for the beginning of the ride, Ryan pulled alongside the other tandems and introduced Melissa and Roger. Roger involved himself in the socializing; he gurgled and waved in response to their greetings. By the time that they arrived at the breakfast location, she had met most of the group. Melissa felt comfortable with Ryan and his low-key cycling friends, mostly young married couples with small children. She savored Ryan's friendship; she did not want to lose it.

They took a seat next to an athletic cyclist who had the rapt attention of several of his table-mates. "Almost ate it on Dead Man's Curve," he said. "Oh… Hi beautiful. Where have you been all my life?"

Ryan said, "Melissa, this is Wayne Cantrell, our club's Lothario in Lycra."

The group erupted in laughter.

"Don't believe a word he says," said Wayne.

"Believe, believe," said a woman across the table.

"Ryan, you are one lucky dog." said Wayne. "Hey, let me borrow your tandem, and Melissa. I'll show her Dead Man's Curve."

"She wouldn't be caught *dead* doing that," said Ryan, evoking another round of laughter.

Ryan turned to Melissa and said, "Wayne was riding in Fox Canyon. It's a favorite place to go off-roading. Dead Man's Curve catches the uninitiated by surprise… A nasty drop off."

"Very nasty," said Wayne. "Say, Ryan, just kidding about borrowing your tandem and your lady. Why don't you take her for a spin through the canyon?"

Ryan shook his head. "She's not ready. This is only her second day on a tandem. She needs more road miles first."

"True," said Melissa. "I've had enough excitement this morning riding on the road. We just had a close golf cart encounter of the worst kind." *Damn, Melissa, you just resurrected Geoff again.*

"Let me guess," said Wayne. "You almost got creamed by a

joker in a golf cart."

"Right," said Melissa. *My ex-husband, the joker of the universe.*

"What'd you do?" asked Wayne.

"I considered the source and avoided a confrontation," said Ryan. Melissa added, "We couldn't have done much. He didn't even slow down, just gave us the one-fingered-salute as he drove off."

Wayne shook his head. "You could have done more. Here's what I would have done. I'd chase him down, grab one of his clubs and threaten to stick it where the sunlight never shone. And then, you know what I would have done?"

"Insert the club where the sunlight never shone."

"No, I'd bend it around my knee and toss it in the bushes. Then I'd tell the guy I was letting him off easy this time, but in the future I'd expect him to observe cyclists' rights."

"That's your style, not mine," said Ryan with a shrug. "The guy would hate cyclists for the rest of his life."

"Maybe so, but he'd be afraid to mess with us."

Once again, laughter erupted from the group.

The conversation drifted lazily from derailleurs to diapers; Melissa joined in when the topics were familiar and became respectfully silent when it flowed back to the world of cycling. A young woman, oozing charm from her crimson lips and voluptuousness from her low-cut jersey, engaged Ryan in conversation. She was "in desperate need of help" with her computer. Melissa suffered an attack of jealousy; but her disquietude faded when she realized that Ryan was enthralled with the topic of conversation, not with his one-woman audience. To Melissa's relief, the group's preparation for departure terminated *Miss Silly Ol' Me's* flirtation.

Roger returned to the trailer without protest, apparently sharing Melissa's enthusiasm for this newfound recreation. She secured him; then glanced at her watch. Ryan asked, "Need to get back for something?"

"Uh huh. It's later than I thought. Remember the friend I was buying the book for?"

"Yes."

"I promised I'd be there by noon." Ryan shook his head. "Tough to do. I estimate we'll hit the parking lot at quarter to."

"Darn! The Hausers are the nicest people, but they have a thing about punctuality. Maybe I could call them and tell them I was detained... No, that wouldn't work. I don't think a bicycle ride would be an acceptable excuse in their book."

"We could stop by their place on the way back. Would that work? Bump!"

Melissa lifted from the saddle, avoiding a painful jar to her buttocks. "It might. They'll get a kick out of seeing me in this bicycle suit."

They exchanged smiles. Melissa was thrilled that their relationship had survived an encounter with Geoff. She retreated into her private thoughts and envisioned that she was riding with her husband and her son and all was right with the world.

Ryan pulled up in front of the Hauser's residence and helped her out of the car. "I'll wait in the car while you visit."

"Why not come in with me? They're dear, sweet people."

"I don't want to intrude."

"No intrusion, come on in with me?"

"Opa," squealed little Roger. Dr. Hauser took him in his arms and led them inside. They threaded their way past an assortment of packing boxes into the family room. "Oma," squealed the toddler. Dr. Hauser held him firmly at a distance from Katrina, propped up on the couch. She roared with laughter. "Well, well, the circus is coming to town and already, here are the clowns."

Katrina's animated laugh conveyed an image of robust health but Melissa sensed that this demonstration was contrived for her benefit. Melissa concealed her disquietude behind a smile. "Katrina, I'd like you to meet Ryan. We've been riding on his tandem bicycle."

"*Mit* little Roger?"

"We pulled him in a trailer. He thoroughly enjoyed it."

Katrina glared at Ryan. "On the roads *mit* cars?"

Melissa said. "We rode on lightly trafficked streets with safe bike lanes. Ryan is a very careful driver."

"*Mit* such a precious cargo, he'd better be."

"I was very careful, ma'am."

Katrina stared at him intently as if she possessed ESP, then a broad smile erupted. She said, "I think you were. You look like a nice young man." She paused to cough; then turned to Melissa. "A fine specimen for you, Melissa. He looks physically fit."

"We just met the other day. You're embarrassing him."

"I'm an old lady and can say whatever I please."

"You do say whatever you please," said Melissa. "But you're not an old lady. Besides, I don't like the sound of that cough. Are you on antibiotics?"

"We're seeing her doctor tomorrow," said Roger.

The conversation returned to neutral topics for a while. Katrina accepted Melissa's gift-book graciously; then let it fall to her lap. Noticing Katrina's increasing fatigue, Melissa bade her good-bye; Dr. Hauser escorted her to the door. She whispered, "She doesn't look well, Roger. I'm worried about her." The expression on his face did nothing to ease her concern. She visualized a hospital bed in which Katrina lay dying, and then forced that thought from her mind. *She's going to get well, Melissa. Convince yourself that she's going to get well.* She asked, "Why not take her up to Hannaford for an independent evaluation. I have a basic mistrust of the IPA?"

"I suggested that to her, but you know how stubborn she can be, that along with her Austrian practicality. She said this is our insurance, we paid for it and we will use it, *das ist alles*."

"I know how she can be. It's up to us to be her advocates then."

"And advocates we will be. There will be no compromise in Katrina's care."

Melissa left feeling somewhat reassured. She and Roger were a good support group for Katrina, she would recover; she had to recover. Ryan disrupted her thoughts. "Nice people," he said.

"The greatest." Melissa smiled at Ryan, then turned to little

Roger. Her concern for Katrina faded momentarily and she fantasized again that they were a complete little family on their way home to a normal house and a normal life. She reflected on the fact that the always-hospitable Hausers had neglected to offer them any liquid refreshment. This intensified her concern; preoccupation with Katrina's illness had invaded their manners.

"You're worried about Mrs. Hauser, aren't you?" said Ryan.

"Very worried. It's one more concern in my life."

"Health is a precious commodity, very precious."

Sadness welled up in Ryan's eyes; she wondered what it was. She said, "I really enjoyed myself this morning, Roger, too. Thanks for taking us."

The sadness faded away. "You're welcome. Kids love riding in a trailer, gives them a chance to see more of the world beyond the confines of their homes." They bounced a smile back and forth. He asked, "Would you like to stop by my place for a cold drink?"

"Love to."

His smile intensified into a wide grin.

Ryan unlocked the door, hastened over to an entertainment unit and thumbed through a collection of CD's. He turned to her and asked, "Do you like classical music?"

"I much prefer it."

Ryan inserted a CD. The speakers began to hum with the sound of violins. Melissa smiled. "Vivaldi's 'Four Seasons.' It's one of my favorites."

"Mine, too. I've replaced most of my old LP's with CDs."

"I have too. It's amazing how much music those little discs can store."

"Other things as well. Did you know that one of these discs can store a whole month's data from your hospital?"

"Everything?"

"Everything from surgical reports, payroll data, down to the number of paper towels in the storage room. When we developed the program, we enhanced it with a robust backup system using

CD-ROM. If you've ever had a hard drive fail, you'd know how disastrous that could be."

She had no idea how disastrous it could be. She also had no concept of a hard drive, but attempted a look of concern. "I imagine it could be." She heard a suspicious rustling. "Whoops, Roger, No, No!" She retrieved a picture from Roger's little hand. "Sorry."

"It's okay. Poor little guy has nothing to play with in here. Say, just a second." He walked to the closet and produced a large red, white and blue beach ball. He rolled it in Roger's direction.

"Ball," squealed Roger. He retrieved it and rolled it back toward Ryan. The game was on.

Melissa replaced the picture on the end table. "Pretty girl."

"Tammy, my sister."

"Does she live around here?"

"Used to. Her husband was transferred recently; Tammy and Bill moved to San Francisco. The transfer turned out to be a godsend. They lost their second child, he was premature."

Roger squealed for attention. "Ball!"

Ryan punched the ball in Roger's direction.

"How premature?"

"Thirty-one-and-four-seventh-weeks, the doctors said. Poor little fellow died two days after birth."

"What a shame. Babies born at that stage have excellent survival statistics."

"Yes. I did a bit of Internet research on the topic. Aside from looking like a spider monkey, the little guy was fine at birth. The doctors told them they'd grow the baby for three or four weeks in the intensive care nursery."

"What happened?"

"He got real sick, went rapidly downhill. I don't know much of the details, except that it was related to some type of birth defect."

"What type?"

"I don't know, other than that it was a fixable one."

"Was this locally?"

Ryan paused to retrieve the ball that Roger scooted somewhat in his direction; then replied, "At Cliffside."

"You mentioned it was her second child. Was their first full-term?"

Ryan stared thoughtfully at the ball. "Yes, he's about the age of your Roger." Roger demanded the return of the ball, jolting him back to the game at hand.

Melissa smiled. "If you don't mind, I'll get the lemonade while you two do your guy thing."

"The lemonade is in the fridge and the glasses are in the cabinet beside it."

Melissa returned with the lemonade and waited patiently for Roger's attention span to elapse. She didn't have to wait long.

She placed Roger on her knee and helped him take a sip. Roger's thirst far outpaced his cup handling abilities. Ryan looked on for a moment; then jumped up. "Just a sec."

He returned with a sipper cup adorned with Mickey Mouse and filled it with lemonade. "Here you go, guy."

"Cup," gurgled Roger.

"I keep it here for my nephew," explained Ryan.

"Roger has really taken to you. You like kids, don't you?"

"I love them. Someday I'll have kids of my own." He furrowed his brow. "The guy in the golf cart... The golf clothes threw me off, he's Dr. Stafford, my nephew's doctor... I tried to get some answers from him—Tammy and Bill were too shook up to talk to him—he was evasive, talked baby talk to me. It was insulting."

"You were entitled to an explanation, a detailed explanation, with medical jargon explained."

"I thought as much... "What do you think of him? Is he good?"

"Trained at Johns Hopkins, very experienced."

"He impressed me as being stressed out, like he has a personal problem or something."

"His job is stressful and he might have some personal problems too. As far as I know, if he does, it doesn't interfere with his work."

"I guess that when something like that happens, one has a tendency to lash out at the doctors, probably unjustifiably. What a tragedy. I hope when I have children, nothing like that happens to me. Going through it with Tammy and Bill was bad enough."

"Most babies aren't born prematurely, and even if they are, most of them do just fine. Your nephew was a fluke. Don't let that hold you back from having children."

"It won't. Only I'm a long way away from having children. I need to find the right person first. I was—"

Her cell phone rang. It was her answering service. Judy Taylor was due; Melissa suspected that she had gone into labor. Her assumption was correct.

"Sorry," she said. "I've got a patient in labor." *Sadly, Judy's the only patient for this month.* "Thanks for everything. Roger and I had a wonderful time, the most fun that I've had in a long time."

"It was my pleasure... Uhh...."

"Yes..."

"I—I could get off early this Thursday. I could get tickets for the summer symphony. It's an all Beethoven evening; we could picnic on the grass beforehand."

She was now certain that the relationship was far from fizzling, it was blossoming. Her mind filled for a moment with the anticipation of a pleasant evening, capped off with an open-air symphony. The momentary image was shattered by her recollection of the Judicial Review Hearing. "I'd love to—I'm a big Beethoven fan—only..."

"What?"

"Only I have a—a meeting to attend, but I'd love to some other time."

"Can I call you?"

"Sure. Now you'd best drive me home so I can shower and change. I don't know if my patient could accept seeing her doctor in a bicycle suit."

"Right, somehow the attire lacks a professional touch... When we met the other day, I was amazed to find that you were a doctor."

She laughed and replied, "I was amazed to discover that you

were a computer programmer."

"Because of my cycling clothes?"

"Partly. I can visualize you dressed for a business day, but you still don't fit the stereotype of a computer programmer."

He escorted her out the door and replied, "A nerdy guy with Coke bottle glasses?

She laughed. "Right."

Vivaldi's music was still playing in her head as they walked toward his car. The music came to mind frequently, along with thoughts of Ryan, for the remainder of the day. After meeting Geoff, Ryan still liked her! But he didn't know the rest.

Chapter 16

Melissa dialed the Hauser's number the following morning. There was no answer; her concern mounted. After arriving at her office, she dialed the number again and allowed it to ring more than a dozen times. A few minutes later the phone rang; she brightened when Jana mentioned Dr. Hauser's name. Melissa snatched up the receiver.

"Pneumonia," he said.

"I was afraid of that."

"So was I. She's being admitted for IV antibiotics."

"Who's her doctor?"

"She's had a slew of 'em. Currently, she's being cared for by a young sprout, Tom Dillon. What do you know about him?"

"Very little, but I'll visit Katrina over the noon hour; then I'll check out Dr. Dillon."

"I'd appreciate it."

Melissa rarely had a patient in need of his specialized services in the field of pulmonary medicine; however, as promised, she would probe fully into the care that young Dr. Dillon was providing for Katrina. If she unearthed any restrictions in Katrina's care for economic considerations, she would do everything in her power to override them.

The last patient of the morning was a plump woman in robust health. She expressed concern over the fact that her menstrual flow had diminished from six to five days and was certain that it was a sign of serious illness. Melissa patiently reassured her; however, at one point, she came close to telling her to be thankful that she was not lying seriously ill in a hospital bed. The woman left the office muttering concerns over her health. Melissa promptly forgot her exasperation as she sped to the hospital.

She pulled into the Doctors' Parking Lot and was distracted from her concern for Katrina by the animated conversation taking place in a nearby parking space. Ken Baker, clad in a rumpled lab coat, appeared distressed as he leaned toward the window of a maroon Mercedes convertible occupied by his wife. She tilted her upper body seductively in his direction, displaying her surgically augmented endowments. Melissa knew that these enhancements were the result of the finest of cosmetic surgery because she had known Andrea when she was flat-chested and worked as a circulating nurse in the OR. Andrea no longer worked in the OR, or even worked at all for that matter. She was now reveling in her status as an affluent doctor's wife. As a circulating nurse, it was her duty to take surgical specimens to the pathologist. After a number of trips to Baker's office, it was rumored, she enticed him into a liaison in the morgue. Shortly thereafter, Ken left his wife of 25 years for her.

Baker's prominent Adam's apple bobbed up and down. "Can't you change your nail appointment? I don't know if I can find a ride at the time I need to leave. I—"

Andrea started the engine and put her car in gear. She gave him a limp-wristed wave. "I'm sure you'll manage... Toodles."

Baker's droopy eyes followed her out of the parking lot; then turned in the direction of Melissa's approaching footsteps.

She said, "Hi, Ken."

"Oh, hi Melissa... Say, you wouldn't happen to be leaving around five? My car's in the shop and—"

"Sorry Ken. I'm just stopping by to see a friend, then going back to the office."

"No problem... I'm sure I can find a ride." Baker, exuding an odor of formaldehyde, fell into step beside her as they entered the hospital. Melissa averted her head in an attempt to escape the odor. He asked, "Say, are you by any chance a member of the La Playa Garden Club?"

Melissa shook her head. "No way, Ken. My life is much too complicated to get involved in that kind of socializing." She winked. "I have it on good authority that they don't do a lick of gardening. They just sit around sipping wine and gossiping at their monthly meetings."

A soft chuckle emanated from Baker's thin lips. "I'm aware of that, but Andrea really wants to join. A lot of the doctors' wives are giving her the cold shoulder."

"Jim Kerr's wife is the president-elect of the Garden Club. Why not ask him to have Janet put in a good word for her?"

"I didn't know that. I'll give Jim a call. We're golfing buddies."

Baker punched the down button adjacent to the elevator bank, Melissa stabbed the up button. "I know you are."

"How do you know that?"

"I was riding on a tandem bicycle yesterday. We were forced to stop abruptly when Geoff charged in front of us."

"So that was you in that silly bicycle suit."

"That was me. We were pulling my son in the trailer."

Baker huffed, "You know, if you were concerned for your child's welfare, yours too for that matter, you'd keep off the roads."

"Where should we ride?"

"The sidewalk or bike paths, not on our roads."

"The roads belong to everyone, Ken. Cyclists have as much right to the roads as cars, more rights to the road than a golf cart. I'm certain that if a car was occupying the space, Geoff would have stopped."

Baker shook his head. "That's different."

"Darn right, it's different. A car would have splatted you, you would have splatted us."

The elevator dinged. Through the closing door, he remarked, "I guess there are two perspectives to most situations, Melissa."

The up sign flashed; Melissa entered the adjacent elevator

and punched the fifth floor button. She reflected on the recent conversation. *He does have a point; there are two perspectives to many situations. That's an ever-recurring theme in my life. I wonder how long it's going to take Ken's little wife to realize that the "La Playa Piranhas" will never stop by with the Welcome Wagon. She can dress in the latest fashions purchased at the finest boutiques, drive a luxury car, have her hair done at the poshest salon, but she'll never be accepted. She didn't pay her dues by enduring the salad years while her husband was in his training. She never attended college, let alone a socially correct one. They've deemed her a predatory fortune hunter and will do their best to exclude her. She hasn't a prayer. Their chance for a happy marriage is somewhere between slim and none. But, hey, look who's talking, little Miss Single Mom.*

The door rumbled open and thoughts of Baker and his young wife vanished. She donned a gown and mask prior to entering Katrina's room. This was a necessary precaution to protect Katrina's nearly defenseless immune system from further attack.

Katrina, her face flushed with fever, was propped up in her hospital bed, staring out the window. The wind-chopped sea was flecked with white bits of "popcorn." A plastic bag labeled "Cefotan" hung on the IV pole. The straw colored fluid was slowly dripping into her vein. Green oxygen tubing snaked across Katrina's face, emitting a low hiss. Her breathing was unusually rapid, a condition with the medical definition of tachypnea. Despite her illness, Katrina maintained her dignity. The chemo had taken her thick head of hair; however, she had replaced it with a wig done up in a style similar to her neatly-coiled bun. She smiled. "*Liebling,* how good of you to come. I was looking at the sea. It looks angry today, don't you think."

"The weatherman is predicting a storm. Would you believe a storm in July? How are you doing?"

"The sea is full of life, but I'm dying."

"Stop that talk. How do you expect to get well with an attitude like that?"

Katrina nodded, smiled meekly. "*Ja, ja.* You're right. To get well I must think of the good things. Good things, like *mein Liebling* has finally found the right man, *dein Mensch.*"

"*My* man... Ryan's very nice, but we just met."

"I saw the way he looked at you. He's the right one, I repeat, *dein Mensch.*"

"I do trust your judgment, Katrina. You fully approve of him, then?"

"*Ja, völlig.* He's the right one; much better than that *Esel* you married."

"You never said anything negative about Geoff before, let alone calling him an ass."

"*Jawohl*, but you know me well already. I don't like to say bad things about people. I always look for the good."

"Did you ever find any good in Geoff?"

"*Nein.* No good in the ways that count, the important things. Your Ryan is good in the things that count."

"Like your Roger."

"*Ja*, like *our* Roger. I want you to promise me something—*cough*—if something happens to me, take care of my Roger."

"Nothing's going to happen to you, Katrina. Stop that talk."

"*Ja,* I will keep the good attitude already. We are just like family and have much happy times to come."

"You and Roger are quite precious, I love you dearly."

"*Ja, und* you're our daughter. The—*cough*—daughter we lost. Lisa would have been a fine doctor, just like you." Katrina's eyes sparkled. "I never saw my Roger happier than the day you graduated from medical school." The sparkle faded. "His only sad day after that was..."

"What?"

Katrina raised her arm and drew it across her brow. "*Ach*, me and my big mouth. He wanted so much for you to take over the practice, but—*cough*—it wasn't meant to be."

"It should have been, but I made a big mistake."

"*Nein, nein.* No talk of mistakes..." A long convulsive cough overtook her.

A rumbling noise interrupted. A tech rolled a portable x-ray machine into the room. The young woman smiled at Katrina and said, "I'm here to take a picture."

Melissa reached out to grasp Katrina's hand, then remembering the reverse isolation precautions, withdrew it. As a substitute, she blew her a kiss through the surgical mask. "I'll be back to see you later. Now, I'm going to bird-dog that doctor of yours and make sure you get the proper care."

Melissa strode to the Nurses' Station, found a vacant phone, and asked the operator to page Dillon. He answered promptly. "I'm in the Doctors' Dining Room. Why don't you come on down?"

Melissa entered the Doctors' Dining Room and, much to her dismay, encountered Geoff, who smirked in her direction. Seated on either side of him like a pair of incongruous bookends were Rachel Hornbeak and a striking redhead. Melissa prided herself in her ability to recognize a fellow physician, regardless of age or sex. This glitzy woman, exuding perfume-laced sensuality, did not look like a doctor or even a nurse, for that matter. Dillon waved in her direction. Seated beside him was Tara Linsey. Melissa selected a small salad from the buffet and took a seat at their table.

Tara asked, "How are you doing?"

Melissa shrugged. "Surviving."

"You know I'll help you in any way that I can."

"I know, but you're not in much of a position to help."

Tom appeared indifferent to Tara's comments. Melissa was certain that Tom was fully aware of her plight and appreciated his politeness. She turned to Dillon. "Tom, you're taking care of a good friend of mine, Katrina Hauser."

"She talks my arm off about you."

"How's she doing?"

"As you know, her white count is dangerously low. We've got her on a second generation cephalosporin. She should improve. Statistically, she definitely will recover. We've had a run on mortality lately."

Tara said, "If you flip a coin, heads is as likely to come up as tails. Percentages don't make an iota of difference in an individual situation. We've lost a lot of preemies lately, but that doesn't mean the next one we get in NICU has any better chance of survival... Ultimately, though, things should balance out."

"They should," said Tom. "In my humble opinion, mortality definitely is up on the seniors we're admitting recently."

Melissa said, "Interesting—preemies and the elderly—the biggest utilizers of the healthcare dollar. The businessmen in our IPA are the only ones who would be pleased by this situation. They'll gloat over the money they're saving."

"Probably just a temporary cluster," said Tom. "According to the last quarterly report, our stats are one of the best in the nation."

"If they're accurate," said Tara. "In my opinion, they're unbelievably good, too good to be true. We just lost a thirty-two-weeker two days after birth. He was on a vent, and given time, should have recovered. It's almost unheard of to lose a thirty-two-weeker."

Melissa said, "That was my experience when I rotated through peds during my internship. Three to five weeks in the NICU, and *voila*, a healthy baby with all his or her potential intact."

Tom said, "*Voila*, an industrial-strength hospital bill. In addition, there are the 'million dollar babies' with multiple congenital problems. Literally, millions are spent on these babies and some wind up with little or no potential."

Tara nodded. "Cerebral palsy and other long-term problems. When these kids are born, we have to make a commitment of whether to go for it or not. It's hard to predict outcome and know where to draw the line. Whether a newborn has a one-percent or ninety-percent chance of normalcy, there's still a chance. You deal with the same problem with the elderly, Tom."

"Right you are. "I've experienced numerous examples of the resilience of seniors. I've had patients that I've come close to writing off one day; the next day, they're sitting up in bed and discussing the news of the day. Many others, though, have a dismal outcome. We bring them through a crisis and the end result is a live patient in a chronic vegetative state."

Melissa winced at the words, *chronic vegetative state.*

Tom muttered, "Whoops, sorry." He turned to Tara and said, "Neonatology has the lion's share of long-term admits; I rarely have a patient hospitalized over a week."

Melissa said, "Me neither. The IPA pushes for one day after delivery for a vaginal birth and two days for a C-section, you have to fight tooth and nail for an additional stay. Some of my moms can barely walk when the powers-that-be deem that they should be discharged."

"I can see the other side of the coin," said Tom. "A hospital is an expensive hotel. People who are well enough for discharge should go home. The problem is, in most cases, a third party is picking up the tab and the patient wants the best service. Non-IPA patients stay longer and run up a bigger tab."

"The IPA isn't footing the bill for those patients," said Melissa. "These patients bring more profit to the hospital... Say, here's a gruesome thought, have either of you noticed whether IPA patients have a lower survival rate than non-IPA patients within these hallowed halls?"

"Haven't paid much attention to it," said Tara.

"Me neither," added Tom. "I see no evidence of them scrimping once a patient has been admitted. A case in point, Melissa, is your friend, Mrs. Hauser. We're giving her state of the art care, including thousands of dollars of antibiotics. Before that she received the latest in chemotherapy."

Melissa glared. "Chemotherapy that reduced her white count to zippo."

"Actually, her white count has bounced back."

"What is it?"

"Fourteen thousand."

"That's encouraging, but I just came from her room. She's definitely not over the hump".

Tom replied in his best doctor voice, "Given time and antibiotics, she'll pull through."

"Who gave her the chemo?"

"Jim Kerr, he's very good."

"Lives very well too," said Tara. "Has a big mansion on the bluffs, owns a fifty-foot yacht, and a Rolls. He's doing very well in these austere times."

"He's near retirement," said Tom. "He made a fortune when medicine was more profitable. He's probably just practicing medicine as a hobby, doesn't really need the income anymore."

"*Au contraire,*" said Tara. "He's a gambling man, quite the high roller I hear. He probably has to continue in practice to cover his gambling losses."

"Maybe he wins," said Tom.

Tara shook her head. "I heard he lost more than $200,000 last year, sold his boat, and his Rolls. He's in a world of hurt."

"Not hurting that bad," countered Tom. "Have you seen his new Beemer in the parking lot, must have cost at least 80 K."

"Didn't notice it," said Melissa. The scraping of chairs distracted her. Geoff and his two female cohorts rose, the redhead leaving a pungent trail as they exited. Melissa said, "I thought this was a Doctors' Dining Room. We're being invaded by administration and—who was that perfume factory?"

"Jean Iverson," sighed Tom. "A pharmacist. She could fill my prescription eight days a week, but unfortunately, she's your ex's main squeeze. But someday..."

Tara shook her head. "Oh brother."

Tom beamed. "She makes the patient's day when she wiggles up to the oncology floor with her little bundles of meds."

"Yours too," said Tara.

Tom nodded. "Can't blame me for being interested. She's beautiful and rich. She drives around in a red SLK convertible."

"Must be nice," said Tara. "I drive an aging Honda, which is in chronic need of CPR. I'd stay away from her, Tom."

"Why?"

"My female instincts. She wiggles around the NICU too. The little men in there pay her no mind, me neither."

"If her wiggles impressed you, that would concern me," said Tom. "In that case I'd never have a chance of getting to first base with you."

"I'm a happily married woman, Tom, and I'm deeming your last pitch a strike. You've well surpassed your limit of three, by the way. Nothing about her impresses me."

"You ought to heed our feminine intuition and stay away from the woman," said Melissa.

"I'll take heed of your warning," said Tom. "But if he tires of her, I'd be happy to console her and tool around in that slinky SLK of hers and, hooh hah!"

Tara shook her head. "It's a tossup, who's slinkier, she or her SLK. Poor little Tommy is thinking with his second brain again."

"You ain't just whistling Dixie," said Tom.

"Don't you wonder how she affords a car like that?" asked Melissa.

"Maybe she has a side business," said Tara. "She looks a bit like a professional girl to me."

"Meow, Meow," said Tom. "Cut it out, Tara. She's rich and beautiful and has a nice set of wheels." He threw his hands back and sighed, "I could love that woman and her magnificent wheels."

"You're hopeless," said Tara.

"That's me, a hopeless romantic."

"Not exactly," said Tara. "You're a hopeless idiot."

"Maybe so, maybe so." He turned to Melissa. "Maybe your ex bought the car for her."

Melissa shook her head. "No way. I know the man too well. He'd only spend that kind of money on himself. He's the ultimate narcissist."

"Now, now," said Tom.

Melissa glared. "He's a real bastard."

Tom raised his hands. "Sorry." He glanced at his watch. "I've got to go. Not to worry, Melissa, I'll give Mrs. Hauser the best of care. She's going to do just fine."

After Tom left, the two women realized that they were the sole occupants of the room. Tara turned to Melissa. "Tom will never change. He's the type of guy who'll never give up his hobby. I pity whoever he marries… If he ever does."

"If he ever does," said Melissa.

"Despite his hobby, he's a good doc. His overtures provide me with comic relief, he's totally harmless."

"As you notice, he doesn't pester me although I'm single and above his minimum standard of attractiveness. But then again, at least he talks to me. Ever since my problem, many of the docs regard me as a leper." Melissa deflected her gaze away from Tara.

"It's rough, isn't it?"

"Uh huh."

"I wish I could help, I really do. You don't deserve what has happened. For what it's worth, I think you're a terrific OB."

Melissa smiled. "Your opinion means a lot to me. Unfortunately, you're in the minority around here."

"Most people can be fickle, our colleagues included. Frankly, I've about had my fill of this place, Stafford in particular."

"Does he still have his problem?"

"He's getting worse, subject to mood swings, acts schizzy. I'm thinking of resigning."

"Where would you go?"

"A lot of places."

"I wish I had that option."

"I know."

Melissa heard the approach of footsteps and beheld Jim Kerr, impeccably dressed in an Armani suit complemented by a "power tie." He selected some items from the buffet, approached them, and flashed a haughty smile. "Mind if I join you two lovely ladies?"

Melissa forced a smile in return. "Please do." After he was seated, Melissa said, "I understand that you did the chemo on Katrina Hauser."

Kerr stared upward. "Hauser, hmm, the name is vaguely familiar.

I do a lot of chemo, you know."

"I know. She's been admitted with pneumonia. The precipitating factor was a low white count. I was wondering if you could enlighten me on her situation. She's a dear friend of mine."

A flicker of recognition formed on Kerr's face. "Hauser, ah, yes, I remember now, German lady, wonderful woman."

"She's Austrian."

"Same difference."

"Not really." Melissa gave him a visual grilling. "So there was nothing unusual with her chemo?"

Kerr's fork was poised midway between plate and lips. A gravy-laden bit of meat plummeted from his spoon and scored a direct hit on his tie. From there it came to rest on his trousers. "Oh no," he blurted. He dunked his napkin in his water glass, and dabbed furiously.

Melissa said, "Too bad, you've incurred a bad stain. Hopefully the cleaners can get it out."

Kerr ignored her and continued to dab. She watched for a moment; then said, "Have you considered a bone marrow transplant in Katrina's case?"

Kerr dropped the napkin on his lap and glared. "We'll cross that bridge when we come to it. We've got to get her through the pneumonia, first things first... Are you questioning my medical judgment?"

"No." *Actually, doctor, I am.* "Katrina is quite precious to me and I want to be assured that she is getting the best of care. I don't want to see her disappear down the managed care drain."

"I can assure you, Dr. Morrison, my colleagues and I are giving her the finest of care, the finest of care."

"I'm glad to hear that. Now, please excuse me. I must be going... See you later, Tara."

Tara said, "You didn't touch your salad."

"I'm not hungry."

Chapter 17

The following morning, Melissa entered Katrina's room, hoping to see improvement. Joy overflowed, lighting up her face. The oxygen tubing was gone; Katrina's breathing had slowed. Melissa said, "Wow, what an improvement."

"I'm going home tomorrow."

"Great, just great. You're from sturdy stock."

"*Jawohl. Danke schön* for talking firm to this old woman. You made me decide that my time had not come already. I have much to do in this life. I will be dancing at your wedding. *Nicht wahr?*"

Melissa smiled. "So you have me married already. I've known Ryan less than a week."

Katrina wagged her finger. "I am right. It will happen, wait and see."

Kerr and his haughty demeanor entered the room, erasing Melissa's thoughts of Ryan. Oozing artificial friendliness, he said, "Well, well, we're doing much better, aren't we. The wonders of modern medicine."

"The wonders of a strong constitution," said Melissa. "In my humble opinion, that has as much to do with her getting well as antibiotics."

A frown flickered momentarily on Kerr's face; then the arrogance reformed. "Perhaps, perhaps, well I must run. Dr. Dillon will be in tomorrow to see to your discharge Mrs. Hauser. Good Day Dr. Morrison." He executed an about face and marched from the room.

"Do you like him?" asked Melissa.

"*Nein*, a pompous *Esel*."

Melissa chuckled. "Right... The important thing is you're getting well, going home tomorrow. Melissa turned from Katrina and gazed out the window. The sea's mood was the same as the previous day, angry and threatening. The storm was still hovering off the coast waiting to strike. Melissa attempted to will the white-flecked expanse into tranquility; then abandoned the futile effort. The sea and Kerr's visit had dampened her cheerfulness. She shrugged off the negative feelings. Katrina was getting well. She turned to Katrina. "I'd best go now, and let you rest. I'll be back tomorrow."

"*Morgen*... Before you go *Liebling,* you've heard the word *Gemütlichkeit;* do you know what it means?"

"Warmth, coziness?"

"More than that, much more. *Gemütlichkeit* is what Roger *und* I, *und* you *und* little Roger have *zusammen*—together. *Verstehst du?*"

"I understand, *Gemütlichkeit.*"

"*Auf Wiedersehen.*"

"*Auf Wiedersehen.*"

Exiting the room, Melissa spotted Kerr approaching from the opposite end of the corridor. She attempted eye contact; he averted his gaze and ducked into a patient room. She was certain that he had seen her. Her disquietude returned.

Despite Katrina's rally, foreboding loomed over Melissa for the remainder of the day. Perhaps it had something to do with the impending storm. She could never recall a rainstorm in July. *That's it. The weather has put me in a blue funk. Katrina is getting well.*

Chapter 18

Katrina was in Melissa's thoughts as she began yet another night of fitful slumbers. A loud thunderclap awakened her. It was five a.m. She lay listening to the intermittent thunderclaps and the patter of the rain on the roof. A flash illuminated her bedroom in a surrealistic glare. She reached for the phone. "Fifth floor please…"

"Fifth floor, Unit Secretary Carole speaking."

"Carole, this is Dr. Morrison. Could I speak to Katrina Hauser's nurse?"

"One moment, I'll get Rita for you." Melissa winced in response to another thundering boom.

A nurse's voice displaced the tinny Muzak. "How's she doing?" asked Melissa.

"Pretty much the status quo during my shift. She's resting comfortably, afebrile, vitals are good, still a bit tachypneic. Anything else?"

"No… Thank you very much. I'll be by to see her in a few hours."

"*Achhoo.*"

"*Gesundheit.* Do you have a cold, Rita?"

"No, just my allergies kicking up. Happens every time that red-headed bimbo comes on the floor. She must buy the stuff by the gallon."

"The pharmacist."

"*Achoo.* Right."

After hanging up, Melissa thought, *Red-headed bimbo. Rita tells it like it is. My kind of woman.*

Melissa dozed intermittently until the alarm jarred her to full wakefulness. She could not shake her apprehension during breakfast or the short drive to the hospital in the light rain. She opened her car door and reached for her umbrella. It wasn't there. She dodged through the puddles in the parking lot and shrugged off the forgotten umbrella as a matter of little consequence.

The overhead page assaulted her ears as she entered the hospital. "CODE BLUE IN ROOM FIVE-THIRTY-TWO, CODE BLUE IN ROOM FIVE-THIRTY-TWO. Please avoid using the elevators until the all clear is given."

No, that's Katrina's room. She dashed for the stairwell and charged up the five flights. Her chest was heaving as she entered the room.

Dillon hovered over Katrina's frame. "Stand clear everybody... Let's give it another go." Katrina's body convulsed. An eerie beep emanated from the cardiac monitor. He stared at if for a moment; then gave the "stand clear" announcement again. Another convulsion; the monitor displayed a flat line. "Damn, we've lost her." Dillon tossed the paddles into the cart and shook his head. As he passed Melissa, he muttered, "Sorry."

Melissa stared through her tears out the window. The sea's anger had increased. She heard running footsteps and labored breathing. Roger rushed into the room. "Is she?"

"Yes," whispered Melissa; she turned to embrace him.

The assemblage of techs and nurses exited, leaving them alone in the room. Roger pulled away from Melissa, cradled Katrina's body in his arms and sobbed quietly. The resuscitation efforts had dislodged her wig revealing scattered wisps of hair. Melissa replaced it. For a fleeting moment she imagined that if she could restore Katrina's hair to its former state, life would be restored to Katrina as well. Realizing the futility of this fantasy, she stroked Roger's hair. The IV was still running. The label stated: Cefotan—

Hauser, Katrina—A367218—Rm. 532. She reached up and turned the thumbscrew. *A lot of good this second generation cephalosporin did her. For all the good it did, it might as well have been plain water... Stop it, Melissa, that's a sinister thought, an unbelievably sinister thought. But what if?* She unhooked the plastic container from the pole, detached it from the connecting tubing, and secreted it in her purse.

Melissa waited patiently while Roger grieved. Finally, he rose and she led him from the room. "Why?" he asked. "Why?" She couldn't answer him because she had the same question.

The rain had abated to light drizzle. Melissa drove Roger to her condo totally convinced that the rare July storm represented an anguished cry from heaven for her beloved Katrina. She seated him on the couch and cradled him in her arms. When his soft crying ceased she rose, walked to the telephone and dialed her office.

Jana began crying. "Joan from Dr. Young's office told me. She was a wonderful lady. What a tragedy."

"I know... It shouldn't have happened."

"Do you want me to cancel the patients?"

"Just for today. I'll be in tomorrow morning, but don't schedule past noon. I've got the hearing in the evening."

"No problem. Is there anything I can do for you or Dr. Hauser?"

"No... As a matter of fact there is."

"What?"

"Could you drive something up to Hannaford for me? I know it's a big imposition, but—"

"No problem."

Jana sat with Roger and Melissa. Not knowing what to say, she said nothing, which was the appropriate thing to do. Melissa reached in her purse, extracted the plastic pouch and handed it to Jana. "Take it to Dr. Woods in pharmacology. Don't leave it with anyone else. I've called and he's expecting you."

Jana nodded and left. Melissa deflected her gaze toward Roger.

He looked older and frailer. This rock of a man had crumbled. Little Roger awoke from his nap; she hastened upstairs to retrieve him from his crib. His innocent cheerfulness served as a welcome tonic; thank God for little Roger, thank God for both her Rogers.

Chapter 19

Anticipatory dread of the Judicial Review Hearing and Katrina's death competed for attention within Melissa's troubled brain. She dispatched her morning load of patients with atypical indifference. A day's worth of patients was easily scheduled in the morning hours. Ever since the newspaper article had hit the streets, she could count the daily patient load on one hand. By 11:30 the last one was seen. She stared upward out the window, toward the clouds. She saw angry faces. Jana buzzed her. "Ryan on line one." His voice cheered her. "How are you doing?"

"Hanging in there."

"I really admire your stamina, holding up under everything."

"I'm amazed at that fact myself."

"How's Dr. Hauser?"

"He's taking it hard; they had a long and very loving marriage."

"In the brief time I knew her, she made an enduring impression, and I know full well what she meant to you... Is there anything I can do to help you or Dr. Hauser?"

"No, nothing. But thank you for offering."

"When's the funeral?"

"Saturday morning."

"May I come?"

Melissa brightened. "Would you?

"Only if it wouldn't be an intrusion."

"It wouldn't be an intrusion; I'd appreciate your company."

After hanging up she deflected her gaze back toward the clouds. They seemed friendlier, just a little friendlier. *Gemütlichkeit*, she thought.

Jana interrupted her thoughts. "How about lunch? My treat."

They dined at the little deli where Jana had taken her on the day she began private practice as Rachel's associate. The two friends ate without speaking; Melissa reflected on how much their relationship had blossomed while other things had fragmented since that first day. *Gemütlichkeit*, she thought. *Thank God for Gemütlichkeit.*

Jana dialed the answering service upon their return to the office and asked for the messages. She reached for a pad of paper. She extended the pad to Melissa. "Dr. Woods at Hannaford."

Melissa dialed the number. "Dr. Woods, Melissa Morrison."

"Melissa, good to hear your voice. How are things?"

"Complicated, very complicated.   Did you analyze the solution?"

"I did, Melissa. And I must tell you, I'm perplexed. There was enough potassium in the bag to put down a mule." His words struck like a loading dose of anesthetic solution, rendering her speechless. He continued, "And, despite the label, there was no Cefotan, just some yellow dye. What is going on, Melissa?"

"Something terrible... Would you be kind enough to send me a written report?"

"No problem, but I don't understand—"

"I told you my life is complicated. I'm in the midst of something terribly bizarre."

"Can you enlighten me?"

"I will... As soon as I sort a few things out."

"Promise."

"I promise."

"I'll get the report out to you in today's mail."

"Could you fax a copy as well?"

"No problem."

"I'll look forward to receiving it. Thank you again."

Tears welled up in Melissa's eyes. "They murdered her. The

bastards murdered her. The IV contained a lethal dose of potassium...
And no Cefotan."

Jana's eyes widened. "Why?"

Melissa had the same question. She took a seat in an attempt
to bring her anger under control. She was overcome by a strong
urge to hit something or throw something; she told herself that she
was a civilized human being, not an animal. *Don't get mad, get
even.* She dialed the police. A woman answered. Melissa spoke in a
machine-gun staccato. "My dear friend, Katrina Hauser, they killed
her with potassium, there was no antibiotic in the IV, they killed her,
they—"

"Hey, lady, slow down, you're leaving me in the dust.

"Sorry, but a dear friend has been murdered."

"What is your location? I'll send somebody out."

After giving the requested information, she dialed Becky's
number. Melissa's voice had its same rapid intensity. "They
murdered Katrina. They gave her IV potassium."

"Easy Melissa." Becky spoke in a soft tone. "Take some long
deep breaths, you're hyperventilating."

Melissa thought, *Dr. Becky. She's talking to me like a patient...
She's right.* Melissa took a few moments to calm her breathing; then
related the facts to Becky.

"Who's they?"

"I don't know, but I'm damn sure going to find out."

"How can you be certain about the IV solution?"

"Dr. Woods did the analysis; he's a highly respected
pharmacologist at Hannaford. Katrina's IV contained a lethal dose
of potassium.

"Potassium."

"It stops the heart, and there was no antibiotic, it has to be
deliberate."

"Did you request a written report from Dr. Woods?"

"Yes; he's faxing it. Do you want to know something else? I
think they gave her too much chemo, set her up for an infection;
they killed her, dammit!"

"If what you're alleging is true, that hospital is truly diabolical. This is unbelievable."

"I've called the police, they're sending someone over."

"You say you secreted the IV in your purse; then gave it to Jana to hand-deliver to the pharmacologist... Chain of evidence."

"What?"

"Despite the seriousness of the event, your evidence has limited value. Any evidence obtained in such a manner is suspect. The hospital will allege that you tampered with the solution."

Melissa's breathing increased. "She gasped, "Why would I do such a thing?"

"I know you wouldn't, but it's a no-brainer to predict the hospital's response, the police, too. Look Melissa, have a cup of tea, calm yourself down. I'll be right over."

After pouring the cup of tea, prescribed by Dr. Thatcher, Melissa twirled the Rolodex and dialed Rucker's number. After some delay, he came on the line. His condescending "hello" grated on her ears. He had not used that tone before. Could this be the same man who had won her confidence? She said, "Mr. Rucker, I've had a number of recent stresses in my life. I don't know if I'm prepared for this evening."

"Requesting a continuance at such a late date will antagonize the opposition."

"I couldn't care less about that."

"We don't want to ruffle their feathers, do we?"

Melissa did not reply.

"Dr. Morrison."

"Yes."

"Look, the evening will be taken up with the presentation of their case against you; all you'll have to do is attend the hearing and listen."

Melissa's voice rose a full octave. "Listening to the slings and arrows of their outrageous attacks."

Rucker soothed, "Try to maintain your composure. Don't go off the deep end on me and retreat into a Shakespearean tragedy."

"This is not a Shakespearean tragedy; modern, day possibly, but not Shakespearean. I can assure you that I'm not going off the deep end... I'm mentally sound. Look, if you'd endured just some of the things that I have over the past few days, you might be a candidate for a rubber room."

"Try to keep cool, Dr. Morrison. Let's not have any more talk of rubber rooms. We'll meet at quarter to six"

"I'll see you then."

Melissa replaced the receiver. *What has happened? He's a hand holder wallowing in artificial friendliness. I need an advocate, dammit, not a conciliatory weasel.*

She located Kerr's number, and placed the call. A crisp voice told her that he was with patients and would return the call shortly.

Jana entered. "A policeman here to see you."

"Ask him if he'd like a cup of coffee, I'm waiting for Becky."

Exiting, she said, "Will do."

Several minutes later, Jana returned. "Another policeman is here, a detective."

"Ask him to wait with the other one."

"I did. No dice. He wants to see you immediately, he's a 'just the facts, ma'am' kinda guy."

"Give me a minute."

As she took her last sip of tea, Jana showed two officers into the chamber, a reed-like man who appeared to be a good six-foot-six, and a short, ovoid man. The tall one introduced himself, in a military voice, as Detective Derek Anderson; the short one followed suit. "Officer Carlos Mendoza, doctor."

To Melissa's relief, Becky entered the room.

"Who are you?" asked Anderson.

"Dr. Morrison's attorney."

Anderson arched his eyebrows, "Hmm."

After Melissa recounted her tale, Anderson spoke. "That's quite a story, doctor. A bit unbelievable."

"Unbelievable, but true."

Anderson turned to Becky. "I'm sure you're aware of the

problem."

"The evidence."

"Right."

"I can assure you that my client would never consider evidence tampering. What would be the purpose?"

"Just playing the devil's advocate." He turned to Melissa. "Doctor, you and the hospital aren't exactly on cozy terms."

"No but—"

Anderson held up his hands. "If what you said is true, the hospital's not going to roll over. The burden of proof is on you." Melissa shook her head. Anderson continued. "What you should've done is this. Shoulda called us from the hospital room. We would have sealed off the room, impounded the IV, and any other evidence... And made it a coroner's case."

Becky said, "There's enough here to make it a coroner's case, unless..." Anderson added, "Unless an autopsy's already been done."

Melissa buzzed Jana. "Call path at Cliffside, see if they've done a post on Katrina." Melissa blanched, began to sob.

Becky rose. "I'll get some more tea. Anybody else?" The officers replied in unison, "Coffee."

When Beck returned, Melissa slouched over her cup of tea, taking small sips. Anderson gulped down his cup. "Good coffee... If you don't mind, doctor, we have a few more questions. I understand that you're in the midst of a malpractice situation with the hospital."

Becky replied, "That has nothing to do with this situation."

"Maybe, maybe not. Can you enlighten us?"

"Dr. Morrison had some patients who incurred bad outcomes, it's being investigated. That's all we care—or need to—say at this time."

The intercom interrupted. After a brief conversation, Melissa hung up the receiver. She whispered, "The post was done yesterday, report's not available yet."

Anderson said, "We'll request a copy... I want to say something, doctor; this is indeed an unfortunate situation."

"Will you investigate?" asked Melissa.

"Of course... Well, we'd best be going. We'll be in touch." Anderson rose, Mendoza snapped to his feet; the duo marched from the room. Becky's cell phone rang. Melissa finished her tea, staring out the window.

"Sorry, I've got to run," said Becky. She gave Melissa a hug.

"Thanks for coming."

"Don't even mention it. I'll call you later."

Melissa dialed Kerr's office. A woman answered. "He's left for the day."

Jana entered, placed her hand around Melissa's shoulder. "There are no more patients for the day and you have a nasty evening ahead of you. Why don't you get out of here and try to de-stress?" Melissa shook her head. "I can't de-stress. I've got to tell Roger about Katrina's murder." Jana hugged her. "That's going to be terribly hard." Melissa pressed her teeth against her lower lip. "Terribly hard."

Chapter 20

She rehearsed her words repeatedly during the drive home to fetch little Roger. She dressed him in his Winnie the Pooh overalls, and said, "Let's go feed the ducks."

He squealed, "Ducks," waddled to the pantry and fetched a box of Cheerios. She poured a generous amount into a bag. He grasped the treasure and tugged her toward the doorway. For a moment she was caught up in his exuberance, but it vanished by the time she entered the highway. She engaged Roger in a lesson on colors, using passing automobiles as examples. Her attempt to escape into a child's world failed. His cheerful, one-word responses could not ease her melancholia. Yesterday's storm had passed. The sun was shining, but it could not warm her.

Dr. Hauser was slumped on a bench, gazing vacantly at the lake. He smiled weakly in their direction.

"Opa," whooped little Roger.

Dr. Hauser's smile brightened as the toddler charged into his arms.

"Where Oma?" asked little Roger.

Dr. Hauser trembled, attempted to blink back his tears, and held the child firmly against his chest. He whispered, "Oma's gone bye-bye."

Melissa took a seat on the bench and embraced her two Rogers.

Little Roger squealed, "Ducks."

"In a few minutes. Mommy needs to talk to Opa."

Little Roger tugged at her. "Ducks."

"Mommy's busy."

He began to whimper.

Dr. Hauser's voice had an edge. "Don't snap at the little guy, he's on another agenda... Let's walk and talk."

They strolled around the lakeshore pausing frequently to allow little Roger an opportunity to engross himself in one of his most beloved pastimes. He alternately placed a handful of Cheerios in his mouth and scattered a second handful to the ducks.

Melissa focused on the blue lake and the quacking of the ducks. Speech eluded her.

Dr. Hauser said, "It's a nice day, the storm is over."

The anger from within welled up and took command of her voice. "No it's not, it's raging."

"What?"

Tears streamed down Melissa's face. "They murdered Katrina. There was no Cefotan in the IV; instead, it contained a lethal dose of potassium."

Shock, then the anger of an incensed grizzly welled up. For several minutes his rage deprived him of the ability to speak. Finally, he asked, "Who? Who did this to my Katrina? I'll kill him with my bare hands if it's the last thing I do."

"And I'll help you—"

"Who?"

"I suspect the oncologist, Kerr, may be involved; at this point it's only a hunch. I called the police, but—"

"But what?"

"I snuck the IV bag out of the room, had it analyzed by Dr. Woods at Hannaford. I should have called the police from the hospital..."

Dr. Hauser placed his arm around her shoulder. "I'm amazed that you had the presence of mind to do what you did. In any event, it's obvious something rotten is going on at Cliffside."

"We'll find out who's responsible... And punish them."

"Kerr never impressed me much, an arrogant society doctor. I know that type well; they're prone to negligence."

"This goes far beyond negligence. I've arrived at a theory that they first gave her an overdose of chemo, and when she got pneumonia, they pretended to give her antibiotics."

"But they must have given her antibiotics, she was getting better. And then, and then." He reached for his handkerchief.

"People recover from infection without antibiotics. Katrina has a tough constitution. She was getting better despite their scheme. My guess is someone made the command decision to give her potassium, make it look like a heart attack."

He shook his head. "Hard to believe. The physician in me refuses to accept your theory. Negligence, I can accept; purposeful, willful murder, I can't. Why would they do such a thing?"

"To save money."

"To save money?"

"Rumor has it that the death rate is up for the preemies and the elderly. My ghoulish premise is that they're hastening the demise of the heavy utilizers of healthcare."

"Do you have any evidence of other such incidents?"

"No, just Katrina. But I'll bet my last dollar that there are others, and I can assure you, I'll get to the bottom of it."

He clasped her hand. "You've got all these problems in your life; how can you fit this in?"

"I'll fit it in. This is very important to me."

"How can I help? I've got time on my hands and I'm filled with grief, and now, anger. I..." Tears streamed down his face.

"Ducks," said little Roger. He extended his bag, now half-empty, toward Dr. Hauser. He took the gift, and little Roger, into his arms.

She left Dr. Hauser seated on the bench and drove home. She had several empty hours at her disposal, and needed to hear a friendly voice. She dialed Ryan's office. "Ryan MacKenzie, please. This is Dr. Morrison."

After a belief delay, she was informed that he was out of the office for the day. She tried his cell phone, got his voice mail. She was disappointed. She also was curious about what he was doing. She knew little about his work. But, she rationalized, her rudimentary computer knowledge would prevent her from understanding his explanation.

Apprehension for the upcoming hearing marched up like a sentinel relieving another's watch. There was only enough room for one of them in her kiosk at a time. Perhaps that was how she kept her sanity. If all of them piled in there at once, she wouldn't be able to cope with them. The Judicial Review Hearing sentry was now on duty.

Chapter 21

The Judicial Review Hearing took place in Cliffside Medical Center's Board Room. The chamber reminded Melissa of Roach and Graber's conference room. She stared at the wall and concluded that it was her lot in life to be tormented in oak-paneled rooms. A court reporter sat at one end of the long table; her bright, flowered dress imparted a wisp of cheerfulness to the somber atmosphere. Melissa sat staring at the panel composed of six of her peers; they were seated on the opposite side of the table. Jim Bridges had been offered, and approved, for the OB/GYN representative on the panel. She had a nodding acquaintance with Jim, but had never had any professional contact with him. The hospital attorney, Herb Sempres, next presented the evidence against Melissa beginning with her first case and moving on to the second, and much more serious, medical misadventure. Initially his words stung and she listened intently to them. *Another weasel,* she thought. *This one looks exactly like a weasel with his narrow-set eyes, his weasel-shaped face, and pointy nose.*

After a while, she either had developed a sensory numbness to his oration or had fallen victim to his droning. The drone brought Melissa's Biology 120 class to mind. The professor spoke in an identical monotone. The class was right after lunch. He dimmed the lights and droned through his slide show, instantly narcotizing Melissa and most of the class. Despite this, she got an A in the course. For a moment, she was back in the lecture hall; then she reminded herself that she was not a college girl and was not getting an A in this class. She found herself staring at Sempres, wondering how much of his drone she had tuned out.

Sempres' monologue had come to an end; perhaps that was why she had been roused back to alertness.

The current OB Chairman, Ken Brandon, began to speak. He explained to the panel that the OB Core Committee had carefully reviewed the cases, and the majority of the physicians had recommended revocation of Dr. Morrison's privileges. The matter was referred to the Medical Executive Committee, where it had been concluded that all of Dr. Morrison's staff privileges should be terminated.

Sempres next called in their star witness, Dr. Rachel Hornbeak. Melissa mused, *Rachel is probably just about as dangerous as a witness against me, than she would be as a panel member. Probably more dangerous.*

"How long were you associated with Dr. Morrison?" asked Sempres.

"Two years."

"What was your initial impression of Dr. Morrison?"

Her voice lacked inflection, as if she was reading a script for an undesired role. "Good credentials, very good educational background."

"Has that opinion changed since that time?"

She continued on with the script reading. "I still feel that she is an intelligent physician... Very book smart. Unfortunately, she has difficulty putting that book knowledge to practical use."

"Could you explain that statement?"

Inflection returned to Rachel's voice; it became authoritative and raspy. "Her first patient, after joining my practice, is a good example. She misdiagnosed an ectopic pregnancy with serious consequences for the patient. As you all know, her second glaring episode of indecision resulted in severe brain damage for a mother and child."

Sempres tried to force an aggrieved look to materialize, however his facial muscles failed to comply. "Were there other examples of Dr. Morrison's indecisiveness?"

"Yes, but they were relatively minor, and more importantly, did not harm a patient. Dr. Morrison often came to me with medical questions that I felt to be trivial; I tried to help her apply her medical knowledge and guide her down the proper path. She seemed to falter when confronted with a diagnostic situation. She could not sense the subtle nuances that indicated the possibility of a potentially serious problem."

Melissa gasped. *She knows that isn't true. I'll match my diagnostic acumen with hers, or any other OB/GYN at Cliffside, any day of the week.* She stared across the table. All the panel members were listening intently to Rachel's discourse.

Sempres continued with his questioning. "Why did you maintain the association for two years in view of Dr. Morrison's shortcomings?"

Rachel's abrasive voice took on a melodramatic tinge. "I felt sorry for her. I hoped that, given time, she could mature into a competent physician. Besides she had personal problems to overcome."

"What type of personal problems?"

"She went through a messy divorce and shortly thereafter became a single mom. Those are tough personal problems and I had hoped that she could work them out. It was a strain on me, too—believe me—she often took time off for frivolous reasons with little or no notice. I tried to shoulder the load and be more supportive."

Melissa shook her head. *Unbelievable! She's portraying me as an airhead. She certainly knows that she saw to it that I shouldered the lion's share of the work load. And what about all the times the hospital couldn't find her? I never once complained about covering her.*

Sempres referred to his notes; then droned onward, "You mentioned that the association terminated after two years. How did it end?"

Rachel forced a pained expression on her face. She was much better than Sempres at this technique. "I terminated her."

"For what reason?"

Rachel attempted a sigh, but a bullfrog-like rasp emerged. "At the end of two years, our contract called either for a stepwise partnership or a severance of relations. I did a lot of soul-searching and concluded that Dr. Morrison was much more of a liability than an asset. In the end, I had to place the welfare of the patients in the forefront."

"Thank you, Dr. Hornbeak. No further questions."

George Rucker began his cross-examination. Melissa was bitterly disappointed in what ensued. He plodded through his questions with no real enthusiasm. She reflected, *This is not how I envisioned he would perform. I expected much more than this lackluster representation. Much, much more.*

Contrasting Rucker's abominable performance was Rachel's answers to his questions. At every opportunity, Rachel continued to convey the image of Melissa as an indecisive physician who was a menace to her patients.

The next witness was Dr. Brookhurst. He informed the committee that he fully concurred with Rachel's assessment. He went on to explain that in the ectopic pregnancy case, Melissa's lack of diagnostic abilities had almost cost a young woman her life. He then described the details of the Sanders case, and outlined Melissa's deficient surgical skills and histrionic responses.

Rucker declined to cross-examine.

A date of one week hence was proposed for the next session; however, two of the panel members had a conflict. Sempres grudgingly agreed to a date two weeks in the future; then informed the panel that the third session would occur one week after that. No excuse short of death or grave illness would be acceptable.

Entering her car, Melissa glanced at her watch—it was ten p.m.—her mind went fuzzy with exhaustion. She expended her last bit of energy on the drive home.

She tiptoed upstairs and checked on Roger, sleeping soundly in his crib. She sat quietly staring at her magnificent child and willed her love for him to displace her frustration and despondency. She kept little Roger's peaceful image in her consciousness while she soaked in the tub. Then she went to bed and mentally reviewed the wretched evening. The responses of Rachel and Brookhurst were expected; however, Rucker's performance was abominable. *He went through the motions of defending me. Has somebody approached him? Has he been bought off? Melissa, tomorrow you're going to find a new attorney. You'll go down the drain with this guy. You need help in the worst way, and that's exactly what you're getting.* Her mind churned relentlessly. Sleep eluded her.

Chapter 22

Melissa awoke the next morning with an agenda. After jump-starting her fatigued brain with two cups of coffee, she headed for the hospital. She rode the elevator to the fifth floor. She had no need to stop on the postpartum floor; she had no patients in-house. Approaching the nurses' station, she asked, "Has Dr. Kerr been by yet?"

Connie, the unit secretary, replied, "Not yet."

Melissa fetched yet another cup of coffee from the utility room. After the first sip, Kerr strode past. She said, "Dr. Kerr, may I have a word with you."

Kerr turned to her and glared. "I'm quite busy."

Melissa glared back. "I just need a moment of your time to discuss Katrina Hauser. Please step in here and talk to me."

Kerr entered the small chamber. "What's there to discuss, she arrested."

Melissa raised her voice, "How can you be so callous?"

A nurse entered, quickly filled a cup of coffee and sped from the room. Kerr's eyes pierced her like a laser. "My dear Dr. Morrison, situations like your friend's are common in my practice. Bad outcomes are commonplace; those in my profession must learn to live with it."

"But she was doing so well when I last saw her. She's never had any heart trouble."

Kerr shook his head. "Are you questioning my care?"

"Most definitely."

He wagged his finger, invading her personal space. "If I were in your current situation with this hospital, I'd be much more cautious about questioning those with long, impeccable careers on staff here." He continued talking as he exited. "The incompetents get weeded out in short order."

Melissa controlled an urge to run after him and give him a firm slap; instead, she poured her cup of coffee down the sink, and left.

Upon arriving at her office, Melissa phoned Rucker's office. His secretary asked her to hold; then told her he was tied up with a client. During a second call, she was informed that he would be in court all day. Melissa's suspicion rose; she summoned Jana to her consultation room. "Try this number," said Melissa. "Tell them that you're a doctor in need of urgent legal assistance. If the creep comes on the line, hand me the phone."

A minute later Jana winked and handed over the phone.

Icicles dripped from Melissa's tongue. "Good Morning, Mr. Rucker. Dr. Morrison here."

"Er—umm—Good Morning."

"I thought you were in court."

"Er… It was cancelled at the last minute."

"I see. I'm extremely disappointed in the events of last evening, your performance in particular." His initial embarrassed tone was replaced with the now-familiar condescending voice. "I'm sorry you feel that way. I did tell you that this session was their defense."

She snapped, "I realize that, but you could have bolstered my case during the cross-examination. You did a terrible job cross-examining Rachel, and you never bothered to cross-examine Brookhurst."

He snorted, "*Doctor*, are you trying to tell me how to practice law?"

She replied, "No. Just my perception of how it should be practiced."

"Well, *my dear*, the cross-examination was not helping your case. I cut it short in the interests of damage control."

Her anger was escalating along with her vocal volume. "Damage control. You were damaging my case with your questions. Why didn't you ask the questions that I suggested? Through a good line of questioning, you might have been able to get them to admit that their portrayal of me as an inept airhead was simply not true."

"Again, doctor, I must admonish you on trying to tell me how to practice my profession. At the next session, we can bring out all your good points. You'll see me in action, and believe me, you'll be impressed."

"I think not. I can't afford to take another chance on you fumbling the ball. My medical career is on the line here. I want to tell you something that really bothers me, Mr. Rucker. You appeared extremely capable when I first met you; then something happened. You seem to have lost interest in my case; as if you were asked to throw the fight."

"What are you insinuating?"

"I'm not insinuating anything, just giving you my opinion. In any event, I do not wish to retain you any longer. After I get off the phone with you, I'm going to find a new attorney."

"Well. If that's the way you want it, that's the way you'll get it. I'll send you a withdrawal form *and* a final bill for my services. Once you sign and return it, my representation will cease."

"By that time, I will probably have obtained new counsel."

"I think not."

"And why not?"

"The Hospital Bylaws prohibit it. Clearly stated therein is a clause that reads: 'In cases where patient welfare is of grave concern, substitution of consul after the hearing commences is not allowed.' Your case falls under the category of grave concern for patient welfare."

"I know of numerous examples where clients obtained new attorneys during a trial. It happens all the time."

"Maybe it happens all the time in our court system, but not at Cliffside. I told you, they operate under their own rules."

She gasped. "In other words they can do as they please."

"Quite true. Well I must go."

"Just one other comment, Mr. Rucker, and then I'll let you go. They're fast-tracking this kangaroo court of theirs, aren't they?

"Of course they are. They want to get rid of you. Goodbye, Dr. Morrison."

Melissa retrieved the bylaws and found Rucker's statement to be correct. She consulted with Becky who concurred. Melissa then resolved that she would act as her own attorney. Worst case scenario, she could defend herself much better than Rucker the sandbagger. She promised herself that she would begin preparation after the weekend. Tomorrow, she had a funeral to attend.

Chapter 23

At Katrina's behest, instead of a eulogy, a pianist and a violinist performed Beethoven's Sonata Number Five, Opus 24, "The Spring Sonata," or as Katrina would have described it in her native German, *"Frühlingsonate."* Melissa sat and visualized Katrina as the violin sang to her and added her own lyrics: *Why did it happen? Why did it happen?* Beethoven was one of Melissa's favorite composers and she was familiar with many of his works. However, she did not recall hearing this one before. Katrina was speaking to her through Beethoven's music from wherever she was right now, and at present Melissa sensed Katrina's presence. Spring symbolized youth and rebirth. Although she was in the spring of her medical career, it was being attacked by winter winds. She looked down at little Roger with virtually his whole life ahead of him. She clutched him firmly as Geoff's custody demand jolted her consciousness. She turned to Dr. Hauser seated beside her. He was listening intently with moistened eyes. He was embarking on a new spring; a life without Katrina. Hopefully, he could survive without the strength of her love. Melissa vowed to devote as much time as possible to helping him through this difficult time. Ryan was seated on her other side. He smiled softly when she turned in his direction. Ryan had definitely breathed a refreshing spring into her life. The warmth of his friendship served as a much-needed counterbalance to all the things that had gone wrong in the past few months.

After the service, Melissa and the three men in her life returned to her condo. The somberness of the occasion had not penetrated young Roger's comprehension. Upon entering, he squealed, "Casper."

Melissa looked toward the patio door expecting to see the dog leaping for entrance; Casper was nowhere in sight. She opened the back door and called. "Strange," she said. "Casper!"

She found Casper lying in the side yard lying near the gate, on his side with a protruded tongue. She gently prodded him for any sign of life, but found none. She ran back inside, and announced, "C-A-S-P-E-R is D-E-A-D."

Dr. Hauser asked, "How?"

"I don't know. Come have a look with me... Ryan, could you handle little Roger for a minute?"

"Sure. Hey champ, how about a ball game."

"Ball."

Dr. Hauser crouched down beside Casper's body. Melissa sobbed, "He was fine when I left this morning, just fine."

"Do you have any bad news neighbors?" he asked.

"No, they're all pleasant. Why?"

"A few years back, somebody poisoned our neighbor's dog, a reincarnation of Attila the Hun."

"Casper wouldn't hurt a fly. Who would want to poison him?"

Ryan appeared, and stared at the corpse.

Melissa asked, "Where's Roger?"

"Tucked safely in his playpen." You have a phone call."

Melissa heard little Roger cry and sped for the door. The others followed. She fetched her son from the playpen.

"Come to Opa," said Dr. Hauser, snatching him from her arms.

She picked up the phone. "Hello."

The husky voice said, "How's your little dog?"

"Who is this?"

"Quit prying into hospital affairs that don't concern you."

"They concern me a great deal, others as well."

"Let me give you some advice, doctor, life-saving advice, you might say... Too bad about the dog, but worse things can happen."

"What do—"

"Roger Podger and Roger Codger."

"What—"

Click!

She ran to her Rogers and clasped them. "Whoever just called me told me that he poisoned you-know-who."

Dr. Hauser asked, "Why?"

"He told me that what happened out there was a warning." Tears overcame her. She took a deep breath. "H-he threatened to harm you and little Roger if I didn't back off."

"Back off from what?"

"He must be referring to me contacting the police... Hmm." She reached for the phone and dialed *69. The phone rang more than a dozen times. A nasal voice, which in no way resembled that of the previous caller, came on the line. "Yeah."

"Who is this?"

"Hey lady, it's your nickel. I just got tired of hearing the phone ringing off the wall."

"Would you mind telling me where you are?"

"I'm at a pay phone next to the john at the Good Times Saloon. I'm here to take a leak. Is that of interest to you?"

"Somebody just called me from there. Is anybody else around?"

"Nah lady. Hey, nice chatting with ya, but I gotta go—really— ha ha." Click!

Melissa dialed the police. A man answered. Melissa asked, "Is Detective Anderson in?"

"Hold on a sec... No he's off duty this weekend."

"Officer Mendoza?"

"Hold on... He's off too. Can I help?"

"I am reporting a poisoning."

The voice expressed concern. "Do you know the identity of the victim?"

"Casper, my little dog."

The concern faded from the voice. "You need to contact Animal

Control."

"Will they investigate?"

"Doubtful… But they will pick up the remains."

Melissa snapped, "Look, maybe you don't think this is serious, but it is. I've also received a death threat directed toward my son and a dear friend."

A tinge of interest formed in the voice. "Any idea who made the threat?"

"I have some suspicions, but I don't know for sure."

"Is this the first threat?"

"Yes."

The voice continued in an officious monotone. "Most of these types of calls are from cowards who have no intention of acting upon them. Do you have caller ID?"

"No."

"Call the phone company and get it. If you receive another call, it can be traced."

Her voice became shrill. "I used star-sixty-nine. The call was from a pay phone. Caller ID won't help. My dog is dead."

"I'm sorry, but this department has homicides to handle, homicides of people, not dogs."

Melissa struggled to modulate her voice, but failed. "Well, my son might be one of your next homicides, my friend, or me. Please inform Detective Anderson and Officer Mendoza about my call."

"Certainly, ma'am." Melissa slammed the receiver down. "He didn't take me seriously, told me to call the phone company to get caller ID. And as far as C-A-S-P-E-R...." Dr. Hauser asked, "What?"

"He told me to call Animal Control to—to pick up the remains."

"Anybody who would do a thing like that is a coward, a despicable coward."

"That's what he said."

Little Roger began howling for his lunch. Melissa averted her gaze so that he couldn't see her tears. Ryan fastened Roger in his high chair, scanned the pantry, and found a jar of food. He began spooning the contents into Roger's mouth, and said, "Melissa, I'm really concerned about you and this little guy here, but I agree with Dr. Hauser, your caller is most likely a coward who's just trying to scare you."

"I hope you're right. I sure hope you're right." She turned to Dr. Hauser. "Do you still have that place up at Santa Theresa Lake?"

"I do."

"Why don't you take Roger up there with you? Ada, too. You'll be safe there."

"That sounds sensible, but what about you? Why not come with us?"

Melissa shook her head. "I still have a few patients... I'm responsible for their care. Besides, with all that's going on in my life at present, I need to be around. I'll be okay."

Ryan said, "I could stay with you."

"That's a good idea," said Dr. Hauser.

Ryan blushed, turned to Melissa and asked, "Do you have a spare bedroom?"

"I have a hide-a-bed in the study."

Packing her son's things saddened Melissa, but she got through the task in short order. Ryan placed his little suitcase in the trunk while she secured little Roger in his car-seat.

She gave both Rogers a final good-bye kiss. They rolled down the driveway in Dr. Hauser's vintage Mercedes. Melissa marveled at the vehicle; although it had to be at least 20 years old, it appeared as pristine as the day it was driven off the showroom floor. Little Roger was not the least upset by the separation; he smiled and waved in anticipation of an automotive adventure. "Bye-bye car."

"You're going to miss him," said Ryan, joining Melissa in a return wave.

Melissa bit her lip. "Both of them, both of them."

Ryan glanced downward, picked up an object. "Keys. Do you know who they belong to?"

"Oh dear, Roger forgot his keys."

"How'd he start the car then?"

Melissa laughed. "These are little Roger's keys. He was fascinated with mine so I made up a set of old keys for him. They're one of his favorite toys."

"My nephew has a thing about keys, too. Say, I'll need to run out to my place and pick up a few things."

He didn't need to ask her to accompany him. She could not be alone; human companionship was essential, particularly his human companionship. During the drive to his condo, she attempted a retreat into her fantasy world of a normal little family: Mommy, Daddy, and Little Roger; however, the absence of her son prevented this retreat into her happier place.

She sat and stared at his seascape while he packed, focusing on one of the seagulls struggling against the stiff ocean breeze.

His voice startled her, "I'm all set."

She turned from the painting to Ryan and envisioned him as a fellow seagull soaring skyward. She felt a little better.

Ryan placed his suitcase in the trunk, and secured his tandem on the roof rack. He handed a rectangular object to her and asked, "Mind holding onto this?"

"Sure. Ah, your laptop."

"I never leave home without it."

"Your laptop and your bicycle, two of your most prized possessions."

"I have lots of prized possessions. I..."

"What?"

"I—er—say, want to stop by someplace for dinner?"

She shook her head. "My eyes are all puffy. Let's eat in... We'll need to find a market; I don't have much at home."

She walked beside him down the supermarket aisles. She felt a much higher degree of comfort with Ryan than she had ever felt with Geoff. This sensation prevailed after they returned home. He fired up the barbecue and skillfully cooked the chicken while she prepared the remainder of the meal. With the first bite of the chicken, she discovered something new about this man, he was a terrific cook.

Geoff's few attempts at barbecuing had been total disasters. He always had a glib excuse, which in no way incriminated the chef.

After dinner, despite the likelihood that it would doom the fruition of their relationship, Melissa decided that it was time to apprise Ryan about her multitude of problems. She was searching for the courage to begin; the doorbell rang. She considered ignoring it; then rose. Melissa opened the door and shuddered—it was the social worker, Grandolfo. "May I come in?" she asked.

"Would it matter if I said no?"

"Not really."

"Well come in, but make it brief. I have company."

As they entered the room, Ryan rose to greet Grandolfo. While Melissa made the introductions, she signaled Ryan with a gagging expression. Grandolfo asked, "May I see the child?"

"He's not here… He's on a little vacation with his Opa."

"Opa?"

"Opa, grandfather."

"According to my records, both grandfathers are deceased."

"He's a very close friend, and is, for all practical purposes, Roger's grandfather."

"I see. Is his wife accompanying them?"

"She's deceased. Her funeral was this morning."

She began scribbling in her ubiquitous notebook. "Let's see if I have the facts correct here. You've entrusted your son to a distraught man who just buried his wife. Aren't you concerned how he will manage a small child all by himself?"

"My housekeeper accompanied them. They'll manage just fine."

"How long will they be gone and where are they?"

"I don't know how long and I'll check with my attorney as to whether I have to disclose their whereabouts."

"Why so secretive?"

"My dog was poisoned and I received a phone call threatening my son and my friend, Dr. Hauser. We decided that leaving the area would be a prudent thing to do."

"I must say that you live in a strange world, poisoning, threats, head concussions, and lord knows what else." She glared at Ryan. "Is that your suitcase in the entry?"

"It is."

Grandolfo wrote furiously in her notebook for several minutes; then said, "Well, I'll be leaving now. Sorry to have interrupted your romantic weekend, Ms. Morrison."

Melissa shut the front door, turned to Ryan, and said, "That miserable woman and her surprise home visits. She comes at the worst times and draws all the wrong conclusions."

"What right does she have to come here?"

"It has to do with Geoff's custody request. According to my attorney, she's within her rights."

"You certainly are being inundated with problems."

"I am, and that's not all of it. Have a seat on the couch and I'll fill you in on the rest."

"I know. A co-worker told me about that piece of yellow journalism in the paper. You don't fit the description one iota."

"Let me explain…"

When she finished her convoluted chronicle, he said, "I believe your version. I've heard of people getting the axe in the business world, but I always felt that medicine was held to a higher standard."

"I thought so, too… Until all this happened. It's a nightmare, a horrible nightmare."

"It is, but I admire your stamina. I wish I could help. I've always prided myself in my problem-solving abilities, but I have to admit this is out of my league."

The warmth of his words instilled her with calmness. With the calmness came fatigue. She stifled a yawn.

"Tired?" he asked.

"Sorry, I've run out of steam."

"Want to call it a day?"

She nodded.

After situating him in the study, she departed for her bedroom and attempted to will her body into slumber. Despite her fatigue, she could not sleep. When she finally dozed off, an irritating voice called out to her.

Geoff was standing beside the bed smirking. Next to him was Anita Grandolfo. *Oh no, she has little Roger.* Little Roger, whimpering, reached for her. Grandolfo pulled him away and strode for the door. "Bad Mother," she said.

Melissa attempted to rise.

Geoff restrained her. "Bad doctor," he said.

The more she struggled, the harder he gripped her.

Melissa yelled, "Let go of me."

She sat up in bed, drenched in sweat.

She heard a knock on her bedroom door. "Are you okay?"

"What. Oh yes, Ryan... Just a stupid nightmare. I'm okay." *Roger, I must check on him.*

She sprung from her bed, found her robe, and opened the door to the hallway, nearly hitting Ryan. He jumped back; then stood red-faced in his boxer shorts. Melissa said, "Sorry, I need to check on Roger,

"He's not here."

"What?.. Oh, right. I forgot." She inhaled Ryan's musky lemon scent. Her arm brushed against his, sending a strange tingle down her spine and into her pelvis. His blue eyes mesmerized her. She felt an overwhelming urge to kiss him. "Sorry I woke you."

"No problem."

"Well, we'd best get back to bed," she whispered; then made a purposeful step through the door before her emotions took control.

She curled up in bed, hugged a pillow, and imagined he was beside her. *Ryan, I need you.*

She slept fitfully for the remainder of the night.

Chapter 24

She was sound asleep when a knock roused her. "Huh?"

"It's Ryan. Sorry to bother you, but I thought you might be up for a bike ride."

Darn, I was sound asleep, a rarity for me. A bike ride? Not a bad idea, I always feel better after one, gets the old endorphins going. "Sure, just give me a few minutes."

She pulled the toucan jersey over her head and inspected her face in the mirror. The puffiness was gone. Her improved appearance and the big-beaked bird lifted her spirits.

She descended the stairs and was greeted by the aroma of freshly brewed coffee. Place mats were set on the table, a glass of orange juice on each. He smiled and filled her mug. "I hope you don't mind. I took the liberty—"

"Mind? I appreciate it, I really do. Would you care for anything else?"

"No thanks. I can't eat much before riding, slows me down. How about you?"

"Juice and coffee is fine. What kind of ride do you have planned for us today, Mr. Bicycle?"

"Nothing heavy duty, just a moderate-paced ride. I want to help you de-stress, not wear you down."

The word *Gemütlichkeit* came to mind. This concept prevailed during their simple meal and the drive to the ride start.

The pack of riders left at a leisurely pace. An amazing wheeled thing came abreast for a moment; then pulled ahead. Ryan exchanged greetings with the riders—four, soon to be five from the looks of the woman occupying the third seat of the monster bike. A muscular young man occupied the front seat. Between the two was a child. He was pedaling some sort of geared arrangement connecting his small legs to a chain ring below. Behind the woman was a single-wheeled contraption, attached by a yoke to the rear seat-post. A young girl was pedaling furiously.

"Now I've seen everything," said Melissa. "What was that?"

"A triple bike with an Alley Cat attached."

"That thing on the back?"

"Right."

"Amazing, simply amazing. Four on a bike, real family togetherness."

"They almost got dumped on Coast Highway a couple of weeks ago."

"Managing that contraption must be tricky."

"That wasn't the problem—a car full of surfer dudes pulled alongside and screamed 'boo.' Thought it was hilariously funny when the bike almost wobbled over."

"Not funny."

"No, and they didn't think it was funny either, after the pack caught them at the light. We engulfed them, made them wait through three light changes. One of the guys unloaded a water bottle—"

The tandem shuddered violently. "Flat," yelled Ryan. He pulled to the curb. "It's your tire that went flat, your half of the bike. You'll have to fix it."

She gasped, "What?"

He laughed, "Just kidding, mind holding the bike?"

"Sure."

Ryan detached the wheel and proceeded with the repair. He was soon finished, but the pack was long gone. He said, "I guess we finish the ride on our own."

She mounted the tandem. "Not a problem. We can just take a

leisurely cruise and enjoy the scenery."

He propelled the bike forward. "Group riding is more competitive, that's for sure. Safer too. A pack is much more visible than a single rider."

"A case in point being when I doored you." He laughed. "Right. You probably would have noticed the whole pack."

"I don't know. I'm pretty stressed out lately. I might have opened my door on a whole pack of riders with disastrous consequences. I suspect that some of them wouldn't have been as nice about it as you were."

"Right you are. You met Wayne Cantrell last week."

"The guy who 'almost ate it in Fox Canyon.'"

"That's the one. He got doored a few months ago. He methodically kicked in the whole side of the guy's car."

"What did the guy do?"

"Sat in his seat, cowering in fear. When Wayne is angry, he's a force to be reckoned with. He has a black belt—"

A mechanical growl welled up from the rear. She screamed, "Ryan, look behind us!" Ryan averted his gaze backward; then yelled, "Bump."

Melissa barely had time to respond to the warning when the tandem veered sharply to the right and jolted over the curbing. She felt the wind force and squeal of tires from the black Hummer that passed by inches from them. Ryan raised his fist and yelled, "Idiot." He steered back onto the pavement; the bike coasted forward on the downward incline.

Melissa reached for a water bottle and took a long pull from it, her heart pounding from a combination of fear and exertion. "That guy must have been drunk or high on drugs."

"He must have…"

"I've never been more terrified in all my life." *Well, maybe one other time, but that was a different kind of terror, the terror of rape versus the terror of death.* "I think I'm coming down with paranoia."

He shook his head. "You're not paranoid when an idiot runs us off the road… That's reality." He pointed to an intersection dead ahead. "Say, if you want more excitement, I could show you Fox Canyon, it's off to the right."

"The hell ride that Wayne mentioned. Thanks, but no thanks."

"Just kidding."

She laughed; then glanced rearward. "Oh no," she gasped. "That idiot in the Hummer is behind us."

The tandem veered sharply to the right as they came abreast of Fox Canyon Drive. Melissa realized that Ryan was taking evasive action and applied pressure to the pedals. A moment later, the massive vehicle squealed around the same turn. Ryan yelled, "Hell ride here we come… Bump." The tandem lurched off the road. "Steep downhill dead ahead, hang on."

The bicycle rapidly gained speed as it tacked down the embankment. Ryan maneuvered the bucking tandem, narrowly avoiding an assortment of rocks, ruts, trees, and other obstacles. Melissa clenched the bars, experiencing a sensation much like skiing down a steep mogul run. She eased up on her grasp after the terrain leveled off. As the terrain rose, they applied force to the pedals, keeping a brisk pace. She released her grip on one of the bars and wiped the grime stained perspiration off her brow. "Wow. That certainly qualifies as a hell ride."

"That's the worst of it. It'll be fairly level for a while, then a bit of a climb, a short downhill, and…"

"Dead Man's Curve."

"The one and only. It's not that bad, really."

"Have you done it before?" She heard the now-familiar sound and turned. "Oh no! Here he comes again."

The Hummer was charging down the embankment, headed directly toward them. They concentrated on their pedaling, aided by a surge of adrenaline. Despite its off-road abilities, the Hummer slowed and was forced to change course numerous times to avoid obstacles too large for it roll over. For the moment, the tandem's increased maneuverability compensated for its slower speed. They were perspiring and panting as they began their ascent. Melissa heard a ping from a nearby boulder. She screamed, "He's shooting at us!" Another adrenaline rush surged into their legs and the tandem's speed increased. The vehicle was gaining upon them rapidly as they rounded Dead Man's Curve. Melissa felt the tandem slide outward toward the edge of the drop-off. She gripped the bars tightly and attempted to twist them, and the tandem, safely around the curve. She prayed that the tires would maintain their hold on the gravelly surface. The engine and wheel noise of the Hummer increased as it loomed behind them. She heard a loud grinding noise and glanced backward. The Hummer's right front wheel had slipped over the embankment. The frame was in contact with the earth, churning up a plume of dirt. The brakes squealed momentarily; the grinding intensified as the Hummer canted over on its side and plummeted down to Fox Creek. It struck a rocky section of terrain, sending up a shower of sparks. Ryan braked to a stop; they dismounted and stared down at the vehicle, which was sliding to a halt on its side adjacent to the creek.

Ryan said, "I wonder if he survived the crash?"

"Unlikely, but possible. I don't see how we could get down to him, and even if we could, we must bear in mind that he tried to kill us."

"Hey look, it's on fire."

Flames began licking upward from the rear of the vehicle, then spread rapidly to a puddle of fuel. Accompanied by a loud whoosh, the Hummer disappeared behind orange flames and black smoke. Melissa put one shaking hand over her mouth, turned from the wreckage. She trembled violently; Ryan held her close. When her shaking waned, he fetched his cell phone from his jersey pocket and dialed 911. In a controlled voice, he calmly recounted details of the incident to the dispatcher.

In a matter of minutes the first emergency vehicle arrived, followed by several others. The most urgent matter was containment of the fire, which had spread to surrounding shrubbery. While the firefighters were launching their assault on the flames, a police officer approached. They both began speaking in a rush.

"Slow down please. One at a time, okay?"

Melissa turned to Ryan. *You do the talking.*

He picked up on her non-verbal go-ahead and said, "Whoever that was tried to kill us." The officer raised his brows above his aviator's glasses and asked, "You sure?"

"We're sure," they replied in unison.

"You'll need to come down to the station and make a statement in that case. Can you show me some ID?"

Ryan withdrew his driver license for inspection. "We can be there in about an hour. We need to ride back to my car."

The officer returned the license. "You two look pretty stressed out. Be careful on that bike."

Ryan held the tandem; Melissa hopped on and gripped the handlebars firmly. As they began to roll, she concentrated on pedaling. They rounded a bend and the crash site disappeared from her view; however, recent events were indelibly etched in her memory. Soon, a paved road came into view. With it came the recollection of the Hummer barreling toward them. A wave of panic attacked her; then she stared at Ryan's sinewy back and the sensation eased. He made her feel safe and secure. She thought, *As long as I'm with him, nothing bad can happen to me, nothing at all.* This thought prevailed during the short drive to the police station.

She asked for Detective Anderson; then recalled that he was off duty. They were escorted to a cubicle; minutes later, an officer entered, extended his hand. "Detective Cunningham." Ryan shook his hand. "Ryan MacKenzie. And this is Dr. Melissa Morrison." Cunningham did not extend his hand; instead he fixed his gaze on Melissa, instantly irritating her. *Why is he looking at me that way? He looks like a bit of a lecher with those beady eyes and scraggly mustache. A trim would help; so would a toupee.*

"Pleased to meet you, said Cunningham, "Say, you look familiar." He scratched his bald pate.

Melissa irritation was transformed to tension. *I'm sure he saw that newspaper photo.*

Ryan disrupted Cunningham's staring. "We're here to make a

statement about an attempted murder."

Cunningham chuckled. "I guess we won't be able to hear the other side of this particular story. Rice Crispies can't make statements—heh, heh—any idea who the guy in the Hummer was?"

Ryan said, "No. Have you identified him?"

Cunningham shrugged. "The vehicle was stolen. The body was badly burned. It's gonna take some time. We may never know. What makes you think he was trying to kill you?"

Ryan said, "He ran us off the road on Elm Drive. I hopped the curb to avoid him. He came back after us again. I turned onto Fox Canyon Drive. He followed. I went off-road. Again he followed."

Cunningham scribbled on his clipboard. "I see. Maybe it was just a coincidence?"

Melissa glared at Cunningham. "It was no coincidence. Somebody poisoned my dog yesterday and then called to tell me he'd kill a dear friend of mine and my son if I didn't back off."

"Back off from what?"

"I reported a murder the other day. Detective Anderson and Officer Mendoza came to my office."

"Hmm, what day was that?"

"Last Thursday."

He punched the intercom. "Sue, can you check Anderson's reports for last Thursday... A *lady* doctor, name's Morrison.... Thanks." He turned to Melissa. "I'll have the report in a minute. Where did the homicide occur?"

"At Cliffside."

Cunningham tapped his pen against his teeth. "Oh boy... Cliffside is a fine hospital. My wife had her kids there, treated her like a queen. Murdered, you say, like somebody broke into her room and shot her."

Ryan said, "Nothing like that. What's important for the moment is that she has well-grounded fears for her safety. Whoever was driving that vehicle was deliberately trying to run us down."

Cunningham focused on Melissa. "I know why you look familiar. You're the malpractice doctor. You look different in a bicycle suit than a bikini—heh, heh—you looked darn good in that picture."

Melissa snapped, "We're not here to discuss that. That guy in the Hummer took a shot at us."

Cunningham tapped the pen against his teeth again.

Melissa stared at the pen. *If he taps his teeth with his pen again, I'm going to snap it in half and throw it in the wastebasket.*

Cunningham repeated the teeth tapping. "We didn't find a weapon."

Melissa grimaced. Ryan said, "In an accident like that, a weapon could wind up almost anywhere... Maybe it went down Fox Creek."

"Possible... Or maybe there is no weapon... Dr. Morrison, are you under a lot of stress these days? Your picture in the paper, being sued and all." He stared at her, and initiated another tapping sequence.

Melissa clenched her fists, successfully preventing her hands from grabbing the offensive pen. "I'm under a lot of stress, but I'm coping with it. I am not hallucinating about people trying to kill me."

Cunningham said, "Look, Doctor, I'm just trying to look at all the angles, noodle things out logically. Anyway, here's another explanation. Mr. Rice Crispies steals a Hummer, goes for a little joy ride. Maybe he indulges in a little booze or drugs. He goes off-roading, crashes, and offs himself... Wouldn't be the first time."

"What about my dog?"

"Maybe the dog had a heat stroke or maybe a neighbor had it in for the animal. Things like that happen."

A young woman entered, handed Cunningham a file. "Thanks Sue."

He absorbed himself in the material. Finally, he looked up and said, "Things are falling into place here."

Melissa thought, *He's going to take us seriously.* She asked, "Has the hospital been contacted?"

"Indeed it has. We have a bit of a conflict here, more than a bit."

Melissa asked, "What?"

He held up a form. "This is the preliminary autopsy report, says the antibiotic levels in the deceased checked out. Here, see for yourself."

Melissa grabbed the document. The words jumped out: "... adequate Cefotan levels." She gasped, "Baker's in on it too.

"What?" asked Cunningham.

"Ken Baker, the hospital pathologist, he signed off on the report."

"As I said, doctor, things are falling into place. The report also contains a statement by Mr. Shackleton." Melissa emitted a soft groan. Cunningham continued, "According to Shackleton, your hospital privileges are under review, also says, in his opinion, 'you're coming unhinged.' He stated that unless you cease making ridiculous allegations against the hospital, they will be forced to bring charges."

"Based on what?"

"Theft of hospital property and evidence tampering."

Melissa broke down. Ryan comforted her; then said, "Despite what's in that report, we're both certain that the driver of the Hummer was trying to kill us."

"I understand, but there's always more than one version of a story."

"Will you continue to investigate?"

"Yeah," said Cunningham. "Look, I know the two of you have had a bad day, but at present we have nothing to substantiate a purposeful attempt to harm you. We need to establish probable cause."

Melissa said, "Probable cause. What about improbable cause?"

He shook his head. "No such animal. Look, here's my card. We'll continue to investigate, and if you come up with any more information, give me a call."

Melissa placed the card in her jersey pocket, feeling certain that she would never be calling Detective Cunningham. She also doubted that further discussion with Anderson would be in any way fruitful.

As they exited the parking area, Ryan asked, "What do you think?"

"I think Cunningham has concluded that it was just a joy rider with no purposeful intent to harm us. He also finds Geoff more credible than me. And another thing, I'm surprised that Baker would check post mortem Cefotan levels. It's not usually done."

"What about potassium?"

"No point. Potassium leaves the cells after death, serum potassium goes sky high."

"You're the expert."

Melissa gave him a wistful look. "You believe me, don't you?"

Of course I do... I liked your improbable cause comment, it fits the situation perfectly. Despite Cunningham's *more probable* explanation, that guy was trying to harm us, or at least trying to scare the hell out of us."

"He definitely succeeded in scaring the hell out of us."

"If it wasn't for the threatening phone call, the events could be attributed to random occurrences.'

"They're all connected. I'm sure of it."

"I am too. I guess, in addition to Geoff the jerk's statement, our cycling outfits detracted from our credibility. We probably came off to Cunningham as a couple of cycling geeks."

Melissa laughed. "Right. We need facts to back up our credibility, hard data..." She stared out the window. "Hard data. Say, you told me that the computer system you set up can do everything but brew the morning coffee."

"That could be programmed into it too. There's an extensive manual explaining it all, on-line help too."

"I never read the manual. I told you I just use it for labs and op reports. Anyway, could the computer sort out hospital deaths by type of insurance. For example: IPA versus non IPA?"

"Of course it can. It's called a query."

"We need to stop by my office."

Chapter 25

The monitor crackled to life. "What's your password?" asked Ryan. Tears prevented her from replying. He placed his arm around her and asked, "What's wrong?"

"C-Casper."

He inputted the password. Morrison, Melissa, M.D. Security Level: 0, flashed on the screen.

"That's funny," she said. "I used to be a two, now I'm a zero. I assume that's the lowest level."

"Correct. They go from zero to five. Let's see what we can get anyway. You select 'medical records' from the menu... Next you enter the query, 'deaths.'" The computer beeped and a caricature of a policeman appeared with the notation: Access denied.

Ryan said, "I was afraid of that. Anything else you want to try?"

"Payroll figures might be of interest but I doubt if we can access those."

"Probably not, but..."

The policeman reappeared, reinforced by the message: Access denied.

"What if we sign in as if we're somebody else?"

"Might work. Do you have someone in mind?"

"Rachel, Dr. Rachel Hornbeak."

"Do you know her password?"

"No."

"Any guesses? You used your dog's name."

"She's a female dog. Try 'bitch.'"

"Are you serious?"

"Just kidding. Try 'Golden Boy.'"

"Bingo! Who's Golden Boy?"

"Her horse. Say, she's a level five. You mentioned that five is the highest level, access to everything."

"Uh huh. Now watch how quickly the query will retrieve the data."

The computer beeped its denial: Access denied. Host computer is level 0. Only level 0 information available.

"Damn," said Ryan. "I forgot about that feature."

"What happened?"

"You only have level five access on Dr. Hornbeak's computer." An impish grin formed. "I was an Eagle Scout and I can't believe what I'm thinking."

"What?

"Do you have a key to her office?"

"You're suggesting that we sneak into her office?"

"I am."

"I was a Girl Scout, but what you're proposing is equivalent to the proverbial Boy Scout helping an old lady across the street."

"You don't look like an old lady to me, but I'd be happy to help you across the street any time."

"Thank you for your chivalry, kind sir, but getting back to your question, I don't have a key. I gave it to her when I left." Melissa stabbed the power button. "Let's get out of here."

"You shouldn't do that."

"What?"

"Turning the machine off without exiting the program. You could wind up with lost clusters of trash on your hard drive."

"I couldn't care less about that at the moment."

"I know."

She pouted on the drive home, unable to respond to his gentle attempts to cheer her. Gloom descended upon him as well; he lapsed into silence. She unlocked the door to her condo and stared at her keys. "Keys," she exclaimed. She sped to Roger's toy chest, and rummaged through a pile of assorted balls, blocks and toy trucks, strewing them about in the process. She looked up at him. "Don't worry, I'm not losing it." She returned to her rummaging. "Ah, here it is." She dangled a key ring in his face.

"Roger's keys?"

"Yes. I had a spare key to Rachel's office, forgot all about it. This one is it! Let's roll."

"Maybe we ought to shower and change before we go."

Melissa laughed. "Right you are. I can envision the headline, 'Burglars in bicycle suits break into physician's office.'"

Caught up in the humor of Melissa's comment, they laughed themselves upstairs. During her shower Melissa reflected on what Rachel's computer might disclose. *I think we're on to something with this computer query but what if we get caught? That's all I need to complicate my life further, being arrested for breaking into Rachel's office. Actually, compared to everything else, so what.*

In anticipation of the break-in, Melissa dressed in the drabbest outfit she could find. Laughter erupted when she noted that Ryan was similarly clad.

"What's so funny?" he asked.

"Our burglar suits," she replied. "Is youse ready?"

"I is," he said with a laugh. "Is youse?"

They continued to distract themselves with burglar-speak during the drive to Rachel's office. The sun was applying an orange paint job to the clouds scudding over the Pacific Ocean. Ryan helped Melissa out of the car and pointed out the spectacle. They paused briefly to admire it; but important business was at hand. They engaged in nervous chatter as they entered the office building and continued with this activity in the elevator. The door snapped open; they reverted to silence and slunk down the hallway. Melissa reached in her purse for the keys; they slipped from her grasp and clanked on the floor. Ryan retrieved them. "Don't be nervous. There's nobody here." Melissa inserted the key in the lock. It refused to turn. "Maybe my

streak of bad luck is never-ending. I bet she changed the locks."
Ryan took the key. "Let me give it a try. He gave the key a firm
jiggle. The lock yielded.

Melissa flipped the light switch. "I can't believe we're doing
this, we're sneak thieves."

"But for a good cause... Aha, there's the computer." The machine
whirred to life; Ryan input Rachel's password. After a few more
keystrokes, Search in progress flashed on the screen accompanied
by a Sherlock Holmes character with a large magnifying glass. A
minute later, the following appeared:

> 412 items match search criteria. Enter any additional delimiters?
> Yes. Age < 1 and IPA member.
> 84 items match criteria. Another query?
> Yes. Age < 1 and not IPA member.
> 36 items match criteria. Another query?
> Yes. Age > 50 and IPA member.
> 210 items match criteria. Another query?
> Yes. Age > 50 and not IPA member.
> 82 items match criteria. Another query?
> No
> Quarterly Summary?
> Yes

After a brief delay, the following appeared:

Hospital Deaths:

Quarter	Age<1 and IPA	Age<1 and not IPA	Total
Jul - Sep	12	10	22
Oct - Dec	10	9	19
Jan - Mar	9	9	18
Apr - Jun	53	8	61
Total	**84**	**36**	**120**

Hospital Deaths:

Quarter	Age>50 and IPA	Age >50 and not IPA	Total
Jul - Sep	30	17	47
Oct - Dec	29	22	51
Jan - Mar	24	21	45
Apr - Jun	127	22	149
Total	210	82	292

Hard copy?
Yes

The laser printer whirred to life. Ryan looked at Melissa and said, "Do you know what this means?"

"Yes. Deaths have gone up dramatically in the last quarter. IPA Preemies have a death rate seven times higher than non-IPA Preemies. It's even worse for the seniors, ten times higher."

"Geoff came to power just before this last quarter." Melissa nodded. Ryan continued, "Even before he was in command, the non IPA members had a better survival rate than IPA members, but the April to June Quarter is indicative of something terribly wrong in the hospital."

"Deadly wrong."

"You mentioned payroll figures. Want to search that?"

"Definitely."

A minute later an alphabetized listing of names appeared.

"Try Shackleton," said Melissa.

Shackleton, Geoffrey   Admin. $7,100 monthly.

"Jean Iverson."

Iverson, Jean   Pharm. $4,200 monthly

"Darn," said Melissa. "I thought the figures would be higher. How can Geoff afford a new Ferrari and a waterfront condo on that salary? How can his girl friend afford a new SLK?"

"Amazing," said Ryan.

"No, there's got to be an explanation... Hmm... The IPA pays quarterly bonuses based on how good a team player you are. Let's check bonuses."

Ryan entered the query. The computer replied, Please Wait. A white rabbit, watch in hand, hopped across the screen.

Melissa said, "Clever, very user friendly."

"We stole the rabbit from Lewis Carroll."

"I think Mr. Carroll would be pleased."

"Did you get bonuses from the IPA?"

"No. I often got docked for ordering too many tests and procedures. I was more interested in maintaining quality of care than getting kickbacks for being frugal."

"Here we go," said Ryan. He entered Geoff's name. When the information was displayed, they both gasped. Ryan said, "I don't believe it, his bonus for the last quarter was $500,000."

Melissa shook her head. "Up from zero for the previous three quarters. Looks like he treated himself to a hefty bonus when he took over... What's this? He's 'car qualified.' I bet that means the IPA is paying for his Ferrari."

"I'll be damned, R-H-I-P."

"Right, rank hath its privileges. Let's try his girl friend." They both gasped again.

Iverson, Jean   Pharm.
Quarterly Bonuses Current Fiscal Year:
Jul - Sep: $0.00
Oct - Dec: $0.00
Jan - Mar: $0.00
Apr - Jun: $100,000.00

Total: $100,000.00
Car Qualified: Yes

Melissa said, "Try the Utilization Nurse, Bridget Middlemas."

Middlemas, Bridget, R.N.   Nursing
Quarterly Bonuses Current Fiscal Year:
Jan - Mar: $50.00
Oct - Dec: $43.00
Jul - Sep: $60.00
Apr - Jun: $130.00

Total: $283.00
Car Qualified: No

"Rachel Hornbeak."

Hornbeak, Rachel, M.D. OB/GYN
Quarterly Bonuses Current Fiscal Year:
Jul - Sep: $1,300.00
Oct - Dec: $1,450.00
Jan - Mar: $900.00
Apr - Jun: $2,100.00

Total: $5,750.00
Car Qualified: No

"That oncologist. What's his name?"
"Kerr, Jim Kerr."

Kerr, James, M.D.   Hem/Onc
Quarterly Bonuses Current Fiscal Year:
Jul - Sep: $1,150.00
Oct - Dec: $800.00
Jan - Mar: $850.00
Apr - Jun: $250,000.00

Total: $278,000.00
Car Qualified: Yes

"Tara Linsey."

Linsey, Tara, M.D.   Neonat.
Quarterly Bonuses Current Fiscal Year:
Jul - Sep: $152.00
Oct - Dec: $210.00
Jan - Mar: $180.00
Apr - Jun: $243.00

Total: $785.00
Car Qualified: No

"Larry Stafford."

Stafford, Lawrence, M.D.   Neonat.
Quarterly Bonuses Current Fiscal Year:
Jul - Sep: $900.00
Oct - Dec: $1,200.00
Jan - Mar: $1,100.00
Apr - Jun: $250,000.00

Total: $253,200.00
Car Qualified: Yes

"Tom Dillon."

Dillon, Thomas, M.D.   Pulm.
Quarterly Bonuses Current Fiscal Year:
Jul - Sep: $300.00
Oct - Dec: $120.00
Jul - Sep: $235.00
Apr - Jun: $600.00

Total: $1,255.00
Car Qualified: No

"Quite a discrepancy in bonuses, don't you think?" said Ryan.

"An incredible discrepancy." She glanced around. "Let's print it and get out of here."

The printer hummed; a small stack rapidly formed in the tray. Melissa snatched up the pile. A key grated in the lock. Melissa towed Ryan toward the opposite doorway in one quick motion. Exiting the room, she flipped the light switch.

They were sequestered in an exam room moments before the office door opened. Footsteps approached. *We're going to be caught. What will she do?.. Probably swear at us and call the police.* The footsteps passed the door. She heard the chart rack swing open, the shuffling of papers, and muted swearing. Melissa began to relax; then tensed. *Whoops, we left the computer on.*

They heard the beeping of a pager; footsteps clumped to the phone. Rachel's voice boomed through the wall. "Hi Grace. I'm glad it's you and not another damn patient in labor. I've been working my ass off... The IPA is the investment of the century... The stock should go up, up, up.... Me? Of course. I've got my pension plan in it... Grace, you and I are two of a kind, no better than ditch diggers who get paid for digging a hole. I work my buns off to care for a patient, and you do likewise to sell a house... Yes indeedy... If the bubble doesn't burst—there's no reason it will—I can retire to the horse ranch of my dreams and feed Golden Boy his oats out of a gold bucket.... Goddamm right... Geoff's given me some inside info; they're going to split the stock in a few months. At the end of the year, he plans to sell the whole enchilada at a big profit, that's when the big money comes in... He also told you... I see... Diversify? Hell no. This IPA is the greatest, a goddamm money machine... I thought so... Damn, my computer's on..." Melissa tensed. Rachel continued, "Goddamm girls left it on again. Just can't get good help these days... Right... See you soon."

Footsteps approached; then receded. The lights went off and the door slammed shut. Melissa exhaled in relief then flipped on the exam room light. Ryan turned and bumped his hip against a stirrup.

"Ow. What's that?.. So this is a gyn room. The lady puts her feet in those things, and..."

Melissa giggled. "And I do the exam seated on that little stool... Ryan, I do believe you're blushing."

"N-no. It's just stress. What was she doing here?"

"Probably needed to review a patient's chart. Despite her abrasive personality, she is a reasonably good physician and does care for her patients. Anyway, let's get out of here."

They sat at the kitchen table and sifted through the computer printouts. Melissa shook her head. "All these bodaceous bonuses began after Geoff came to power. Geoff's bonus can be explained on the basis of administrative greed. I understand many IPAs are top-heavy in administrative costs, but what's going on at Cliffside is obscene. There's only one explanation for the fact that some physicians receive a huge bonus and others a pittance. One has to ask oneself how an airhead pharmacist can be reaping a huge bonus. I bet she mixes IV solutions and conveniently leaves out the antibiotic. She may also add things like potassium or insulin to other IV solutions."

"What would insulin do?"

"Like potassium, another subtle way to kill people. They're focusing on the elderly and premature because they are the highest utilizers. In addition, they're profiteering from it with huge bonuses and luxury cars. The first rule of medicine is to do no harm..."

"Harm... My nephew... My nephew may have been one of the victims. I bet they killed him."

"Was your sister an IPA member?"

"Yes. I recall them grousing about the restrictions of the plan at dinner one evening... What should we do with this information? Should we go to the police, the State Medical Board, or what?"

"I think we better discuss this with Becky."

"Can you reach her tonight?"

"I don't have her home number. I'll call her first thing in the morning."

"Darn! I'd really like to get her input on this."

"Me too, but I guess there's nothing else we can do for the moment."

"Right. Getting back to basics, do you realize that all we've had to eat today is a glass of orange juice and a cup of coffee? Want to go out for something to eat?"

"Uh huh... Just something light. There's a Chinese place nearby, nothing fancy, but good food. It's a family place... Do you mind kids in h-high chairs?" She bit her lip and looked away. He placed his arm gently on her shoulder. "You miss your little guy, don't you?"

"I do. But I know he's safe right now... That's the important thing. Anyway, is Chinese okay with you?"

"Fine."

They sat at a corner table. Melissa was soothed both by the warmth of the tea and Ryan's company. The waitress shuffled up with their meal and the savory aroma rekindled her appetite. Melissa was deficient in her skills with chopsticks and in her fumbling attempts to bring food to her mouth found that Ryan was no more proficient than she was. She laughed, handed him a fork, and fetched another for herself. This evening, she was in no mood to improve her Asian dining techniques. She quickly reduced her platter to a few bits of rice. Noticing that Ryan's plate was equally bare, she reached for the fortune cookies and handed one to him.

He smiled. "Ladies first."

She cracked hers open and extracted the slip of paper. "Well?" he asked.

"'Trust your heart and true love will be yours.'"

He blushed and smiled at her.

She said, "Your turn."

He opened the cookie, laughed.

"What's so funny?"

He extended the paper. "Help! I am a prisoner in a Chinese Fortune Cookie Factory."

Their laughter was interrupted by the return of the waitress. She asked, "More tea?" They both nodded. After she padded off, they concurred that Melissa's fortune was by far the better of the two. Melissa was certain that her fortune was meant for both of them. She sipped her tea and lapsed into her fantasy world where all was right. The din of the restaurant increased, distracting her from this indulgence. "Ready to go?" he asked. She nodded.

They did not speak on the drive home. Melissa was grateful for the silence, and concluded that he was of the same mind. They were so compatible that they could communicate without speaking. Upon their return, he followed her upstairs. He was close enough to touch and she wanted to touch him. She turned to him. "It's been quite a day, hasn't it?"

"An unbelievable day."

"Ryan."

"What?"

"I want to thank you for your support. I really appreciate it." He flashed his little boy smile. "Glad to do it."

She looked at him; she knew that he wanted to kiss her. She leaned forward and their lips met. They embraced, folding into each other. "I love you," he said.

"I love you." She pressed her lips against his again. After a while, he drew back slightly and gazed at her. She pulled him toward the bedroom. He remained rigid for a moment; then relented. They stood beside the bed; she began carefully unbuttoning his shirt. She looked up at him with yearning and said, "Go slowly."

He reached for the buttons on her blouse. "Very slow and very easy."

When they were both fully undressed, he stared at her without reserve. "You're so beautiful." She ran her hand down his chest and torso. "So are you." She followed her fingers down his body and his knee came into view. "Your knee is almost healed; I don't think it'll leave a scar." He looked at her softly. "Almost healed and no scar... You've been hurt badly, haven't you?" She nodded. He ran his arm down her back. "You've been hurt and scarred... I'll try to heal your scar." She drew him down to the bed. He kissed her softly and then began stroking her erect nipples. He reached between her thighs and began rubbing in soft circular motions. She exhaled in soft, quick pants; then her body exploded. She drew him to her and he became one with her. She was floating on a cloud, totally enmeshed in his gentleness.

When the throbs of pleasure faded, she stared intensely into his eyes. "Fireworks."

"What?"

"Fireworks. Thanks for the fireworks... Can we do it again?"

He smiled. "Give me a few minutes."

She slept peacefully, immune this night to her customary nightmares. She awoke first and stared at this handsome man that she loved so deeply. She whispered, "I love you."

His eyelids fluttered open and he said, "I love you so much." He stared at her quietly for several minutes and then asked, "Will you marry me?" She began crying. What's wrong?" he asked. "I can't."

"Why not?"

"You're the nicest, dearest man in the universe. I can't involve you any further in my mess of a life." He rubbed her shoulders and stared intently at her. "I'm a big boy—I can handle it. You're smart and beautiful, the most amazing woman I've ever known. I can handle the mess, I want to help you." She bit her lip. "It's a huge mess you'd be wading into. I'm being sued for malpractice. The settlement may exceed my insurance. I'll probably lose my hospital privileges, even my medical license. If that happens, what's left of my career will go down the tubes. You'd be saddled with a wife with no job and a huge financial obligation. Besides, there's little Roger."

"Roger's not a problem. He's a terrific little guy. He needs a dad."

"That's part of the problem. Geoff is suing me for full custody."

"Remember the toucan jersey?"

"Uh huh."

He kissed her forehead. "Two can. Together, we can fight all your problems. Isn't that what marriage is all about, for better or worse?"

"There's a lot of worse in my life right now."

"Look, my eyes are wide open, and I'm looking at the most beautiful woman in the world. Her problems pale in comparison. Two can. Okay?"

She did not reply, gazed tenderly at him.

"I love you. Will you marry me?"

She made a faint nod.

He asked, "Is that a yes?"

"It's a yes." She drew him to her and gave her body to him completely. She had found the real thing; not the illusions from her imaginary world, which paled in comparison. She was no longer a frightened woman dreaming of love, she was experiencing it. This treasure of a man wanted her as much as she wanted him.

Afterward, she began to cry. "What's wrong?" he asked.

"Nothing. Nothing is wrong. At this moment everything is right in the world."

Chapter 26

She drove to her office humming along to a piano rendition of "Moon River," playing on the radio. Ryan's love had made her invincible. This was true love; she was sure of it. She patted the sheaf of papers in the seat beside her. Life was beautiful.

Entering the office, Melissa was greeted by a quizzical stare from Jana. "You look happier than I've seen you for a long time, have a nice weekend?" She drew her cupped hand to her mouth. "Oops— sorry—I forgot that you began the weekend with a funeral."

"It's okay, Jana. My weekend began with a funeral and then all sorts of things happened."

"Good things?"

"Some good, and some terrible. It's been an incredible weekend."

"Tell me about it."

"In a few minutes. I need to make a phone call first."

Melissa retreated to her consultation room and dialed Becky's number. Her secretary answered. "She's on the other line. Do you wish to hold?"

"Yes."

After several minutes, the secretary came back on the line and said, "Sorry, she's still tied up. Do you wish to continue to hold?"

"No. Please have her call me back."

Jana placed a cup of coffee on her desk and said, "Well." The phone rang in the front office; Jana left to answer it. Melissa stared at the telephone, hopeful that Jana would buzz her. She didn't.

The phone rang again. This time the call was from Becky. Melissa grabbed the receiver. "Becky, I have some amazing news to share—"

"I have some news too, not good. I hope your news is bettrt."

"It is, but let's dispense with the bad news first."

"I just got off the phone with Herb Sempres."

"The hospital attorney. What did that little weasel want?"

"He advised me to admonish you for bringing false accusations against the hospital."

"I'm not surprised. Guess who responded to the police investigation... Geoff."

"I know. I have a copy of the police report." Melissa thought, *I'm not losing Becky, too. Dear God, please tell me that Becky's still with me on this.*

Becky interrupted her thoughts. "I've never come across anything so diabolical... Murdering people in the hospital, killing dogs, running cyclists off the road—"

Relief flowed throughout Melissa's being. "You believe me, then."

"Of course."

"Do you think they'll press charges against me?"

"Just saber-rattling at this point, but if they so desire, they could pursue that tactic. Now, what's your news?"

"Let me bring my evidence over to you. You're going to be amazed, simply amazed."

After hanging up, Melissa sped from her consultation room. Jana said, "Fill me in on your weekend."

"Sorry, Jana. I've got to go. Later."

Jana frowned. "I'm dying of curiosity."

"I know. It's a long story and an incredible one. I'll fill you in later today. I promise."

"You sure?"

"I promise."

Driving to the law office, Melissa maintained a positive outlook, focusing on the computer printouts and their ramifications.

Melissa stared expectantly at Becky while she scanned the documents. When Becky finished, she shook her head. "I have never come across anything so diabolical in my whole life."

"We have them dead to rights."

"Yes and no."

"Why yes and no?"

"Let me explain. You illegally entered Dr. Hornbeak's office and illegally accessed her computer to obtain this information. The information is not admissible and furthermore, you have committed a crime."

The abrupt transition from hope to despair left Melissa shaking. "I can't believe it. This isn't fair. They're killing people in that hospital, but I'm a criminal for breaking into Rachel's office. What a wonderful legal system we have."

"I know, I know. Our society is governed by laws, laws made to protect the common welfare. A society without laws is anarchy."

"A hospital that murders people is the epitome of anarchy."

"I know."

"What can we do?"

"It appears from the amount of bonuses Dr. Hornbeak is receiving that she's not involved."

"Probably not, other than chastising physicians with a high C-section rates. An OB would not be in a position to help them in their cause, killing preemies and the elderly. Rachel is a disgusting woman, but I seriously doubt that she would be involved in a murder scheme."

"What if you went to her and asked for her cooperation?"

Melissa shook her head. "We're not on speaking terms. I doubt if she would give me an opportunity to explain."

"We'll keep her in mind as a possibility. Do you know anybody else who might be able to access that information?"

Melissa stared upward for a moment. "Tara Linsey... I don't know what security level she has."

"Check that prospect out. Tomorrow, we're deposing your ex-husband and Nurse Middlemas. Maybe we can get some information from them to go forward. Do you think either them are aware of what's going on in that hospital?"

"Middlemouse is not on the payola according to the information I found. She might have an awareness of what's going on. If she does, my guess is that she's been threatened to keep silent."

"Your ex-husband?"

"I bet that he does. The man has an inner evilness. He's capable of being in on the scheme. On second thought, he's capable of masterminding it. Yes, that makes sense. I bet Geoff hatched this whole scheme."

"Well, I'll do my best to lead him down the garden path, then fang in for the kill. It's an uphill battle though."

"I know. Geoff is smart and clever, he'll be a tough nut to crack, a tough nut to crack indeed."

Melissa's cell phone rang. She smiled upon recognition of the voice. "Hi, Ryan."

"Jana told me you were with your attorney. I hope I'm not intruding at a bad time."

"No, not at all."

"First off, I want to tell you again that I love you."

"Me too."

"Did you show her the computer printouts?"

"I did, and I have some bad news. The computer data isn't admissible."

"Why?"

"It came from Rachel's computer and therefore not admissible evidence under our wonderful legal system."

"Well, in all honesty, I have to agree. We did break in, but I thought the ends would justify the means..."

"Bad news, every day is more bad news. Remember that old line? 'Cheer up, things could be worse.' Well, I try to cheer up and things keep getting worse."

"Remember the friendly little bird with the big beak?"

"I know, two can."

"Continuing on with the cheer up motif, are you free for dinner tonight?"

"You know the answer to that one."

"I made a reservation at Pascal's, figured that you were long overdue for a nice night out." A wide grin formed on her face. "I'd love a night out, but Pascal's is expensive."

"You're worth it and I'm trying to put some bright spots into your life."

"You certainly are."

"I love you."

"Me too."

Becky stared at Melissa and said, "You're glowing, you're definitely glowing."

Melissa smiled back. "I am."

"Please enlighten me."

The intercom interrupted. "Mr. Rudolph on line three. Don't make him wait." Becky scribbled a number on a piece of paper and extended it to Melissa. "Enlighten me later. Here's my home number. Call me if you have any last minute revelations. If not, I'll see you there at quarter to ten." Becky picked up the receiver. "Good morning, Mr. Rudolph."

Melissa rose and quietly left. Instead of returning to the office to await her first patient, scheduled at eleven, she formed an agenda.

Baker's basement office was empty. A tech passed by, specimen vials jingling in his carrying case. Melissa asked, "Where's Dr. Baker?" The tech muttered, "Doing a post."

"What's the key-code?"

"Do you have authorization?"

Melissa glared. "Do I have to go to your supervisor? Give me the code."

"Umm, two-three-nine-five."

Melissa stared at the door. Gross anatomy and pathology had been difficult med school course for hers. She recalled the path session where she had earned a new nickname. She sat in the upper tier, as far away from the corpse as possible. This corpse was particularly bothersome; it bore a resemblance to her father. Dr. Samuels held up the heart, filleted into neat sections, and noted the cause of death: acute myocardial infarction. The recollection of her father's death, coupled with skipping breakfast had been too much. Dizziness overcame her; she plopped forward into the next row. For some time thereafter "Victoria Swooner" replaced "Ice Maiden" as the epithet snickered behind her back.

Her Victoria Swooner days were long gone. She punched the keycode and entered the tile chamber. Her eyes were assaulted by the overhead glare; her nose was attacked by the stench of formaldehyde and decay. Baker was hunched over a corpse. He extracted a purple liver, riddled with yellow-white nodules, from the gaping abdominal cavity and placed it in a scale.

Melissa reflected that this may have been the same table where the alleged sexual encounter between Baker and his trophy wife had taken place. "Metastatic cancer—colon?"

He turned with a start. "What... Oh hi, Melissa, didn't hear you come in... Right you are, no sign of a recurrence in the colon, but widespread metastases."

"That's the nasty thing about cancer; it starts in one place, then spreads, planting evil seeds of destruction."

"Umm, right."

Ken, you did the post on Katrina Hauser." Baker lurched forward, nearly stumbling over a footstool. He shucked off his gloves, extracted a cigarette from a pack in his coat pocket; he inhaled deeply. "Mind if I smoke?"

"No." *Actually, I do, but you already are, and the way this room smells, it makes little difference.* "I understand that you found adequate Cefotan levels in the post mortem serum.

Baker took another drag, smoke exhaling with his soft reply. "I did."

"Isn't it a bit unusual to order antibiotic levels?"

"Mmm, yes."

"Why in this case?"

Baker stubbed out his cigarette, and lit another. "Jim Kerr asked me to."

Melissa glared. "Anything for a friend?"

"What do you mean?"

"I didn't know you smoked."

Baker took another deep drag. "I quit for ten years, and—"

"Recent stresses."

Baker took another drag; then stubbed it out. "Nasty habit."

Melissa said softly, "Nasty business."

Baker lit another cigarette as she exited. As the door closed, she heard a crash. It sounded like a fist striking something.

Melissa's next stop was the administrative annex, a dilapidated structure hidden behind the pristine facade of the main hospital. She had never visited Bridget's office, and had trouble locating it down a side corridor. Bridget was seated at small steel desk, piled high with papers and manuals. She cowered behind a pile of papers.

Peek-a-boo, thought Melissa. "Hi Bridget."

"Oh hi, Dr. Morrison... Umm, what can I do for you?"

"I didn't get a copy of the new utilization guidelines, wondered if I could pick one up."

Bridget reached into a box next to her desk, and extracted a manual the size of a small textbook. "Here you are."

Melissa accepted the item. "Thanks. Well, see you tomorrow."

"What?"

"At the deposition."

Bridget's left arm flailed forward, dislodging a pile of papers; they rained to the floor.

Melissa helped scoop them up. "There, that's the last of them. You could use a larger office, Bridget. You're packed to the gills here."

"Right... Umm, I thought I'd just be talking to attorneys." She pleaded, "Why will you be there?"

"I have every right to be there, this is about my career." Melissa stared at her, forcing a response.

Bridget sighed. "I've never been to a deposition before. I'm real scared."

"Nothing to be scared of. All you have to do is tell the truth."

Melissa turned and exited, carrying her extra copy of the utilization guidelines. Her next stop was the neonatal intensive care unit, located in the new wing.

She always experienced a sense of awe when she entered the NICU and viewed the array of isolettes containing tiny beings clinging precariously to life. A frieze of yellow ducklings ran around the wall, softening the techno-machine atmosphere that prevailed in the room. The little birds had a cheering effect on the adults in the NICU; however, the infants were far too young and too sick to respond to them. Tara was hovering over an isolette; its occupant, which appeared full-term, contrasted sharply with the multitude of premature infants in the room. Standing near Tara were a young man and woman, watching her every move. A nurse approached and said, "Time to leave."

The woman blew the child a kiss, and the man gave the top of the isolette a pat. Tara turned in the direction of Melissa's approaching footsteps. "Oh, hi Melissa."

Melissa peered into the isolette, noting the IV attached to the baby's head. To the uninitiated, that would be horrifying; however, Tara and Melissa were accustomed to the use of scalp veins for infants. Melissa said, "He's cyanotic... Congenital heart disease?"

"Right. Baby Miller has Tetralogy of Fallot. We're also working him up for possible sepsis."

"Thank God for modern medicine. His problems are fixable and he can lead a normal life."

Tara softly stroked the baby's back as she spoke. "His parents were shocked when I told them the diagnosis but were quite relieved after the cardiac surgeon discussed the prognosis following corrective surgery. They were concerned over costs. They jumped for joy when I informed them that the IPA would pick up the entire tab."

"Open-heart surgery is expensive, beyond most people's means without insurance."

"That's for sure. What brings you to the land of the little

people?"

Melissa stared around the unit. She spotted Stafford at the other end of the room; he was facing the opposite direction. She whispered, "I wonder if I could look up something on your computer?"

"Is yours down? And why the whispering?"

"I've happened upon something, and accessing your computer might help."

Tara draped her stethoscope around her shoulders and adjusted the IV flow. "Okay, it's down the hall in the NICU office."

Heralded by her perfume, Jean Iverson sashayed through the door carrying a basket of pharmaceuticals. The door closed behind them.

Melissa said, "Well, if it isn't Little Red Riding Hood coming to visit the Big Bad Wolf."

"Who's the Big Bad Wolf?" asked Tara.

"Stafford."

Tara gave her a perplexed look and opened the door to the NICU Office. A nurse was seated at the terminal. Melissa waited impatiently while she finished her input. Finally, the nurse rose, gathered up several sheets of paper from the printer and left. Tara entered her password and was greeted with: **Linsey, Tara, M.D. Security Level: 2.** Melissa felt momentarily encouraged; she entered the medical records query. The computer beeped its reply: **Access Denied.** "Darn," said Melissa. "I was hoping..."

"Hoping what?"

"Hoping I could find information about something terrible that's going on in this hospital."

The door opened; Melissa winced. Stafford entered. "Dr. Morrison, what brings you here?"

Melissa jabbed the keyboard, erasing the policeman and his message from the screen. She hoped her voice would not reflect her tension. "Just going over a patient with Tara."

Dark circles accented Stafford's piercing eyes; his hands had a slight tremor. "I didn't know you had a patient in the unit."

"I don't. It was back a few weeks, the Adams baby."

He snapped, "That baby went home more than a week ago."

She flashed an innocent smile.

He glared. "Playing on the computer I see."

"Right. Playing on the computer."

Stafford continued to glare. "If you'll excuse us I need to discuss a patient with Dr. Linsey, a sick patient, not one that's gone home."

Melissa nodded. "Certainly... See you later Tara."

As she approached the hospital exit, the overhead page blared, "Code Blue in NICU. Code Blue in NICU. Dr. Linsey, stat to NICU. Dr. Stafford, stat to NICU." Melissa considered going back to the unit; then abandoned the idea. *I'd just be in the way.*

Driving to her office, her mind was filled with a frightening image: Iverson handed Stafford a syringeful of poison; he smiled while he rammed it into an infant's head. Upon her return, Jana's inquisitiveness displaced this vision. Melissa had ample time to apprise her of the weekend's events before the first patient arrived. When the woman arrived, Melissa found that she had more time for the patient than the patient had for her. After the woman departed, proclaiming that she had to pick up her kids from day care, gloom attacked again. The intercom buzzed, "Dr. Linsey on line one." Melissa reached for the phone. "Hi Tara, What's up?"

"I quit the hospital."

"What happened?"

"The Miller baby arrested. Stafford came down on me with all fours. That baby was doing just fine. It certainly wasn't my fault. Anyway, that was the last straw with that man, he's a psycho."

"That's terrible Tara. I'm sure it wasn't your fault."

"It wasn't, but Stafford has a lot of clout in this place."

"True, he does."

"He's not the only one, Kerr's another."

"I agree."

"Speaking of Kerr, guess who else resigned today?"

"Who?"

"Tom Dillon. He had some sort of run-in with 'Crazy Kerr,' as he called him. Apparently Kerr blamed him for some bad outcomes, including Mrs. Hauser's."

"I have no criticism of the care Tom gave to Katrina. Others in these hallowed halls, but not him. Let me explain my suspicions to you."

"Suspicions of what?"

"I was hoping to get some substantiating information from your computer. Unfortunately you don't have a high enough security level. I suspect that the IPA is killing off the elderly and the sick neonates to boost profits up."

"You're kidding."

"I wish I was." Melissa explained her findings to Tara, including Woods' analysis. Tara said, "You have proof then."

"Yes and no. Baker, amazingly, found appropriate levels of Cefotan when he did the post."

"That's incredible... Cefotan in her blood, but not in the IV. Doesn't make sense."

"Baker's involved in this thing."

"What thing?"

"I think I've uncovered a conspiracy."

Tara's voice took on a motherly tone. "You're under a lot of stress these days. Doctors couldn't do such a thing, a disgruntled aide, maybe. I recall something in the paper a while back. An overworked nurses' aide hastened the demise of patients to lighten the work load, did it under the guise of mercy killing."

Melissa snapped, "Believe me, Tara. Doctors are killing off patients right and left."

"Incredible."

"I've identified the key players: Stafford; Kerr; Baker; and a little Angel of Death, Jane Iverson. They're killing people."

Tara gasped. "You can't be serious?"

"Deadly serious... No pun intended."

"Explain to me what happened to the Miller baby."

"They probably put potassium in the IV, like they did with Katrina."

"Are you sure? I still have trouble accepting all this; it's horrible, beyond belief."

"I know, but hopefully I can ferret this all out... If they don't kill me first."

"Try to keep calm, Melissa. Okay?"

"You don't believe me, do you?"

"One side wants to; the other side doesn't. Maybe you're in need of professional help."

"Stop it," snapped Melissa. "Granted, I've suffered enough stress recently to wig out, but I haven't. I'm stressed out, but I'm coping."

"Sorry. You've impressed me with your resilience over the past few months. I don't know if I could hold up as well... Anyway I'm outta here."

"Where are you going?"

"I interviewed with Stanford recently. I gave them a call and they offered me a position."

"Well, good for you. When are you leaving?"

"Immediately, if not sooner. I've had it with this place."

"My sentiments exactly, but wait and see. I'm going to get to the bottom of this thing."

The light patient load allowed ample time to reflect on Tara's words. *Should I go public with the information? Yeah, right. Tara doesn't really believe me. The police have been no help. I would come across as a nut-case. I need proof. But how? Ryan might have some ideas, but not tonight. Tonight I'll tune this all out, enjoy his company and a gourmet meal.*

Chapter 27

The waiter presented the bottle; Melissa gasped, *"Dom Perignon... Oh Ryan, it's too expensive. You shouldn't have."*

"Yes I should. You're worth it."

The waiter poured a sample for tasting. Ryan was oblivious to him, captivated by Melissa. She stared back with equal affection. The waiter cleared his throat.

"Sorry," said Ryan; he lifted the tulip. "Excellent!"

The waiter poured the two glasses and departed. They clinked glasses. "To us," said Ryan.

"To us." She took a sip. "Mmm, delicious. She leaned forward and kissed him softly. She took another sip; then she placed the glass on the table and stared at the rising bubbles.

"You're thinking about your problems, aren't you?"

"I'm sorry, but I seem to be thwarted at every turn. I stopped by the NICU to see Tara... She's a level two and can't access any of the information we need."

"Tara?"

"My friend, the neonatologist."

"We checked her out on the computer."

"Right, she's not involved."

"Did you inform her of your suspicions?"

"We were interrupted by," her voice dropped to a whisper, "one of the murderers. That's one of the reasons I'm so upset. An infant with congenital heart disease arrested. Stafford blamed Tara and she resigned."

"That's too bad; she might have been helpful in unraveling this situation."

"Yes and no. Tara's a good friend, but I got the feeling that she thought I was going paranoid from the stress of everything."

He patted her hand. "I know that's not true. The only crazy person in this room is me. I'm crazy about you."

Melissa clasped his hand. "I'm crazy about you, too. I just wish we didn't have all these problems. It's a bit overwhelming."

"More than a bit, but things will work out. Your ex's deposition is tomorrow. Do you think your attorney can trip him up?"

"Probably not. Geoff is smart and clever. It's a shame about that computer evidence."

"And the bogus path report."

"Falsifying records, destroying records, they're morally bankrupt."

"Chart records or computer records?"

"Both."

"Ripping a page out of a chart is one thing but erasing it from the computer isn't so simple."

"Well, they've done it. When I unloaded my tale of woe on you the other night I left out a sore point. It makes me so furious… My whole malpractice case is based on my discharging a sick patient. I fought to have her admitted and they denied it. When the patient returned to the hospital after experiencing a seizure, they created a cover-up."

"How?"

"I made a note in the chart that I wanted to admit her, and I dictated a discharge summary. I became suspicious when I didn't receive a copy of my dictation. The computer usually spits them out within a day. When I called the transcription department, I was told that there was no record of it. I also checked the computer, it wasn't there. I re-dictated the note, but it was after the fact."

"Most likely the transcription had been taken off the tape before the patient returned to the emergency room in dire straits."

"Right. Whoever set me up must have deleted my dictation."

The waiter reappeared. "Are you ready to order?"

"No," snapped Ryan.

After the waiter left, Ryan said, "I told you, you can't delete anything from the computer. There are safeguards—"

"Oh yes you can. A few months ago, I dictated a history and physical before some labs came in. When they arrived later that day, I deleted the original and re-dictated the whole thing. I thought that would be cleaner than adding an amendment. I brought up the first report and selected 'delete.' It went away."

Ryan shook his head. "No it didn't, and neither did your discharge summary. As a safeguard to information tampering, deleted files stay in the system."

"I don't understand. I looked for my discharge summary on the computer, it's not there."

"You told me you never read the manual."

"Uh huh."

"Whoever deleted that record probably didn't either, at least not in depth. Your file is still on the server and can be restored by a simple command, and do you know what else?"

"No."

"The electronic signature of who deleted it will be on there too."

"Wow!" Her eyes danced with excitement; then she furrowed her brow. "Oops, major problem."

"What?"

"I'm a level zero. To get that kind of information, we'd need to break into Rachel's office again only to obtain more inadmissible evidence."

"No you won't. I reviewed the various computer levels as prescribed by the hospital—I never felt a need to pay any attention to that stuff before—a level zero user only has access to information that he or she generated. You generated the information and can access it."

"Are you sure?"

"Positive."

Melissa grinned; she began to twitch. "We'll need to go by my office tonight."

The waiter returned. Melissa's twitching increased; she began shuffling her feet. Ryan turned to the waiter. "Check please?"

The waiter gasped, "*Monsieur,* is something wrong?"

"No. The champagne is excellent. Please share it with the staff, with our compliments. The lady has developed a medical emergency, we must leave."

"Nothing serious I hope."

"Yes and no, depends on one's perspective."

"*Oui Monsieur.*"

Melissa had to admonish Ryan to slow down several times during the drive to her office. After he parked, they raced to the office.

Melissa stared impatiently at the monitor. *User friendly, please, dear little computer, be user friendly and find my file.*

The message appeared: File does not exist. A cartoon librarian shook her head. Melissa's apprehension increased. She prepared herself for another disappointment. "Watch this," said Ryan. His fingers attacked the keyboard; he entered: Search.

Search for? Deleted Files.
Physician: Morrison, Melissa
Subject: Discharge Summary
Patient: Sanders, Victoria
Restore? Yes

The report appeared on the screen.

Ryan asked, "Is this it?"

Melissa whooped, "Yes. That's it."

"Let's print it out." The laser printer extruded a copy into the tray. Ryan pointed to the upper right hand corner of the document. "Well, well. Look who deleted the file, Geoffrey Shackleton."

"That's no surprise," said Melissa. She reached for the phone. "Becky, Melissa. I am holding in my hot little hands a very valuable document."

"Can we discuss it a little later? I just stuck a steak on the barbecue."

"This can't wait. We were sitting down to dinner, too, when Ryan's revelation occurred."

"Ryan's revelation, it sounds biblical and I do want to hear all about it. How about a couple of hours from now? I missed lunch."

"Dammit, Becky, this can't wait. Take your steak off the coals and eat it tomorrow. As far as tonight goes, I'll fix you a dinner at my place."

"A gourmet repast?"

"Most definitely."

After she hung up, Melissa thought, *I lied to Becky about the gourmet meal. Oh well, after she digests "Ryan's Revelation" it won't matter. This is going to knock her legal socks right off.*

Melissa was correct in her expectations. Becky carefully read the document a second time; then looked up at them and smiled. "We've got it. I really think we've got it."

Melissa pulled Becky from her chair and danced her around the room. "We've got it 'enry 'iggins, we've got it."

Ryan looked on at their exuberance with a smile. After their cavorting ceased, they returned, panting, to the table. When Becky's breathing slowed, she said to Melissa, "Say, you pulled me away from dinner. Is your offer for a meal still good?"

Melissa smiled. "Of course." She strode to the refrigerator and assessed its contents. She shook her head. "I'm sorry Becky, I fibbed to you about the gourmet repast, not much here. Nothing to replace your barbecued steak."

Ryan peered in the refrigerator. "I can whip up a mean mushroom omelet. Would that be okay?"

"Fine with me," said Becky.

"Me too," said Melissa. She turned to Becky and said, "If Ryan ever tires of programming, he could launch a second career as a chef."

Ryan smiled; then began selecting the ingredients. "Kindly exit the kitchen while Chef MacKenzie prepares his masterpiece."

Melissa saluted. "Yes boss."

The two women sat and watched Ryan deftly flip the omelets. He placed one on each of their plates and said, "Don't let them get cold. Mine will be up in a minute."

Becky took a bite, "Mmm, delicious." She whispered to Melissa, "He's a hunk. In addition, he's a gentleman and a fantastic cook. If you tire of him, let me know and I'll go into my predatory female mode."

"Do you have a predatory female mode?"

"No, but for him I'd develop one."

Ryan returned with his meal and took a seat. "What are you two whispering about?"

Melissa smiled and planted a kiss on his lips. "Just protecting my turf. Becky here has taken notice of your masculine appeal. I was just about to inform her that you're already taken."

Becky gasped, "When did this happen?"

"Quite recently. I was going to tell you this morning, but we were interrupted."

"Interrupted," said Ryan. "Where's my jacket?"

Melissa pointed to the garment, draped over a nearby chair. He sped to it, groped in the pocket and retrieved a small case. He returned to Melissa's side and extended it in her direction. "Our dinner was interrupted. I planned to give you this at Pascal's over a gourmet meal, together with a carefully rehearsed speech. Only, only we're having omelets and I forgot the speech." He blushed.

"Open it," squealed Becky.

Melissa extracted a ring from the box and gasped, "Oh Ryan, it's lovely. When did you—"

"Today. I took the afternoon—actually the whole day off—couldn't concentrate anyway—just would have made spaghetti code."

Becky gestured with her fork toward her plate. "If your spaghetti code is anywhere as good as this omelet, I bet it's delicious."

"Spaghetti code refers to—"

Becky interrupted, "I know. I took a couple of computer courses in college and I was a master chef at spaghetti code. Anyway, congratulations you guys. This calls for a celebration. Melissa, do you have any celebratory libations around here?" Melissa shook her head. Becky said, "Well, I'm going to finish this delicious omelet— my compliments again to the chef, by the way—then I'm off to find some libations."

Becky returned, extended a bottle and said, "The advantages of living in an upscale community. I found *Dom Perignon* at the market down the road."

"What a coincidence," said Melissa. "We enjoyed a glass a little while ago."

"Drink it all the time, it's our favorite table wine," said Ryan.

Becky laughed; Melissa left to fetch the glasses. Upon her return, she placed three cut-crystal tulips on the table. "These were a wedding gift from the Hausers, one of my prized possessions. I've saved them for an occasion and this certainly is an appropriate one." She reflected on the one previous occasion that she had prepared them for use, the night she told Geoff about her pregnancy. This was a much more appropriate inauguration of this special gift; she was pleased. She was certain that Katrina had picked them out. Katrina would have been pleased as well.

Ryan popped the cork and filled their glasses.

Becky raised her glass. "Here's to two very special people, to their forthcoming wedding, and long happy future together."

"I'll drink to that," said Ryan.

"Me too," said Melissa. "Here's to our wedding and our future and to someone else's funeral and non-future."

"Who might that be?" asked Ryan.

"You know the answer to that one."

After taking the last sip from her glass, Becky's demeanor changed abruptly from festive to resolute. She turned to Ryan. "I want you to give me a crash course in the hospital computer system. Security levels, backup system, document retrieval, the whole nine yards."

Chapter 28

The deposition took place in Cliffside Medical Center's Board Room. Melissa felt at ease in this room for the first time. Geoff glared cockily at Becky and Melissa from across the table. Herb Sempres appeared bored as he stared downward at his legal pad. Becky began by asking Geoff if he understood the penalty for perjury, then continued with questions about Geoff's education and occupational history. Geoff doodled on a scratch pad with a pencil and repeatedly glanced at his watch.

Melissa thought, *You're a rat—no, strike that—this legal mumbo jumbo is rubbing off on me—you're a weasel in a Skinner Box—an especially large one designed for weasels like you. The rat, or in this case, the weasel, either gets a reward or a painful stimulus. Unfortunately for you, you're about to receive an unusually painful stimulus, you poor little weasel.*

Melissa was pulled from her thoughts when Becky asked, "Do you have a computer terminal in your office?"

"I do."

"What do you use it for?"

Geoff continued with his doodling. "Administrative reports and review of hospital information."

"What sort of hospital information?"

Geoff smirked. "The IPA and the hospital are intermeshed. I am constantly receiving information from and disseminating information to the hospital. It's my job."

"I see. Tell me, do you ever delete records on the computer?"

The lead snapped in Geoff's pencil. "No... On second thought, I have occasionally deleted memos."

"What sort of memos?"

"Just trivial, interdepartmental memos. Occasionally, new information supersedes the previous before the memo is disbursed."

"I see. Have you ever deleted medical information of any sort?"

He dropped the useless pencil. "Never."

"I see. I have here a hospital memo on successful VBAC rates. Did you produce this memo?"

Geoff scanned the document and said, "I did."

She asked, "How do we know that you produced it?"

He pointed. "My name is on it, right here."

"How does your name get on the memo? Do you type it in?"

"No. This is the computer era. My name comes from an electronic signature."

"Electronic signature. Please enlighten me. How does the electronic signature work?"

Geoff shook his head. "I guess you're not that computer literate. Well, I type in my password and the computer knows it's me. I input the password and the documents I produce have my name displayed in what is termed an electronic signature."

"I see. Does anyone know your password?"

"No. It's private."

"Could somebody look over your shoulder and spy on you when you type it in?"

"No. If you'd ever used a computer, you'd know that when you type in your password a row of asterisks—little stars—appear on the screen."

"Thank you for enlightening me." Becky retrieved a sheet of paper from her briefcase and extended it in Geoff's direction. "I have a discharge summary. Have you ever seen it before?"

"Yes. It's the summary Miss—er—Dr. Morrison produced three

days after the tragic incident."

"What tragic incident?"

"You know. The double brain damage case."

"The Sanders case?"

"Yes."

I see. For the record, I'm marking this discharge summary 'Exhibit A.'"

Sempres snapped to attention, stared at the document, then at Geoff. Geoff shrugged his shoulders. Becky produced a second sheet of paper and said, "For the record, I am labeling this document 'Exhibit B.' Mr. Shackleton, would you please identify this document?"

Geoff studied the sheet of paper. "It's the same as the first, a discharge summary for Vicky Sanders."

"Look at it closely, Mr. Shackleton, and compare it to 'Exhibit A.' Do you notice any differences at all?"

Geoff placed the two sheets of paper side by side. "Now that you mention it, the wording is a little different."

"What about the date?"

"Hmm, the dates are different."

"I see. What is the date displayed on Exhibit A?"

"March nineteenth."

"And the date on 'Exhibit B?'"

"March twenty-second... But I—"

"Could you read the information displayed in the upper right hand corner of 'Exhibit A?'"

"It says..." His face blanched.

"If you're having trouble reading the information or are experiencing an aphasic episode Mr. Shackleton, I'll read it for you. Displayed in the upper right hand corner of 'Exhibit A' is the notation: 'Deleted by Shackleton, Geoffrey March 20 (Electronic Signature).'"

Geoff slumped in his chair and pressed his hands on his temples. Sempres dropped his pen on the legal pad, arose, and said, "We need to take a break."

Geoff followed him out the door looking much like a puppy that had been caught in the act of soiling the carpet. Becky and Melissa exchanged smiles. The court reporter rolled her eyes. After the door shut behind Sempres and Geoff, the court reporter chirped, "That's why I stay in this business, typing away on my little machine. This is our first depo together, Ms. Thatcher. I'm looking forward to more of them."

"I'm sure our paths will cross in the future."

"I'm sure. This computer stuff is interesting. I just bought my ten-year-old a computer and she's a whiz on it I must say. She makes the thing do nip-ups and..."

Becky sat and feigned interest in the idle conversation. Melissa perched on the edge of her chair, eagerly awaiting the return of Geoff and Sempres. Finally, the door opened. Sempres entered alone, looked meekly at Becky and said, "I'm sorry, Mr. Shackleton has been stricken with a virus attack and cannot continue. I'll call you tomorrow to compare calendars."

Becky smiled. "Fine. We have Nurse Middlemas' deposition scheduled this afternoon. In order for me to plan out my day, is there some chance that Nurse Middlemas might be coming down with the same virus?"

"A very good chance."

After he departed, Becky gave Melissa a firm hug. After the court reporter packed up her machine and left, Melissa smiled and asked, "Do you think they'll fold up and admit that we've won?"

"Possibly. I wouldn't be surprised if they don't make a last ditch stand to turn this thing around."

"What can they do at this point?"

"I'm sure they'll come up with something. This whole thing is going south with tremendous implications for a lot of powerful people. Don't forget we're fighting a hospital with vast resources. I'm going to devote the remainder of the day to anticipating their future plan of attack. Could you come by my office tomorrow at nine? There are some things we'll need to go over."

"I'll be there."

Melissa danced through her day and slept peacefully that night––a sleep devoid of nightmares.

Chapter 29

After digesting the newspaper the following morning, another piece of the jigsaw puzzle fell into place. Entering Becky's office, Melissa extended the Metro section of the paper. "Did you see this article?"

Becky took the paper and gestured to a chair. "Have a seat."

"Turn to the second page, third column."

The article was entitled, "IDENTITY OF OFF-ROAD JOY RIDER MADE."

After reading the piece, Becky looked up. "That's the man who chased you on the tandem."

"Right. Look at the description of the next of kin, 'Jeremy Iverson is survived by his parents, John and Joanne Iverson of Chicago, Illinois and his sister, Jean Iverson, of La Playa.'"

"Well, isn't that interesting."

The intercom buzzed. "Mr. Sempres on line two."

Becky pressed the button for the speaker-phone. "Good morning, Herb. How are you today?"

He cooed, "Fine. Fine and dandy. And you?"

"Never better. Are you calling to reschedule those depos?"

"Yes, that, and to share a bit of bad news with you. The hospital computer has gone down. One of those computer viruses, destroyed all the data. What a mess."

"Could this be the same virus that Mr. Shackleton and that nurse were suddenly stricken with?"

"Don't be ridiculous, computer viruses are not the same as human viruses, you know that."

"Of course. Fortunately, we have backup systems, Herb. They're worth their weight in gold at times like these."

"Hmm, I'm sure they can retrieve most of the important stuff. As far as allegedly deleted and miraculously restored files that may be another matter. Besides, I got to thinking after yesterday's depo. All that computer data is on erasable media. It wouldn't be hard for someone experienced with the system to fabricate a file. Erasable data won't hold up in court."

"The courts depend on the written record, things carved in stone."

"Right, right. Too bad that alleged discharge summary wasn't carved in stone."

"I just got a CD burner for my computer, Herb. Those things are really slick. They store 700 megabytes of data, all permanently etched into the disk surface. In a sense the data is carved in stone. Do you know how the hospital backs up their data?"

"I use a tape system in my office. I'm sure the hospital does it the same way, probably a more elaborate system, but the same idea."

"Not exactly, Herb, they back up to CD ROMs... Carved in stone... Herb, are you still there?"

"Hmm, yes—er—I assume these CD's are stored at the hospital."

"No. It's prudent to store backups at a separate location, in case of fire or other catastrophes. The discs were stored at RAM-Tech. However, yesterday afternoon, we took the precaution of moving them to the vault of a nearby bank. Can't be too careful these days."

"No, one can't... Getting back to comparing calendars, I'm hopelessly booked for the next two months."

"I see. I would advise you to free up some time and give this case a priority status."

"Whatever for?"

"I will be deposing Dr. James Kerr, Dr. Lawrence Stafford, Dr. Kenneth Baker, and the hospital pharmacist, Jean Iverson, among others. My secretary can furnish your office with a complete listing."

"You still haven't answered my question... I don't understand..."

"Normally I would not find it necessary to accelerate the discovery process; however, my conscience is influencing me in this matter. Innocent lives are at stake."

"Getting a little melodramatic, aren't we? Suggesting that people might die."

"They are dying and the individuals on the list that I'll be furnishing you with are aware of it. My client and I have hypothesized that your beloved hospital is selectively enhancing the demise of premature babies and the elderly in the guise of cost containment and furthermore taking the profits to enhance their lifestyle."

"That's preposterous. Cliffside is a fine hospital with a wonderful reputation."

"Not any more. I have a message that I'd like you to convey to Mr. Shackleton and the CIPA Board of Directors."

"And what might that be?"

"Inform them that all the vital information to this case has been safeguarded and instructions have been posted to the senior partner of my firm and other selected individuals. In the case of my demise, or that of Dr. Morrison, her son, or Dr. Roger Hauser, this information will be released. Tell them to give it up."

"Preposterous, simply preposterous. You're proposing that members of the hospital administration and respected physicians would commit murder."

"They already have, they already have. Say, I've got to let you go Herb. Have a nice day."

"Wow," said Melissa."

"What's Ryan's cell number?

"555-2737."

Becky punched the telephone buttons. "Good-morning, Ryan....
I thought you'd be in Cliffside's computer room. You mentioned the
data integrity checks the other evening... Great minds think alike...
I thought so.... How long before you can get the computer up and
running and extract the info?.. No, not all of it, just enough to launch
an investigation... Be sure to look up the pathologist, Ken Baker...
Bye, and happy hunting."

"What?" asked Melissa.

Becky punched the telephone again. "I need to speak to
an investigator... Yes, it's urgent.... Hello, my name is Rebecca
Thatcher." Becky rolled her eyes. "No, I'm not making up the
name... I'm an attorney with the firm of Roach and Graber. An
acquaintance of mine has uncovered some disturbing information...
Next week... No, we need to speak to someone this week... Because
innocent people are dying. More will die unless emergency measures
are instituted as soon as possible... Yes, I have proof. Tomorrow at
one o'clock, then."

"Who were you talking to?" asked Melissa.

"The California Medical Board. We're going to blow the whistle
on Cliffside."

"Where's your proof?" asked Melissa. "All we have is the
printouts from Rachel's office."

"By noon tomorrow at the latest, we'll have everything we need
to launch an investigation. They made a big mistake when they
trashed the data on the computer. They played right into our hands.
Ryan will run some data integrity checks. Just random names and
queries. Quite by accident, mind you, he'll uncover some shocking
information and present it to the medical board."

"*The Daily Breeze* might be interested."

"Most definitely."

Chapter 30

Two days later, Jana snapped the appointment book shut. She turned to Melissa and said, "That's it for today."

"Let's both call it a day. You could use an afternoon off."

"That I could."

"See you this evening."

"Wouldn't miss it for the world."

Melissa was immersed in the luxury of posh solitude. She was curled up on her family room sofa, and one chapter into the novel that she had been meaning to start for months. The CD player was loaded with an afternoon's worth of her classical favorites.

A key turned in the front door lock. The novel flew from her hands. She sped to the fireplace to retrieve a poker; then turned to face her intruder.

"Hi honey, what—"

"Ryan, you scared the heck out of me."

He clasped her and planted a firm kiss on her lips. Between kisses, she said, "You told me you'd be lucky to make it here by six."

"I was given the afternoon off... By the hospital security guards. They escorted me off the premises. Somehow I feel we've lost the hospital's business."

She kissed him again. "I'm sorry, I've jeopardized your job."

"Not really."

"You're just being kind."

"We service hospitals throughout the nation, and have other products as well."

"So losing the contract won't hurt your company."

"Not at all."

I feel better. One of these days you need to tell me all about the company you work for."

"I can—"

"Shh—later. Right now I think I need to take you upstairs for some love in the afternoon." She grabbed him playfully. "Roger's on his way back. We have until four."

Afterward, she fell into a deep sleep nestled in his arm.

He jarred her to wakefulness. "It's 3:30."

"Yikes. We better hurry. Greeting Roger in my bathrobe would not be cool."

She was buttoning her blouse when the doorbell rang. Melissa ran to the door and kissed both her Rogers hello. "Mom-mee," said little Roger."

"Roger-Podger, did you have fun with your Opa?"

Dr. Hauser wagged his head up and down. "A wonderful time. He's got the makings of a fine fisherman. I can't wait for him to get bigger. Being around him helps me to..." He averted his gaze; then turned to her. "And you, how goes it with you?"

"Terrific, just terrific. I've had an interesting time for myself since you left. Come on inside and I'll tell you about it."

Ryan appeared and extended his hand. "Dr. Hauser, how are you sir?"

"Fine. I'm coming along just fine. He glared at Ryan with mock sternness. "Did you take good care of my little girl?"

"Very good care."

Melissa held up her ring finger. "Very good care, indeed."

"Well, well, my congratulations to the both of you. My intuitions—and Katrina's—are still fully functional."

Little Roger wiggled from Melissa's grasp and surveyed his surroundings. He plodded toward the door. "Casper, where Casper?"

Melissa blinked. "Casper's gone bye-bye."

Ryan snatched a ball from the toy chest and rolled it in Roger's direction. "How about a ball game, big guy?"

"Ball!"

Melissa asked, "Would you like a glass of lemonade, Roger?"

"That was a long, hot drive. I could use a cold beer."

"Coming right up." She returned with a pewter mug and a bottle of *Edelweiss Weissbier*. He smiled with approval. She said, "Have a seat on the couch, Roger... Do I have a tale to tell."

When Melissa finished her recap, Dr. Hauser shook his head. "I can't believe such a thing could happen in a hospital. Doctors who are trained in the art and science of healing murdering people—including my Katrina—it's beyond human comprehension. Why?"

"I'll tell you why. It has to do with greed and power and chemical addiction. Here's my hypothesis and see if you don't agree. Geoff has always lived in the fast lane. When he was first in a position of authority, he blew it because of inexperience, overconfidence, and two-martini lunches. He later wins a power struggle to become CEO of Cliffside IPA—he's a pro at back-stabbing and double dealing. The IPA isn't doing well; he notices the huge expenditures for preemies and the elderly. The wheels begin to churn in his twisted mind, lubricated by cocaine and booze."

Dr. Hauser nodded. "Makes sense."

"He becomes friendly with Larry Stafford, a fellow coke-head. He uses a carrot and stick approach with him. He offers him a financial reward if he goes along and a whistle-blowing for his drug habit if he doesn't. The other two physicians involved at this point are Jim Kerr, the oncologist, and Ken Baker, the pathologist. Jim's drug is gambling. He's a high roller who's been losing big bucks. He gets involved so that he can maintain his expensive life style and keep all his nice toys."

"The pathologist... Is he involved in drugs, too?"

"Don't know, might be. At this point his addiction is a trophy wife whom he's desperately striving to keep happy. As far as his involvement in this thing, he attested to the Cefotan levels in Katrina's blood and also is on the bonus payola."

The doorbell rang; Ryan disrupted the ball playing to answer it. Becky entered. Dr. Hauser rose. "Ms. Thatcher; how are you?"

"Pleas call me Becky. I'm fine and you?"

"Listening to an incredible story."

"Isn't it?"

"Care for a glass of lemonade?" asked Ryan.

"Love one."

As Ryan returned with the lemonade, the doorbell rang again. Ryan opened the door to Jana. She smiled and waved. "Hi everybody."

"What's this, some kind of party?" asked Dr. Hauser.

Melissa nodded. "I'm hosting a TV dinner party."

Dr. Hauser shook his head. "TV dinners… I didn't think you ate that kind of food."

Melissa laughed. "I don't. We're all assembled here to watch the six o'clock news. Afterwards we'll enjoy Chef MacKenzie's famous barbecued chicken."

Dr. Hauser furrowed his brow. "The chicken sounds good, but what's the deal with the news?"

"Geoff's holding a press conference. We all figure it's a last ditch chance to save his precious backside…" Jana said, "It's traditional for rats to go down with a sinking ship." Melissa laughed. "You got it. Anyway, Roger, we have a few minutes. Let me finish my hypothesis. Assuming that Dr. Woods at Hannaford was correct, do you know how Katrina received an IV with potassium and no Cefotan?"

"The Cefotan is prepared in the pharmacy."

"Great minds think alike. Geoff's girlfriend works in the pharmacy. She received a hefty bonus the last quarter and drives around in a new SLK. A pretty nice perk, don't you think?"

"Nice perk indeed. Did she add the potassium to the IV also?"

"Possibly, or it could have been added after it was hung."

"By whom?"

"An aide, nurse, doctor... Anybody with patient access."

Becky interrupted, "News time." She snapped the TV on, took a seat and poised her pen on her legal pad.

A woman's face with a taut smile blossomed on the screen. "Ladies and Gentleman, we are bringing you a special report, live from the Board Room at Cliffside Medical Center. Some startling allegations have surfaced regarding patient care at Cliffside. In particular the care—or lack of it—provided to members of the Cliffside IPA. Geoffrey Shackleton, CEO of the Cliffside IPA, has called this press conference to explain." The camera panned to Geoff. Seated on one side of him was Ken Baker and on the other side, Bridget Middlemas. Geoff exuded confidence; this aura was completely lacking in the tense individuals seated beside him.

Geoff folded his hands on the table. "Ladies and gentlemen, to begin with, I want to assure one and all that the standard of excellence which has prevailed for many years at Cliffside Medical Center is still present within these walls. Some information was made public as a result of an unfortunate crash of our computer system. During the data restoration process, and—as I understand it—a random data integrity check, an erroneous conclusion was reached by a purported computer expert. This alleged expert, in a moment of over-zealousness took this information to the Medical Board and the media. Unfortunately Cliffside has been thrust prematurely and unnecessarily into the limelight. I, for one, was well aware of the slight statistical fluctuation in our death rate. An investigation was already well under way through the safeguards of checks and balances built into our hospital. An increase in deaths has occurred during the last quarter of this year. These deaths occurred mainly among the severely premature and the terminally ill. It is an undisputed fact that seriously ill people often die and natural fluctuations in death rates do occur. I have some background in statistics and I can assure you that this slight upward fluctuation can be explained as well within the normal limits of probability."

"A seven to ten fold increase?" asked a voice from the background.

Geoff shook his head. "It was nowhere near that high. As I mentioned, the computer went down and after the restoration many of us here at Cliffside feel that this number is incorrect. Once we have sifted through all the data, we will issue the correct numbers to the public. I'm sure they will be much different than the *hacked together* ones that the medical board received."

Ryan shook his head. "Oh brother, 'hacked together.'"

Geoff continued, "Understandably, we are canceling our contract with our information service. Their erroneous findings reflect gross incompetence."

All eyes turned to Ryan. He shrugged.

A reporter asked, "Wouldn't that be the hospital's decision and not the IPA's? I understand they are separate entities."

Geoff flashed a smile. "Of course they're separate, but we share some services, including information technology, and have a close working relationship."

"Mr. Shackleton, what about the allegation of physician's receiving financial rewards for acting as, for lack of a better word, Dr. Death?"

"We have found no substantiation for that allegation. However, we have launched a thorough internal investigation of our own of all staff physicians. Two physicians recently resigned, and preliminary evidence leads us to believe that they, and possibly others, may have been responsible for some loss of life. If so, I want to assure the public that if any wrongdoing by Cliffside physicians is uncovered, the sternest of all possible action will be taken against them. We are working with the medical board on this matter."

"Who might these physicians be?"

"I'm not at liberty to release that information, but I assure you, that as the investigation goes forward, we will release the names."

Geoff, exuding confidence and innocence, went on to expound on the high level of care and impeccable physician standards that prevailed at Cliffside. Becky interrupted her writing. "He's setting the others up for a fall to save his egotistical hide."

"Tara and Tom," said Melissa.

"They're the ones that you told me resigned recently."

"Yes. They're both excellent physicians; they left in disgust."

"I bet the schemers there are busy preparing a paper trail as we speak."

"Wouldn't surprise me in the least. I bet Geoff has plans to implicate his co-conspirators as well."

"Let's listen to what the ass has to say," said Dr. Hauser.

"I am primarily a businessman, MBA from Stanford." Geoff paused expectantly to observe any signs of acknowledgment of his credentials. He furrowed his brow and continued, "I have invited two individuals with medical expertise to help explain the situation: our hospital pathologist, Dr. Ken Baker and our Utilization Nurse, Bridget Middlemas. First, I'd like to call on Bridget." He swept his hand in her direction, "Bridget."

Bridget did not reply; she sat wringing her hands. She stared at Geoff for a moment; then gazed off-camera. She faced the screen again and began to speak in a quavering voice. "My name is Bridget Middlemas. Ever since the first grade, I've been called Middlemouse, and for good reason. I've always cowered in a corner like a little mouse and been told what to do, by my parents, my teachers, and of late, Mr. Geoffrey Shackleton."

"Bridget," said Geoff with an edge to his voice. "Bridget, this––"

"This isn't what we rehearsed." Bridget held up a sheaf of papers. "This canned speech you gave me; I'm keeping it for evidence. I have my own speech."

Geoff stood up and glared at Bridget. "Bridget, you appear distraught."

Bridget pulled a container from her purse and growled, "This is pepper spray. Take one false move toward me, you creep, and I'll let you have it."

Geoff moved in her direction. "Bridget, put the can down. I won't hurt you."

"Oh yeah, you murderer. You've been killing people in the hospital and you've threatened to kill me, too. I'm going to tell these good people all about—"

Geoff's temper took control; he lunged toward her. The spray can hissed, scoring a direct hit on his eyes. He rubbed them furiously; then fell to the floor moaning. Baker rose from his chair, dabbed a handkerchief in his water glass. Geoff wailed, "I'm blind, I'm blind." His flailing arms struck Baker in mid-chest, sending him sprawling. Baker retrieved a water pitcher and hurled the contents in Geoff's face. Geoff rose to his feet sputtering.

A figure approached from off-camera. Herb Sempres said, "Geoff! It's Herb. Keep cool. Have a seat." A soggy and thoroughly disheveled Geoff obeyed the command, took a seat and blinked at the camera through red-rimmed eyes. Sempres faced the camera. "Ladies and gentlemen, due to these unfortunate circumstances, I am terminating this conference."

"Who are you?" asked a reporter.

"Herbert Sempres, the hospital attorney. This lady is obviously distraught and—"

"Let the lady continue," said the reporter.

"Let the lady continue," said Bridget.

"Now, Bridget," said Sempres.

She aimed the can in his direction. "Sit down and shut up you little weasel or I'll let you have it too. You're the one who wrote this bogus speech."

Sempres retreated.

Melissa clapped her hands and whooped. "Right on, Bridget." Becky said, "This is Nurse Mouse's coming out party... Unbelievable."

"Shh, I don't want to miss any of this," said Dr. Hauser.

"Right, much better than the soaps," said Jana.

"Shh," said Dr. Hauser. Bridget continued, "I've heard a lot of rumors circulating in the past few month, hearsay, that weasel in the corner would call it. One of the rumors is that Mr. Shackleton keeps a stash of cocaine in a Ferrari model on his desk. Maybe somebody would like to run across the street and check it out." Geoff reared up. Bridget raised her spray can, prompting him to cower down in his seat. He intermittently blinked and stared in Bridget's direction as she continued, "I want to share a few facts with you, ladies and gentlemen, first-hand facts. Many of you probably saw the article about the malpractice case against Dr. Melissa Morrison. Dr. Morrison is a fine OB doctor—I know—nurses know the good doctors—always do. Anyway, Dr. Morrison wanted to admit a patient because she sensed she was seriously ill... The patient was. As Utilization Nurse I was compelled to follow IPA guidelines. In most hospitals, a physician could override those guidelines, but not at Cliffside. Mr. Peepers here refused her request to admit the patient, and then, when the patient developed her problem, he destroyed the records."

"Can you substantiate that?" asked a reporter.

"I can. I received some documents this morning from a—a friend."

"Why didn't you come forward before now?" asked another.

"Fear, pure unadulterated fear. That man browbeat and intimidated me on many occasions, but after the tragic incident, he threatened my life, and—*sniff*—my poor little Toby."

"Who's Toby?" asked a reporter.

"My little Yorkie." Bridget stifled her sniffling as well as her mousiness. "He, or one of his cronies, poisoned my dog. Then, somebody called up to gloat, said I'd be next if I didn't play ball. I was afraid, afraid until now. I finally found my courage in a room with only a few enemies. I count among my allies the ladies and gentlemen of the press, and..." Bridget swept her hand outward. "All you people out there watching." Bridget gazed into the camera with her newfound confidence.

The moderator turned toward Baker. "Dr. Baker, we haven't heard from you yet. I'm sure our viewers are anxious to hear your comments."

Baker sat limply in his chair much like a marionette with severed strings. He reached slowly for his water glass, took a sip, and cleared his throat. "This is very hard… Thanks to the courage displayed by Bridget, I've decided to rise to the occasion. I'm not going to recite the script prepared by that man over there." The camera panned to Sempres, mopping his brow, and then back to Baker. "I probably shouldn't be talking without benefit of legal counsel but I will say a few words. A dramatic increase in mortality has occurred at Cliffside in the past quarter, mostly seniors and premature infants. I noticed the increase right away. I do the posts—autopsies—on all hospital deaths. I became alarmed and approached this sterling example of administrative ineptitude seated to my left." Geoff glared. Baker returned the glare. "Bridget, keep the spray handy." Geoff wilted down in his chair. "This man used personal information and my loyalty to my colleagues to keep me silent. I refused. He then threatened me with loss of my hospital position, and black-balling. He coerced me into falsifying medical records. For that I deserve to be punished, as I'm sure I will. However, I am not directly responsible for any of the deaths. Others are, and I will cooperate fully with the investigation. That's all I have to say."

The moderator appeared. "Ladies and gentlemen, there you have it, live from Cliffside Medical Center."

"Wow," said Melissa. "Let's hear it for Middlemouse."

"Hooray for Middlemouse," shouted the group.

Melissa rose and snapped the TV into silence. "Poor, poor Geoff. Orange is a terrible color for him."

"Orange?" said Jana.

Becky said, "Geoff will soon be wearing an orange jail suit."

Jana laughed.

"Serves the creep right," said Ryan. A stricken look formed. "Oh no, my chicken." He stormed out the door.

A few minutes later, he returned. "Well folks, I have some good news and some bad news."

"What's the good news?" asked Dr. Hauser.

"Depends on how you like your chicken."

"I like it cooked just right. Moist in the middle, with a slight crispness outside."

"The crispness is more than slight. How about extra crispy?"

"I think not... I have an alternate plan. Let's go to Pinocchio's and celebrate, on me."

"It's okay in the middle," said Ryan.

Melissa kissed him firmly. "I'm sure it is, honey, but in these austere times, one can't turn down the offer of a free meal."

Their waiter was the Mad Hatter again. Little Roger recognized him and said, "Hat." The Mad Hatter contorted his face in a goofy grin, eliciting peals of laughter from the toddler. The Mad Hatter departed; then returned with a Champagne bucket. He presented the bottle to Dr. Hauser who nodded an approval. Melissa glanced at the label. "Well I'll be darned, *Dom Perignon* again."

"What's the matter, don't you like it?" asked Dr. Hauser.

Melissa pecked him on the cheek. "We love it. Thank you so much."

Dr. Hauser smiled and extended his glass. "Here's to the soon-to-take-place union of Melissa and Ryan. May their lives be blessed with happiness." Becky extended her glass. "Here's to the much-deserved resolution of Melissa's legal entanglements." Melissa tipped her glass. "Here's to all of you seated here with me, you're all quite special. I love you all."

Between sips of Champagne, Dr. Hauser asked Becky, "What's your legal prognosis for Geoff?"

"Murder one, most definitely murder one. I'm sure that the DA has wind of this thing and Geoff will be brought in for questioning, the same for the neonatologist and oncologist. Ditto for that little pharmacist. People entrust their lives to doctors and hospitals, that trust has been violated and I'd hate to be in the position of defending them."

"What about the pathologist?" asked Dr. Hauser.

"Falsifying medical records is a serious offense; however, it's a far cry from being punishable by death. In Mrs. Hauser's case, he was involved in the cover-up of a murder, not the murder itself. He will be charged with accessory after the fact. Best case scenario, he's in a heap of trouble."

Dr. Hauser stared into his glass. "This little scheme of theirs lasted three months or so before Melissa and Ryan uncovered it. What were they thinking? They couldn't get away with something like that forever."

"No they couldn't," said Melissa. "Geoff's goal was to keep it going until the end of the year, milking it for all it was worth. Then he'd sell the IPA. Despite the skimming, they'd still look terrific on paper thanks to their gruesome scheme."

"In addition, nose candy has a clouding effect on one's reasoning abilities." added Becky.

"It does," said Melissa.

Dr. Hauser turned to Melissa and Ryan. "Let's turn the topic of conversation to something more pleasant. Have the two of you set a date yet?"

Melissa shook her head. "So much has happened recently, and I'm sure to be involved in upcoming legal events."

"That's for sure," said Becky.

Melissa said, "We'll figure it out over the next few days and when we can clear out a full week, we'll have a wedding and take a much-needed honeymoon."

"Very much needed and deserved," said Dr. Hauser. "Say Ryan, "I'm sorry to hear that your company is losing the hospital contract."

"It's no big deal; we service a number of facilities... And, medical software is a small component of the business. Hey guys, enough shop-talk. Let's enjoy the meal."

The Mad Hatter placed the check in the center of the table. Ryan snatched it up.

Dr. Hauser reached for the tray. "Hey this is my treat."

"No it isn't. I burned the chicken; this is my penance, and my pleasure."

"Nonsense," said Dr. Hauser. "That's a hefty tab for you to pick up. That champagne costs a buck a bubble."

Ryan kept a firm grasp on the check. "I can handle it."

"Look, you need to be careful with your finances. You could lose your job over the whistle-blowing."

"I think not... I'm real tight with my boss."

Melissa glanced at Ryan's credit card. It read: Ryan A MacKenzie. Recognition flashed. "Aha, R-A-M—RAM-Tech."

Ryan grinned, "You found me out."

Melissa returned the grin. "I thought you were a programmer."

He nodded. "I am, but I'm also the CEO."

After the group digested their surprise, Becky queried Ryan about his company. He explained, "We have about 100 employees currently, and are expanding."

Becky asked, "What does your book of business include?"

"Our major thrust is currently with our graphics card. We have contracts pending with IBM, Dell, and Hewlett-Packard."

Dr. Hauser said, "I see that your business has many "*RAM*-ifications.""

Ryan chuckled. "Right. RAM also stands for 'random access memory,' which I'm sure you know is—"

Little Roger's fussing interrupted. Melissa gathered him up from his high chair and said, "We've pushed his envelope for restaurant-sitting. Time to go."

The group returned to Melissa's condo in high spirits. After bedding down little Roger, Melissa returned downstairs and broke out in song. "Happy Days are Here Again." The others joined in, creating a raucous refrain as they paraded around the room. After their exuberance was spent, they sat together in the family room basking in the *Gemütlichkeit*. After a while, Becky made her good-byes and Jana followed suit. Melissa sensed that it would be difficult for Dr. Hauser to be alone. She said, "It's late, Roger. Why don't you sleep over?"

"Good idea... Only the hide-a-bed in the study is occupied by Ryan."

Ryan's face reddened. "I—er—I."

Dr. Hauser affixed a menacing glare upon Ryan. "This little girl is quite precious to me. I hope you haven't taken any untoward advances toward her."

The redness increased on Ryan's face. "I—er—"

A laugh erupted from Dr. Hauser. "I can read you two like a book. This is a different world than the one I grew up in, I fully understand. If it makes a difference, you have my approval."

"It does make a difference," said Ryan. "Thank you."

Dr. Hauser wagged his finger. "Now if little Roger was a little older, I wouldn't approve for his sake."

"Right you are," said Melissa.

Blushing Ryan asked, "Are you up for a bike ride tomorrow morning?" Melissa pondered the thought for a moment; then shook her head. "I think I'll pass. I need to spend a bit of quality time with my son."

Ryan's redness gave way to a pout. Dr. Hauser said, "Say, I've done some cycling in the past, never been on a tandem though. If you don't mind towing an out of shape old man, I'll give it a go."

Ryan smiled. "Sound's good."

Chapter 31

The following morning, Melissa's household was a kaleidoscope of chaos. Little Roger was asking everyone about Casper's whereabouts. Dr. Hauser was searching through Ryan's cycling wardrobe, trying to find something that would accommodate his ample belly. Ada, disgruntled at Melissa's depleted larder, announced that she was off to the market. Ryan delayed her departure by giving her a detailed shopping list. "Ada, we need free-range chicken, not those frozen buzzards, fresh rosemary, some balsamic vinegar—"

Dr. Hauser, bulging out of a jersey with Donald Duck printed on the back, interrupted. "It's 8:30, if we don't hurry, we'll miss our cycling adventure."

"Be right with you. I need to redeem myself from last night."

"Melissa has fully apprised me of your culinary expertise, but we've got to go... Melissa, be sure to lock the door after us."

Halfway through one of Roger's favorite Winnie the Pooh stories the doorbell rang. She ignored it. The bell rang again. She approached the door and asked, "Who is it?"

"La Playa Florist."

Melissa opened the door to a large floral display obscuring the face of its bearer.

"How nice. I wonder who—"

The flowers dropped, exposing the face of the bearer: Geoff. Pointing a revolver in her direction; he growled, "Inside."

"Geoff, don't."

"Quiet, bitch." He forced her backward and shut the door.

"What do you want?"

"You have something I want, my son."

She struggled to control her tears. "In biology only, you bastard."

He aimed the gun at her head. "Move it! Fetch my son. We're going for a little drive to sunny Mexico, *arriba, arriba.*"

Little Roger whimpered while Melissa fastened him in his car seat. She tried to control her terror for his sake. After she completed the task, Geoff barked, "You drive." He took a seat on the passenger side.

"Why are you doing this?" she asked.

"Why, because you cost me millions. Do you have any idea of the money involved?"

"Your plans to sell the IPA at the end of the year."

"How'd you know that?"

"I have my sources."

He poked her with the gun. "Who?"

"Rachel."

"Stupid bitch... Well, it really doesn't matter now that you've screwed up the works... It would have been the sweetheart deal of the century. I'm talking a lump sum payment for the sale of the IPA plus millions more on stock options. The likelihood of a co-chair in the new IPA. My future was set."

"Profits made at the expense of human lives, including Katrina's."

Geoff smirked. "That old fool of a husband killed her. She would have received the standard care until he brought up the topic of a bone marrow transplant... Not at all cost effective in these austere times."

Melissa snarled, "Austere for whom, Geoff? Certainly not for you. You preach austerity to all but yourself. Doesn't it bother you even a little bit for the suffering you've caused?"

"The patients who were liquidated all died relatively quickly and painlessly, sort of like putting old Rover to sleep."

"You're disgusting, totally disgusting. Do you know what it's like to die from a potassium injection?"

"The heart stops."

"The heart stops, but the victim is fully conscious for several agonizing minutes as the oxygen level in the brain drops."

"Gosh, that makes me feel just terrible."

Melissa clenched her fist; he gave her another painful jab with the revolver. She grimaced. "Who made the final decisions on these 'liquidations,' as you call them?"

He jerked his thumb in his direction. "Me. I made the decisions and my pawns carried them out. You must be aware that in today's times, with spiraling costs, healthcare rationing has become a reality all across the nation. Insurers are constantly redefining what is reasonable and necessary. I just came up with my own definition, and carried it a step further."

"A step further, what an understatement."

"Depends upon one's perspective. It was a smooth-running operation until you exposed it."

"If I hadn't found you out, somebody else would have, it was just a matter of time."

He sneered. "Maybe, maybe not. In any event if the liquidation of useless lives came to the surface after the IPA sale, it wouldn't much matter. I'd still be set for life. Furthermore, there's no paper trail to incriminate me. I'm not a physician, just a humble administrator, and cannot be held accountable for medical incompetence."

Melissa shook her head. "But you are responsible."

"Responsible for what? Defective babies and dying, worthless old people. B–F–D. There's not enough room on this planet for the aged and defective."

Melissa reflected that Geoff, the greedy businessman, epitomized the dark side of managed care. In Geoff's world, the quest for profits far outweighed the value of a human life. The thought sickened her.

He interrupted her thoughts. "Thanks to you, the police will soon be on my tail and everything will be exposed." The anger in his eyes intensified. "For your information, I was able to transfer a not-insignificant sum to an offshore account. These funds will allow me to live in splendid luxury."

"Where?"

"Myanmar."

"Where in the world is that?"

"Southeast Asia, used to be called Burma. No worry of extradition. And, the women there are amazing; really know how to make a man happy."

Hopefully one of those little chicky-plums will give you a virulent STD, one that will rot off your equipment. "You're retiring, then? Living in a far-off land with exotic maidens at your beck and call."

"Oh yeah. I get hard just thinking about it. And I have a few ideas for the future, they make me hard too. I'm going to create a fucking empire from there." He pressed the gun barrel into her ribs. "As for you, you'll be vacationing in Mexico while I finalize my plans."

Melissa tensed, fearing that Geoff had a more sinister strategy than detaining her south of the border for a while. He had about as much use for her and little Roger as he did for the set of golf clubs she had given him for a wedding gift, the best that she could afford on a resident's salary. After their divorce, she had reminded him that he had left them in the front closet. He told her to call the Salvation Army, and with a little luck, they'd relieve her of the "sack of shit-metal." He probably needed a hostage. Yes, that must be the reason. After they arrived in Mexico, he would no longer need either of them. And then what? Why would he chance telling her his ultimate destination? Extradition laws are subject to change. She shuddered. *He's only sharing the information to gloat. He doesn't expect me to have an opportunity to tell anybody.* She drove carefully and deliberately, struggling to formulate a plan. *It's Saturday. They start in the parking lot next to Carl's Jr. They exit right, then down Main Street. It might just work.* She said, "You master-minded the whole scheme, didn't you Geoff?"

"Right on, babe. I turned a floundering IPA into a profitable operation in a matter of months. People are so easily manipulated."

"Vicky's nurse, were you behind that?"

"Who?"

"My patient, Vicky Sanders. The one in a coma."

"Yeah, right. Your malpractice patient." Melissa stiffened, but apparently Geoff failed to notice her reaction. He continued, "Piece of cake that little nurse. Fifty grand and she disappeared."

"That's all it took?"

He chortled. "That plus a reality lesson if she had any altruistic notions."

Melissa turned right, rather than left at Bridge Drive. Her fists were clenched tightly on the wheel. She relaxed when he failed to notice the slight detour. The irritating smirk widened on his face as he continued, "Your colleagues, Baker, Kerr and Stafford—brilliant doctors my ass—stupid pawns."

"And your little girlfriend from the pharmacy?"

"Ah yes... Her too. I'll miss her and all the great sex, but there'll be others."

"How nice."

"Yes indeed, many more. All better than you, ice woman. You're the world's lousiest lay."

She mused, *Only for you, you snotty bastard. Hopefully, my White Knight is around the next bend.* The clock on the dash read: 9:18. She rounded the curve; to her relief the pack of cyclists came into view. In the middle of the pack was a familiar tandem bearing a portly man in a Donald Duck jersey. As she drew abreast of Donald Duck, she honked.

Geoff growled, "Cool it. We don't need to attract any attention to ourselves, do we?" He grabbed her arm forcefully, causing her to grimace.

She smiled icily. "I'm just warning them. Didn't you notice that several of them were straying out of the bike lane? Running over a cyclist would certainly be attention-getting, don't you think?"

He released her arm. "I guess."

Despair struck as she passed the pack. The horn had attracted their attention, as she knew it would. But the stoplight ahead glowed bright green, thwarting her plan. She eased up slightly on the accelerator. The green turned to amber; she braked to a stop.

Geoff snapped, "You coulda made that light."

"I thought you wanted to avoid attention. I'm just following your orders."

"Don't get cute with me. I've got a short fuse." He glared at the traffic light. "What the hell are we doing on Coast Highway anyway?"

Melissa shrugged. "It's as good a way out of town as any." She glanced in the rear view mirror. The pack was almost upon them, traveling at a pace of about twenty-five she guessed. An opposing vehicle turned in front of them, signaling the imminent change of the light. A moment later, they were totally surrounded by the cyclists. A dozen of them positioned themselves in front of the car and engaged in a variety of activities. Several took a pull from their water bottles. Two others dismounted and inspected their derailleurs.

The light turned green. "Goddamn," yelled Geoff, leaning over and laying on the horn. The group ignored him. His face turned crimson. A tap on the window distracted him. Melissa noted the familiar tandem. Geoff punched down the window, leaned forward and screamed, "Get the fuck out of the way, you bunch of assholes."

Ryan dismounted and discharged his water bottle into Geoff's face. "Goddamn," he spluttered. Melissa, remembering a self-defense course, applied a karate chop to Geoff's neck. Dr. Hauser wrenched the door open, grasped Geoff by the lapels and pulled him forward. Ryan struck Geoff's forearm forcefully with a tire pump, dislodging the gun from his grasp. Geoff lurched forward in an attempt to retrieve it. Dr. Hauser, exhibiting surprising agility, snatched the weapon from the pavement and leveled it at Geoff's temple. Geoff held up his palm and whined, "Easy, old man. You wouldn't shoot anybody."

"Make one move, you bastard. Give me the excuse I need to blow you away."

Geoff moved forward. "You—"

"I could with pleasure after what you did to my Katrina. Here's a token of my appreciation." Dr. Hauser applied his knee firmly to Geoff's groin. Geoff moaned to the pavement, accompanied by the wail of approaching sirens. Dr. Hauser planted his foot firmly on Geoff's back.

"Hey," gasped Geoff, "I can't breathe."

Dr. Hauser increased the pressure. "Good."

Two officers brandishing shotguns approached. One shouted, "Stand clear everybody."

"He's all yours," said Dr. Hauser.

Geoff rose shakily. "I'm glad you're here, officer. This man assaulted me. I want to lodge a—"

"Give it a rest, jerk," said Melissa. "We have at least 50 witnesses who can testify as to what happened. You're toast."

Chapter 32

The following morning, as expected, Melissa found her name on the front page under the headline, "SHACKLETON IN SHACKLES." She positioned herself at the kitchen table and digested the news. The ringing telephone interrupted her rereading of the article. She knew instinctively whom the call would be from. "Good morning, Mother."

"Have you read the morning paper, Missy?

"Yes, I've seen the paper."

"My god, I'm shocked beyond belief. Is it true what they say? He was abducting you at gunpoint."

"Very true."

"I can't believe it of him."

"Well, believe it because I can assure you that it's a fact."

"It's still hard to believe. Geoff has always been so charming... Charming, hmm." Her voice took on an angry tinge. "He charmed me into investing my last dime in the IPA. Where did I go wrong? I've tried so hard to accrue an estate to leave to you and Ricky."

"It's okay, mother, I have a good number of productive years left. I don't need to rely on you for financial support."

"But poor Ricky," she wailed. "What about poor Ricky?"

"Maybe now you can quit coddling poor Ricky and give him a chance to grow up."

"There you go again lambasting me and criticizing poor Ricky."

"That's my opinion, Mother. Take it for what it's worth."

Grace moaned, "I've lost everything, lost everything in that ill-fated health plan. Why me? I've worked so hard, so very hard."

Melissa said, "I've always heard it's prudent to diversify one's investments."

Grace wailed, "I'm destitute, totally destitute." She paused. "Missy are you there?"

"Yes Mother."

"Poor Rachel—*sniff*—poor dedicated Dr. Rachel. My heart goes out to her."

"She doesn't have a heart to respond back with, her thoracic cavity contains a shriveled lump of coal."

"Don't be cruel, Missy, in your hour of triumph."

"I'm not being cruel, Mother, just factual."

"Well—*sniff*—speaking of facts. Do you really believe all those allegations about Geoff?"

"He's likely to get life, maybe the death penalty."

Grace snapped, "You're just being vindictive. Nothing has been proven yet."

"No, Mother, I'm not being vindictive. Innocent people were murdered in that hospital. He authorized those murders... A jury will decide his future. In any case, it won't be a happy one."

Grace wailed, "Where did I go wrong? I've scrimped and saved and tried so hard. My god, where did I go wrong? I'm sure that you hate me, Missy."

"No, Mother, I don't hate you. You just made some bad decisions along the way. We all have, me included."

"Thank you for putting things in perspective, Missy... That's always been a comfort to me."

Melissa's web of problems began unraveling at an ever-accelerating pace. She was fully caught up in its momentum. Perusal of the morning paper and the clipping of articles relating to "The Cliffside Scandal" became a daily ritual. Among her collection were articles entitled: HOSPITAL BIGWIGS POINT FINGER AT

EACH OTHER IN HOSPITAL SCANDAL; WRONGFUL DEATH SUITS MOUNT TO MORE THAN 100, MORE EXPECTED; and MURDER ONE, STATES D.A. The one in today's paper was the best yet: a picture of Geoff and his girl friend seated in his Ferrari titled: ADMINISTRATIVE REWARDS.

The information that Melissa gleaned from the media was enhanced by the local medical grapevine. Jean Iverson ran off the road in a vain attempt to escape the police. Her SLK overturned and caught fire. The red-headed vixen incurred third degree burns to her face and upper body, leaving her scarred for life, what was left of it. Larry Stafford's suicide attempt was thwarted by modern technology. The day his ex-wife was to return from a European vacation, he consumed half a bottle of scotch, sequestered himself in her (formerly his) garage, and sat listening to the purring of his Mercedes. When the air quality deteriorated, sensors shut down the engine; thus, his life was spared. When he regained consciousness, he informed the media that he would plead guilty to all charges. One step ahead of the police, Jim Kerr fled to Las Vegas where he enjoyed his best-ever winning streak. His joy was short-lived; Kerr was arrested in his suite. The $30,000 he won at the craps table could be used as a down payment for his legal defense. Although Kerr professed innocence, Stafford not only freely admitted injecting potassium into IVs but also attested that Kerr had done the same. Ken Baker's wife, Andrea, left him. She dated Morgan Brookhurst briefly—until his wife, Stephanie, caught them in a compromising position on one of his exam tables. Stephanie sought out a divorce attorney. Andrea moved on to a better prospect, the plastic surgeon who had quadrupled her bra size.

The large gaps in Melissa's appointment book vanished; soon, she was fully booked three months ahead, not including the week blocked off for her honeymoon. To be sure, a portion of the new patients were motivated by an opportunity to get a close-up view of the doctor who had brought a healthcare system to its knees.

After one of her too-busy days, Melissa returned home to enjoy a quiet evening with little Roger. After dinner, she placed her son

on her lap for a bedtime story. The doorbell rang. Ada answered.
Grace made her typical entrance, strolling across the family room
in Ginger Rogers fashion. "Hi Missy, I was in the neighborhood,
and... I hope I'm not intruding."

*You definitely are, but what the hey. Her usual means of
communication is the telephone, haven't seen her in months. She
looks older, more tired.* "Would you like a cup of tea?"

"That would be great... And how's my little man? My how he's
grown." She reached for him. Roger howled, nestling into Melissa.
Ada padded off to fix the tea.

Melissa said, "He's tired. I'll settle him down, be right back."

Grace said, "Mind if I smoke?"

"Sure, in the backyard."

"It's a bit nippy out."

"Ada will fetch you a jacket."

Melissa returned to a smoke-filled room.

Grace said, "My, it was chilly out there."

"Right," said Melissa, opening a window.

"You're letting in the damp air," snapped Grace.

"I'll shut it in a minute, as soon as the air clears."

Ada entered with the tea. Melissa asked, "Would you like
anything with it?"

"Cream."

"Sorry all I have is low-fat milk. Would you like some?"

Grace frowned, shook her head, and took a sip of tea. She
adopted her pseudo-cheerful tone. "I always knew that you'd be
vindicated from those awful charges and would rise proud and tall
from the situation in true Morrison tradition. I've always been there
for you, Missy, helping out when I can." Melissa looked aside, and
rolled her eyes. "Yes, Mother."

"I certainly hope you're going to sue the socks off of the IPA."

"The IPA has gone belly-up, Mother. I'll have to wait in line for
any settlement... The IPA and the hospital are being deluged with
wrongful death suits... The hospital might go down right along

with CIPA."

"Would that make you happy, Missy, bringing a hospital to its knees?"

"Not in the least. Only a handful of people are involved. If the hospital falls, hundreds of good people will be hurt—all dedicated healthcare professionals. Seeing the bad apples get their just deserts is all I want. All the dirty laundry is surfacing. Among other things, evidence exists that Rucker, who ineptly represented me at the hearing, was paid off to lose the case."

"Well, if that's true, sue the bastard's socks off, too."

"I couldn't care less, Mother. I have my reputation back and my malpractice suit has been dropped, the Judicial Review Hearing as well. And most important, Geoff the jailbird is no longer a contender for little Roger's custody. That's all I really want. People lost their lives and at present, I'm only out some money. I can make it back."

Grace's voice cracked. "I'll never be able to recoup my losses; I'm much concerned about my future. And, I feel just terrible about this; I don't have a farthing to contribute to my daughter's wedding... Even though it's her second."

"I know you can't help with the wedding. I don't expect you to."

"The small token that I can offer you for the wedding is my Ralph. He's looking forward to walking you down the aisle."

"Sorry mother, that honor goes to Dr. Hauser, he deserves it. I hardly know Ralph."

Grace sniffed, "Well! Desert your family for casual acquaintances if you must."

"He is by no means a casual acquaintance. You certainly must be aware of that."

"Well, I suppose, but getting back to basics, I've always prided myself on my organizational abilities, and am offering my services for the wedding preparations."

"Thank you, Mother, but I don't need any help with the planning; it's a simple ceremony, about two dozen guests."

"Well, if that's the case and you truly are not in need of my expertise, I'll gracefully bow out."

Melissa stifled a chuckle and made no reply.

Grace broke the silence and asked, "Have you planned a honeymoon?"

Melissa smiled at the mention of the word. "We're going on a one week cruise around the Tahitian Islands; Ryan and I have never been but have heard it's a great honeymoon locale."

"I certainly hope you have a wonderful time and can relax even though others are suffering terribly."

Chapter 33

At the security checkpoint, Melissa picked up little Roger and gave him one last kiss. "Mommy will be back soon. You and Opa will have such a good time."

Dr. Hauser nodded. "This afternoon we're going to the zoo and see the elephants. What does the elephant say, Roger?"

Little Roger gave his imitation of an elephant's trumpeting and gurgled. Melissa returned him to Dr. Hauser's arms. Melissa turned to Ryan and asked, "Where are the boarding passes?"

"In my jacket pocket."

"Give me your laptop."

While he retrieved the passes, Melissa winked at Dr. Hauser and passed him the computer. She grabbed Ryan's arm, and said, "Bye everybody."

The flight attendant presented glasses of champagne as they took their seats in first class.

"To us," said Melissa."

"I'll drink to that." Panic blossomed on Ryan's face. "My laptop, where's my laptop?"

"I gave it to Dr. Hauser for safekeeping. I plan to keep you too busy to use it, my darling." She kissed him firmly.

"But..."

She gave him a pouty smile. "You're not mad at me are you?"

"No. You're much better looking than my laptop."

"I certainly hope so. Much better than a GUI."

"I'm working on the ultimate GUI, a hologram where the user can actually walk around and touch things. You're a quantum leap above that."

"I certainly hope so. Holograms can't kiss, can they?" She planted another kiss.

"No they can't."

She clinked his glass again. "Here's to us and our future. 'real-grams' not holograms."

"To us and our future... Speaking of futures, have you thought out yours in the aftermath of all this?"

"I have. For starters, I want a baby soon. Is that acceptable with you?"

"Quite acceptable." He kissed her again. "What about your career?"

"I don't want to work full time. Young children need a mother. I'm a firm believer in that. I also went to significant trouble and expense to become a physician. I can't walk away from medicine."

"Is it really worth being a physician in today's times? Look what you've just been through. I would think that would leave you jaded."

"It's been an eye-opener for sure, but I've always been a believer in profiting from one's experiences. Cost-effective medicine is here to stay. The type of practice Dr. Hauser had at the onset of his career is gone forever. I'm going to involve myself in managed care."

"I thought you hated it?"

"That was mis-managed care. We can't halt what's going on in medicine today, but we can insure that the quality of medicine is the best it can be. I do believe it's possible to shave costs and maintain quality. That's what I'm going to do. If I can't work within the managed care system and help fix it, then I'll work against it and stomp it down."

"Little old you?"

"Little old me... And a little help from my friends. I'll write magazine articles, books... I'll go on the lecture circuit..."

He interrupted her with a kiss. "Shh, we're on our honeymoon, remember?"

The flight attendant's voice came on the speaker. "Ladies and gentlemen, please fasten your seatbelts and place your seat in the full upright position. We are about to take off."

Epilogue

Our nation is in the midst of a healthcare crisis. In September 2003, the *Wall Street Journal* ran a front page series describing the rationing of healthcare in hospitals across the nation. Decisions are being made on a daily basis on which patients should be continued on expensive treatment. Spiraling costs have forced many of us to explore alternatives to the traditional fee for service medical care. Managed care has been lauded by many as the best solution to this crisis. Other members of our society have condemned this concept as a major step backward in the quality of medical care. The doctor - patient decision loop has been expanded to include the grim reality of economics. This problem does not exist in third world countries with limited resources. The premature and elderly either survive with basic supportive care or they expire. In these nations the constraints are due to lack of availability of medical services as well as economic limitations. In the United States, technologic resources continue to advance, however economic resources are becoming depleted. Advances in medical technology have vastly improved in the past four decades. For example, the premature Kennedy baby that expired in the early sixties would have an excellent chance for survival in the neonatal intensive care unit of today. During that same decade, we landed men on the moon. Subsequently, we abandoned moon landings due to economic considerations.

Economics are an intrinsic part of wars, partnerships and many other human events. In medicine, percentages are often glibly quoted i.e., "You have an 80 percent chance of a full recovery after open heart surgery, Mr. Smith;" "A woman in your age group has a one percent chance of having a baby with Down syndrome, Mrs. Anderson." Rationing of healthcare is occurring at present in our hospitals. If a premature infant has less than one percent chance of a normal life or an elderly person has a slim chance of recovery it is not economically possible to justify the tremendous expense required for their ongoing care. The term "comfort care" is used for these patients. They are kept comfortable and allowed to die as peacefully as possible. The less than one percent case is fairly simple to decide, but what if the chance of recovery is five percent, 10 percent or even 50 percent?

To date, fortunes have been made and lost in the arena of managed care. Assume for a moment that you are a managed care provider and have been given a sum of $50 million to provide this year's care to the "lives" in your plan. What happens if you run out of funds in July? The answer is that you go bankrupt and the "lives" receive no care for the rest of the year. If you turn a huge profit, it is at the expense of denied medical services of the "lives." Some of the "lives" are no longer alive.

Regardless of one's viewpoint toward managed care, traditional fee for service medical care is a dinosaur well on its way to extinction. The positive aspects of managed care are its focus on preventive healthcare—it is far less costly to prevent a disease rather than treat it—and a decrease in unnecessary and often costly medical procedures. The negative aspect is the loss of a human life that could otherwise be saved. We must trim the fat from the medical care system without cutting away chunks of flesh as well.

What can one do when faced with making a medical decision for a loved one or even oneself in the case where reasoning powers are still intact? I suggest that one analyze the situation realistically and obtain input from healthcare professionals. If you question their decisions, seek a second opinion from other healthcare professionals, not relatives, neighbors or magazine articles. The Internet is a good source of information, but review the data with a critical eye, and consider the Web-site sponsor's possible biases. Discuss your wishes in the event of a serious illness with your spouse and children. Reinforce your wishes with a living will. A hospitalized patient needs an advocate in today's medical climate. In the case of a premature infant, the parents can fulfill that role; however, an elderly person is often not so fortunate; however, close friends and/ or relatives can serve as effective advocates, even if they possess limited medical knowledge. Hospitalization without an advocate could prove to be fatal.

Many current health plans of today embrace the concept of managed care. The variety of terms in which they are described is confusing to the medical consumer. When deciding on a health plan, ask for a disclosure of what sort of process one must go through to get approval for medical services. Tailor your questions toward the type of services you might be in need of at present and in the future. If the answers are vague, shop further.

About the Author

Robin Wulffson is a California native and a graduate of the UCLA School of Medicine. He served as a battalion surgeon in the Vietnam War. After completing his specialty training in Obstetrics and Gynecology, he practiced in Orange County, California for 25 years. Since 1998, he has done freelance writing in the healthcare field. He resides with his wife, Carole, and his greyhound, Amber, in Tustin, California. *An Improbable Cause* is his first novel. For further information, access his Website: www.rwulffson.com.